CRITICAL ACCLAIM FOR MORT CASTLE:

Mort Castle "show(s) the promise of becoming (a) big name in the days ahead. . . ."

—*Fangoria*

"Mort Castle is one of the best sheer writers of horror we have with us!"

—J.N. Williamson,
author of *Babel's Children*

"(My) favorite story in the whole book *(Masques II)* is Mort Castle's brilliant 'If You Take My Hand, My Son.' The surprise ending is absolutely perfect. I can't praise this story enough."

—*2AM Magazine*

Mort Castle "is a master wordcrafter . . . Fans know the icy effect of the Castle chill, but not even a jaded horror reader can pre-guess the garotte twist of the Castle kill."

—*The Chicago Heights Star*

ACKNOWLEDGEMENTS

"Thanks to/for": Jane Castle, my own good wife, who first got me interested in the Rom; Mary Williamson, mind-reader and moral supporter; Nancy Parsegian, who long ago told me this one had the makings; Jerry Williamson, Irwin Chapman, J. Peter Orr, Lawrence Person, John Maclay, Robert Lightell, and others who were telling me I was a writer when I was anything but certain; Ray Yates, who convinced me if it's already broken you don't have to worry about breaking it; Jane Thornton, John Littell, the good folks of Leisure Books, for extraordinary patience and understanding; Robert Weinberg, for calling me gentleman and scholar; young Dan Madsen of Northstar, who flatters this aging author; Lewis and Potter, those good dogs, gone now, but in memory always.

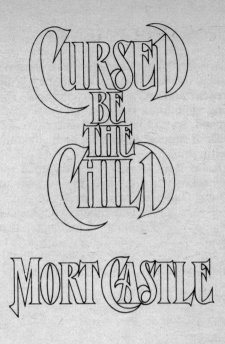

CURSED BE THE CHILD

MORT CASTLE

LEISURE BOOKS NEW YORK CITY

For Lillian and Sheldon Castle,
my parents,
Simply the best

A LEISURE BOOK®

June 1990

Published by

Dorchester Publishing Co., Inc.
276 Fifth Avenue
New York, NY 10001

WAKING ALONE IN DARKNESS

It's only the wind, mothers
tell their children in the night
when upturned leaves rattle on the
    windowpane,
furious and black;

only the wind
when night cries in children's dreams
and children cry out
in the darkness.
                                    —W.D. Ehrhart

From CONNECTIONS

and reconnect
        our
            fading lines

tracing
        our ways
    back
together
            through
the paths

            created
in the night.
                                    —Jane Castle

"O detlene tat o Beng nashti beshen pashasa."

"Neither the spirits of dead children nor the
devil can remain at peace."
                                    —Pola Janichka

Another Word or Two on *Cursed Be The Child*

Though the Gypsy customs and beliefs in this book are based on extensive research, there have been times when I've created a Gypsy saying or fable. Artistic license? It's said that when the film *King Of The Gypsies* was being produced, the Gypsy consultants were more than willing to make up an "old Gypsy tradition" on the spot; I've assumed the same freedom.

Though the book deals with powerful sexual topics—child abuse, molestation, pedophilia and incest—there are no scenes in the book that graphically depict sexual activities between adults and children. More often than not, such scenes are suggested rather than narrated at all.

Mort Castle

PROLOGUE

Late summer, 1918

She was calling.

Sweating, trembling with chill, he heard. He was sitting by the front window at the end of the second floor hall, a small man, feverish cheeks rusted by three days' growth of reddish-brown beard. Suspenders held his baggy trousers up over a dingy union suit. He wore two pairs of heavy socks, feet crammed into leather slippers.

She cried out again.

God, how could he hear her so plainly? She was in the basement. That little whore, voice disguised as a child's—begging, pleading, trying to lure him.

After the last time—yesterday? the day before?—he'd shut her away, slamming the basement door, locking it with the chain and the key.

Or maybe he was merely imagining that he heard her. That was part of the sickness. There were frantic chills that made you quake like you had the St. Vitus dance, blazing fever, a cough to rip your lungs out, and delirium, seeing and hearing things that were not real, things you could hardly bear to see or hear. Delirium and then death.

The Spanish influenza!

He had it. He couldn't lie to himself anymore or try to pretend it was nothing but a cold, that it would leave him in its own good time. He didn't need Dr. Lawson to confirm his diagnosis, and what good would a doctor be anyway? Dr. Lawson was dead, killed by the influenza. Everyone in the world was dying in this modern plague time—society's high and mighty and its dregs, the saints and the sinners.

He peered out the window through the oak and silver poplar leaves whose sharply defined edges seemed to reduce the street below to miniature. In the dusk, no one sat on a front porch, drinking lemonade and stirring the oppressive, humid air with a funeral parlor fan. Three doors down, across the way, Baumer's Model T stood in the same spot at the curb it had occupied for two weeks. Kramer's wagon wasn't making a final grocery delivery for the day. No junkman was singing out "Rags-A-Lye-Own" in hopes of finding one more bit of copper or lead before he had to return his rented nag to the stable. No whistle of the peanut vendor's cart tried to catch customers on their way to Metz's Uptown Kinema. Not a child bicycling, rolling a hoop, racing an orange crate scooter.

No one.

Grove Corner was still. Only the sun moved, slowly, slowly, descending in the west, perhaps forever.

He realized he had been holding his breath, waiting, and when she did call again, he exhaled with the thick, gurgling sound of water swirling down a sluggish drain. Even as he told himself he would not go, he was struggling up from the chair, an effort that made his head spin.

He *had* to go to her, go to the demon child that had destroyed him. Harlot! The sluttishness was in her blood, the birthright of his whore sister.

She called herself a dancer, but he knew better. She'd done her dancing on her back in cheap rented rooms with her skirt up and a man between her thighs. And one of her "dancing partners" had planted his seed, a seed no less wanton than the whore womb that nurtured it, then spat it out to grow, to blossom into a lovely, poisonous flower.

He was dizzy. Halfway down the hall, the floor seemed to pitch and roll under his shuffling slippers. He reeled, tottering against the wall, bracing himself with a hand on the doorframe of the bedroom.

Her room! He peered inside. He seemed to see with unusual clarity and depth perception as though he were looking at a three-dimensional card in a stereopticon.

On the high dresser, gilded by the dying light, were some of the treasures she'd brought with her—a paperweight, a rose preserved for eternity inside a glass ball, and a white china doll, the figure of a seated little girl wearing a bonnet and holding a basket of eggs in her lap. On the washstand were her hairbrush, with a strand of hair curling up from the bristles, flaming in the light, and two vibrant green ribbons.

The room looked like a child's bedroom. The irony was not lost on him. A little girl—innocent, carefree, playful.

A lie! Deception!

Oh, she had been so clever, pretending to be his loving niece who wanted only to please him.

She was always wanting to sit on his lap. Kiss him goodnight. Would he tuck her in . . . *please*?

Gradually she became more brazen. Would Uncle scrub her back when she was in the tub, *please*? She needed help with her dress; she couldn't do all the buttons down the back. *Please*?

And he knew. Perhaps not from the first but from very near the first. He saw it. The way she gazed at him when she thought he was unaware; the knowledge—the desire—in her eyes, eyes that were too calculating and beckoning to be those of a child.

He knew. He heard the true meaning that lay under the words she spoke, words that might have passed for guileless prattle had he not listened so keenly.

And the way she walked, her hips as lazily sensual as a cat's.

And the way she pouted, lower lip thrust out, eyes downcast, long lashes veiling mystery and a pledge of wicked passion.

And even the way she yawned, not an indication of sleepiness but a lewd invitation.

He had known and had tried to resist, but it was useless.

She had won.

Again, he heard her call, tempting him, a siren's call.

She was calling him, and he would go to her.

As he had.

As he must.

She thought she was hungry, but she could not be sure. Her body no longer signaled its wants and needs as it should have. Broken inside, bleeding, her body was attuned solely to imminent death.

Her mind was not.

Naked, she lay on her side on a worn, woolen blanket, knees drawn up to ease the sharp, hot pains in her belly and chest. Her blonde hair was insanely tangled, glued to her forehead in spiky bangs by dried blood. She breathed in rasping, whistling sobs; her nose was crushed, lips swollen and crusted with scab as hard and shiny as a beetle's carapace. A green and purple dome of bruised flesh sealed her left eye shut.

She wondered how long it had been since she had eaten. She could remember Uncle bringing her food, but she didn't know when that had been. He'd brought her food and watched her eat, and for a little while it seemed like he wasn't mad at her anymore because he kept touching her face, calling her "My pretty little girl, so pretty . . ." But then he got angry, and he hit her and hit her and hit her.

She thought she heard something, someone moving up above.

Mama?

No. She had to tell herself once more that she would never again see Mama.

Now that her existence was comprised only of times of pain and times when her mind took flight, fleeing pain, she sometimes forgot Mama was gone. Sometimes it was as though Mama were still with her, here to take away the cold, lonely feeling and the hurting and the fear.

Sing Mama a song, my pretty Lisette, a funny song, one that will make us laugh like we don't have a worry in the world. Sing, Lisette, s'il vous plait.

Rufus! Rastus! Johnson Brown! Whatcha gonna do when the rent . . .

No, Lisette, that new song, the one about this silly old flu thing everyone's so afraid of!

> *There was a little bird*
> *An itty-bitty bird*
> *And his name was Enza!*

But her mama always went away. Mama had to go.

Mama was dead. She was really, really dead. It's terrible to die! I won't die! Not ever!

She heard the click of a door chain, then the sound of a key in a lock, a doorknob turning, the small, sharp screech of hinges, the hush and scrape of leather on wood.

She turned her head, and her one eye peered toward the stairs. She could not see legs or a face, only the ghostly gray white of the top of his union suit floating down through the blackness.

Uncle is coming.

She was afraid but maybe it would be all right now. Maybe he'd take her back upstairs where there was light—she missed the light so very much—and she would never be locked away again and he would never hit her again.

She would be a good girl, a good, good girl to make Uncle love her.

Certainly she had tried to be good, but in some way she did not understand, she had failed. Uncle wouldn't have punished her like this if she had been good.

Uncle will take care of you, Lisette. Mind your uncle, always do what he says. Love Uncle and he'll love you back, just like you were his own little girl.

That's what Mama had said before she died.

No! It was her silent shout against the actuality of her mother's death, against Death itself, against the death filling her up, advancing calmly and inevitably as the blood seeped within her, bypassing channels of life and taking routes through and around torn tissues.

"What do you want? What do you want now?" The voice drifted to her from faraway, but Uncle was close, so close she smelled the oily-brown smell of his slippers and his sweat—and a smell that she sensed was death.

Her tongue felt thick, and she could move her jaw only a little. Her lips were unable to shape a word.

"I know what you want. Lord God, look at me! You're still tempting me! Don't you see? Don't you know we're dying?"

No!

"We're dying, and the world is dying, and you're yet a harlot! Doesn't it end? Doesn't it ever end?"

No!

He squatted down alongside her. A hot dry finger stabbed her ribs. "Want Uncle to play a game with you? Want Uncle to touch you?"

The dim memories came to her, the times when he had touched her and kissed her, kissed her all over in a way that was like some strange kind of playing, a game she didn't understand but that made her giggle and feel warm and funny, and whatever he wanted her to do, she did, even when it hurt her deep inside. But that never seemed to make Uncle love her. He was almost always angry afterward, accusing her, "You're going to tell, aren't you? I know you are. You'll tell the world. I know. Don't lie to me."

I won't tell. Never tell. Not anyone. I promise, I promise.

He never believed her, and he just got angrier and angrier. "You made me do it, you know. You *made* me."

And then he would start hitting her, using his fists on her belly and back and face.

Uncle said, "Not this time. No!"

He rolled her onto her back. "Whore! Slut!" His hand covered her face, fingers spread like a wolf spider on top of a robin's egg. He smashed the back of her head against the floor again and again.

The bony bowl that held her brain shattered.

She was dying as he lurched up the stairs.

No!

The basement door opened and closed. The key clicked in the lock. The door chain metallically slithered.

She drew up her left leg and planted her foot flat.

Her right eye rolled back.

Her heart stopped.

She was dead.

One: *O Drom Le Ushalin*
THE WAY OF SHADOW

The vast body of Romany folk stories and myths, orally passed on from generation to generation, is called Darane Swature. *Like all classic myths, a* swato *is a fable that reveals* tshatsimo; *it tells the truth.*

Long ago, in the old days, the days of ever-golden summer, when the Gypsy caravans traveled the roads, proud horses pulling vurdons *as bright and festive as peacocks, Pola Janichka was regarded by the* Rom *as a gifted narrator of* Darane Swature. *Scarcely more than a child, she was not yet the* Rawnie, *the Great Lady who had the magical power to work all manner of* draba *charm, heal the sick, and even ward off* zracnae vila, *the malevolent spirits of the air. That came later. For the time being, it was enough for her to be able to relate a* swato *in a dramatically entertaining and instructive way.*

Late in the evenings, the kumpania *would gather around the campfire, and Pola Janichka would tell her* swato *to the attentive children, their dark eyes gleaming in the firelight, and to the men and the women.*

This is a swato *of Pola Janichka:*

"Once some people came to a great lake under the cold silver light of Chon, our Mother Moon. The lake was still. Not a bubble disturbed it, not a ripple. In the center of the lake, the reflection of Chon was a huge white ball.

"The shore on which the people stood was the end of the Earth. As we all know, the Earth belongs to the living.

"Beyond the Earth is the realm of the mule, *where the dead dwell.*

"But the lake was the Void, a place between the Nation of the Living and the Dead. Here you might find those souls who had not made the great journey anda l thema, *beyond the waters.*

"Suddenly, far out in the lake, in the center of the waters, something happened! It was a small splash, the very smallest of splashes, and it made the mirror image of Chon shimmer in its own light. The splash caused so soft a sound that you might have thought it made by a pebble, but that was not what did it.

"Could it have been the gentle brush of God's little finger, giving comfort to the dead? Or perhaps was it the breath of Beng, the Old Evil One? Or maybe it was a mulo, *the spirit of one of the dead deep in the lake? Ah, who is to say? Not I. I am a simple teller of stories.*

"Now, who among the people on the shore heard this tiny splash? I will tell you. Only those who had ears that could hear very, very well.

"*Then the tiny ripples rolled away from the reflected* Chon.

"*And who among the people saw these tiny, fluttering waves? I will tell you. Only those who had eyes that could see very, very well.*

Then the waves came to the shore and touched it with the softness of the fragile leg of a butterfly upon a flower.

"*And who among the people on the shore felt the waves touch the shore? I will tell you.*

"*Those who heard the splash and those who did not hear.*

"*Those who saw the waves and those who did not see.*

"*All the people on the shore felt the waves from the Void, the lake of the dead who have not passed on.*

"*As do we.*"

ONE

She was right on time for her 11:30 Monday morning appointment, and, as soon as she took the chair alongside his desk in the small office, she told him she didn't understand the assignment.

"What exactly is it you don't understand?" he asked. He arched an eyebrow. It seemed funny to him now that he was nearing 40 and his brown hair was receding to give him a marked widow's peak that his eyebrows were getting bushier.

"The assignment, you know," she said.

That narrowed it down, Warren Barringer thought. The assignment for Lit and Comp 101 was to read Thoreau's essay "Civil Disobedience" and to write a paper showing that Thoreau's ideas either did or did not apply to the 20th Century. The reading and writing parts obviously were beyond her.

Damn! Miss—what was her name? Only the second week of September, he hadn't begun to learn his students' names. He slipped on his reading glasses and checked the appointment book that lay open on the desk—Miss Luttemeyer, Ellen F. She was typical of the majority of students in his three sections of basic freshman English, typical, as he had to admit, of the students who attended North Central University.

Established 18 years ago, North Central University, some 50 miles south of Chicago in the middle-class suburb of Lawn Crest, was the product of state and federal misspending and the last gasp of the radical educational optimism that had marked the 1960s. When it first opened the doors of the single, huge, octagonal building that was its College of Arts and Sciences, College of Business, College of Education, College of American Studies, etc., it had two basic admission requirements. A prospective student had to be able to prove he was alive and could somehow manage to pay the tuition. Since then, of course, with the end of the education boom and the realization on the part of accreditation committees that NCU was awarding degrees to people who were not quite critically retarded, things had changed. Still, the students who enrolled in NCU were, by and large, not exactly Harvard, Yale or Brown material.

And he was stuck with the dregs of the dregs, Warren reflected, the low man on the departmental totem pole. He was new this term, without a dime's worth of seniority. His doctorate—earned at the University of Iowa's famed Writers Workshop, no less!—and his publications—the three dozen plus short stories, the two novels, read by perhaps twice that number of people—didn't mean a goddamned thing.

Well, that would change, once *A Civilized Man* was published.

"So do you think maybe, you know, you could kind of help me," Miss Luttemeyer was saying.

He studied her face, as round and expressionless as a cream pie. Help her, he thought, perhaps a brain transplant.

"Read the essay several times," he said.

"I'll try," she said, "but I don't know, a lot of it is, well, kinda confusing."

"Just take it slow," he said. "I'm sure you'll get it."

He pushed his chair back on its rollers and rose. She didn't get the message; he had to gesture at the door. "Miss Luttemeyer, why don't you get to work on it and then, when you have a rough draft of your theme, you can bring it in and we'll take a look together. I'm sure you'll have fine ideas."

Fine ideas? He was sure that if she ever had even one idea it would be a first.

"I don't know, I don't know," she kept saying as he showed her out.

"Jesus," he said, after he'd shut the door. What was he doing here at North Central U, anyway? (Why, Warren, you're doing your time on the cross, pal, and paying those dues. You know every great American writer has to suffer!)

Hell, he was being self-pityingly melodramatic, and he knew it. To tell the truth, he was doing all right. Okay, NCU wasn't Oxford, but he had a job, and there were plenty of Liberal Arts PhDs who couldn't make that claim. And Missy—he loved that kid, *his* child. And Vicki—well, she'd stuck with him through the bad times.

All right, there'd been rough waters, and, he had to admit, he bore much of the responsibility for setting them churning, but his life was on an even keel at last, and there was *A Civilized Man*. The novel was going well. It would do for him what *The World According to Garp* had done for

John Irving. It would be his new start.

And as long as he was balancing his personal books, you could add the house to the "Credit" side of the ledger, that old house on Main Street in Grove Corner. Years ago he had read a poem called "Coming Home To A Place You've Never Been," but it had taken that house, to teach him just what that title meant.

Warren took off his glasses, put them in the case and checked his watch. It was nearly noon, and his next class was at two. Time for lunch.

He'd made the mistake of eating in NCU's cafeteria once. He didn't care for egg shell salad sandwiches or coffee that tasted like Mazola oil. He'd go to Milly's Family Restaurant in Grove Corner—Grove Corner, his home, he thought with a smile—only five miles away. Milly's had good food, and he liked that he was getting known as a regular. "Hello, Professor, and how are you today? Coffee? Or would you like something from the bar?"

"Coffee," was what he always said though he always would have liked something from the bar. But that was a problem that was no longer a problem; he was in control. At night, a drink or two after he'd finished working on the book, when he really needed to unwind, and that was it,

To get to the faculty parking lot, he had to pass the art gallery on the main floor. First he saw the posters: *Photographs by David Greenfield*, and then he saw the black and white photographs on the walls, and then he saw David Greenfield.

You sonofabitch, Warren Barringer thought. There was a heavy weight in his stomach like a boulder. How had he missed hearing that Greenfield would be exhibiting at NCU?

Encircled by a dozen or so students, a number of which had cameras dangling from their necks, David Greenfield, in blue jeans and a black, short-sleeved knit shirt, stood at the far end of the gallery. Just under six foot tall, he was a lean, dark man with curly black hair; there were deep squint crinkles at the corners of his intense, anthracite eyes.

He looked like a blow-dried Clark Gable, Warren Barringer thought, Mr. Rhett Butler himself, ready to sweep Scarlett off her feet, up the stairs, and into bed—Scarlett or any other woman. Warren saw Greenfield smile at a young lady who'd apparently asked him a question, a Marlboro man smile without any discoloring tobacco stains on those straight white teeth to shatter the image.

Show him what you're made of, Warren thought.

He knows what you're made of—chickenshit, through and through.

Warren Barringer walked to the far end of the gallery. "Excuse me," he said, and a young man, interrupted in the middle of a question about backlighting, stepped aside.

"Warren," David Greenfield said.

"Hello, David," Warren said, and then he held out his hand.

(And why are you greeting this sonofabitch? Because you've got to do the right thing, that's why. Because if you don't, because if you do what you want to do, do what you really honest to God feel, that lets the monster out, and then, oh brother, you are really fucked. And so you shake hands and you turn the other cheek and bygones are bygones and the world keeps on spinning.)

David said, "Are you teaching here?"

Warren nodded. "First year," he said. "Assistant professor."

"I see," David said.

"I read about you over the years," Warren said. "You seem to be doing well."

There had been two full pages in *Time* magazine's "Art section" a few years ago. Warren had seen that—two pages in *Time*, for Christ's sake! "The mature work of a photographer whose stark simplicity provides memorable insights into all the aspects of the human condition blah-blah-blah." David Greenfield was likely to attain the prominence of an Ansel Adams or a Diane Arbus.

David shrugged. "I'm doing all right. I like my work."

"Good," Warren said. There was a long pause. For a moment, Warren was afraid David would say, "And how's Vicki?" or something like that.

He didn't.

"Well," Warren said, "you've got people who want to talk with you. I have to be on my way." And then, once more, he held out his hand.

When he got to Milly's Family Restaurant, Warren was shown to his usual corner booth. "How are you doing today, Professor?" the waitress asked. He said all right. She asked if he wanted coffee or something from the bar.

He ordered a Bloody Mary.

TWO

In its typically facile style, the *People* magazine story related the problems and pressures of the author of a first novel that had zoomed onto the bestseller charts. In the accompanying pictures, one showing him aboard his newly purchased cabin cruiser, another relaxing in the Jacuzzi with his live-in lover, an aspiring actress and certified acupuncturist, he looked neither pressured nor problem plagued.

And why, Vicki Barringer wondered, did *People* never print articles on the authors of smash flops—authors like her husband.

At 32, Vicki Barringer, slightly built and fair, her short hair a curling halo framing her oval face, looked her age, neither more nor less, and it was an age that suited her. She'd felt awkward throughout most of her 20s and knew that people thought of her as pleasant-looking and wholesome in an era in which chic and trendy were the style of youth. In one of his drunken outpourings of sarcastic bile, Warren had told her, "You look like you stepped out of a Norman Rockwell painting of a PTA meeting. You're the second assistant hospitality hostess, holding a paper cup of lukewarm punch and scared shitless that no one will like the chocolate chip cookies you baked." At that time she'd been so hurt that, though she rarely swore, one of the few welcome remnants from the strict religious upbringing she'd tried to reject, she yelled at Warren, calling him a "drunken asshole dumb bastard fart." That made him shake his head. "Jesus, you even swear like Betty Crocker."

Vicki had come to a time in her life and a state of mind that made her comfortable with her pleasant-looking and wholesome self. And, she'd recently reflected, she was perfect for Grove Corner, a town that Norman Rockwell *could* have used as the inspiration for a thousand *Saturday Evening Post* covers.

She dropped the magazine to the floor at the side of the brown suede chair. It was only 9:30, but she was tired, though not unpleasantly so. It had been a good day, her first on the job at Blossom Time, the florist shop. Afterward she'd raced home to be there when Missy got out of school. Now Vicki felt too logy to take the three steps to bed or even to reach up and turn out the lamp.

She leaned back her head and closed her eyes. Her quilted housecoat felt snuggly warm, a grownup's security blanket, and soon she was floating in the dusky limbo between sleep and wakefulness. Centering her attention on the beat of her heart, Vicki was contentedly at rest. It was even better than the heaviness of sleep, this airy sensation of well-being.

She could barely hear the distant tapping of the typewriter as, downstairs in his study, Warren worked on the book. Good. She'd been concerned about him today. He'd come home from the university at 6:00, with absolutely nothing to say, and had been just as uncommunicative all through a dinner which he hardly touched. Past experience had taught her that his heavy silences were too often a prelude to heavier rages, furies fueled by hard drinking. After supper, he'd gone straight to the study and closed the door, locking himself and his silence away from her and Missy.

But in the past hour, Vicki had heard first the tentative clicks and then the rhythmic tapping of his typewriter. Warren was writing, and that meant everything was okay.

The drinking and the hateful, hurtful arguments that were not disagreements but emotional demolition derbies were all in the past. She could wave goodbye to the past and thumb her nose at it, too! This house was good for Warren, good for the three of them. The old house on Main Street, oldest still standing in Grove Corner, with its sun parlor and a living room as big as a used car lot and the magnificent oak and silver poplar trees all around was their home.

As for the past, all right, she had not been blameless. She had been foolish—not just foolish but stupid. All right, stupid and bad and wicked. Unfaithful. Sinful. No! That word, the heavy, hissing weight of it, the guilt that went beyond guilt, belonged to her childhood, to another time and place, another world. That was her parents' world, but her parents were dead, and it was still her sister's world, her sister Carol Grace who'd married evangelist Evan Kyle Dean, but her sister was a stranger.

Goodbye to the past.

The past was over and finished and done.

On the swirling purple screen of her eyelids, a red rose appeared. It was a memory, the first sale she'd made on this first day at work. "One red rose, please." The customer was an old man with a plaid cap and, as he explained, the need for a peace offering. "The wife and I had a spat, and this should put me back in her good graces."

In her relaxed state, it was easy for Vicki to think of the single rose as an omen of the future. The future was a bright flower, open and inviting. No more trouble with *the* problem. "All writers drink too much, especially if they're stuck with someone as insensitive as you." No more trouble, not *this* time at *this* school. "Bastards denied me tenure. They don't want you around if your mind isn't as fossilized as theirs!"

Mama?

Vicki thought that without realizing it she had crossed the borderline and slipped into slumber and dream. It was a dream voice she was hearing.

Mama!

Blinking, hands on the arms of the chair, she sat up, listening.

Mama? Missy hadn't called her that since playpen and pacifier days. "Mom." Once in a while "Mommy," if Missy craved an extra dose of TLC or was trying to wheedle an extra half-hour until bedtime.

All Vicki heard was Warren's typewriter. No, it couldn't have been "Mama" from that big girl of seven who wasn't afraid of anything as long as the nightlight shone and she had Winnie-the-Pooh.

So it was a dream then.

Still, it wouldn't hurt to check.

Vicki went down the hall, her steps sure even without a light in the house she already felt to be truly their home. She opened the door to Missy's room.

In the outlet above the baseboard, between Missy's table and chair set and the walk-in closet, the plastic face of Mickey Mouse glowed a cheerful pink greeting.

When Vicki stepped over the threshold, she felt the cold.

It had been a warm day, not even hinting at the approach of autumn, and so Missy must have left a window open and now, with a sudden change in the weather, so often the case in the midwest . . .

Both windows were shut.

It didn't make sense, this penetrating chill. Even if the temperature had drastically dropped, the house had new insulation, less than two years-old, the real estate agent had told them, a real energy saver, part of the extensive renovation done by the previous owners. "They didn't have kids, you see, and so they kind of treated the place like their baby." They had central air conditioning, a new furnace, modernized plumbing, new wiring, dropped ceilings, paneled basement family room and no-wax kitchen floors.

But Missy's bedroom was freezing, and, as usual, Missy had waged her nightly war with the covers. They lay in a heap at the side of the bed, Winnie-the-Pooh face down on top.

Vicki went to set things right.

"Mom?"

The stuffed bear fell from Vicki's hand. Then she smiled as a giggling Missy popped up like a Jack-in-the box and swung around to dangle her bare legs off the bed. Missy hated pajamas and insisted on sleeping in her underwear. A thin child and pale—she never tanned—she seemed almost ethereal, as though with blonde hair cascading down her back, she had just slid down a moonbeam from a fairy tale land to the Earth.

Vicki said, "And why are you awake?"

"'Cause I'm not asleep."

"Hmm, that makes sense."

Vicki sat down beside her, slipping an arm around her narrow shoulders. "Aren't you chilly, honey?" Even as she said it, Vicki realized the room was not cold anymore. Then she thought she understood. She had been awakened from sleep by the call for "Mama" she thought she'd heard, and so it took a while for your circulation to get going, for your internal thermostat to adjust.

"I'm not chilly," Missy said. "I'm horny."

The word jolted Vicki. Oh, it wasn't as bad as the Ugly Awful "F" word that Missy, with her first grade reading skills, had learned from a public washroom wall a year ago, but it wasn't anything Vicki wanted her daughter saying.

Quietly, Vicki asked, "Do you know what that means?"

"What? Horny?" Missy tapped herself on the forehead. "Like I have a horn or something, I guess."

"Wrong."

"I don't know. This kid was yelling it in the playground today. He's a big fat slob. He's in fourth grade."

"I see."

Missy said, "So what does horny mean, Mom?"

Every book Vicki had ever read on how to

raise happy, normal, gifted, intelligent, sensitive, well-adjusted, non-homicidal/suicidal children offered virtually the same advice about these situations—tell the truth. Then, in terms the child could understand, you explained that certain words were considered vulgar by many people and why they were not to be used.

Vicki, however, had her own way of dealing with this, one with which she was much more comfortable. "Never mind what it means. It's a dirty word. Don't use it."

"Why?"

"Because I said so."

"You never explain anything to me."

"Check back with me in twenty years. I'll explain then."

"That's a long time."

"Okay, forty years."

"Mom!" Missy squeaked in outrage.

Vicki said, "How about I tuck you in and you go on back to sleep?"

"Uh-uh," Missy said. "I'm really a whole lot awake." She tugged at Vicki's sleeve. "Mom, you want to hear a joke?"

Vicki was used to a seven year old's way of changing the subject. In a three-minute conversation, Missy was likely to cover a half a dozen subjects.

"Is it a good joke?"

"Awesome," Missy said. "What's green and throws rocks?"

"A green rock-thrower?"

"No. Give up?"

"Sure do."

"A lawn. I lied about the rocks."

"That's some joke, all right," Vicki said. "That's a fine note of comedy for you to go to sleep on."

"Hey, I learned a new song. Want to hear it?"

"They taught you a new song at school?"

"No. Not at school. Listen!"

Missy followed an elastically flexible melody set to no fixed rhythm. Her voice was as thin as she was but oddly plaintive.

The song of a lost child, Vicki found herself thinking, and wondered why she thought that.

> *There was a little bird,*
> *An itty-bitty bird,*
> *And his name was Enza!*
> *I opened up a window,*
> *And in he flew!*
> *In! Flew! Enza!*

Vicki lightly applauded. "That's some song, Missy. They don't write them like that anymore."

"Did you like it?"

"Sure did."

"Want me to sing it again?"

"Sing it in your dreams," Vicki said. "Time to take the trail to sleepy town." She rose.

"Aw, Mom!" Missy whined. "I want to stay up!"

"I guess you are chilly after all," Vicki said. "Your behind must be, anyway, because you're acting like you want me to warm it for you."

Missy sniffed indignantly. "I get it!" She stretched herself out on her back and lay as rigid as a plank.

In a moment, Vicki had both Missy and Pooh under the covers.

"You are very mean to me," Missy said.

"I try. Kiss?"

Missy took a second to ponder the question of a kiss for a very mean mother. "I guess."

Vicki kissed the child's warm cheek. The brush of lips she received in return was perfunctory, but was followed a moment later by, "I love you anyhow."

"I love you too, Missy," Vicki said. "Sleep well."

She stood watching her daughter as Missy, eyes closed, rolled on her side and curled up, and then she started toward the door. A gleam of light winked up from the floor, slipping just inside the peripheral boundary of her vision.

It lay on the carpet, Mickey Mouse's nightlight nose pointing at it.

A rose, she thought, picking it up. The round glass paperweight rested on the flattened base of her palm.

She had never seen the paperweight before and wondered where Missy had gotten it. She couldn't ask. The little girl who'd been "a whole lot awake" was already sound asleep. Perhaps this was a keepsake overlooked by the house's previous owners when they were packing.

Whatever, Vicki Barringer did not like the paperweight. That was a feeling she had, not a thought. Sealed in the glass globe, the flower seemed a mockery of what was once alive, as insulting to life as a corpse too perfectly made up by a zealously artistic mortician.

She put the paperweight on Missy's table. In the master bedroom, Vicki went back to *People* magazine but soon discovered she was reading words without comprehending.

Somehow her feeling of optimism, of the future's glowing promise, was gone. Her mind was strangely burdened by ponderous thoughts of life and death.

And of a rose.

THREE

Look at it! He cranked page 68 out of the typewriter, the wrap-up of the dentist office scene, and read it aloud, in a low, flat voice, trying to keep his tone objective:

> Mitchell's eyes crossed as the needle approached, and he braced himself for the pain. But it wasn't so bad, not so bad that he couldn't bear it.
> And it came to him then in a moment of drifting lucidity brought on by the ocean-ic rushing of the nitrous oxide he'd been inhaling that his entire life had been the lengthy learning of pain acceptance, that he could now withstand any pain, bear up and get on, continue with a brute perseverance to live.

Yes, that was writing! That was solid. That was revelation and insight captured in words, and he, by God, he Warren Barringer, author, had written those words.

Not that it had been easy. Writing was never easy. It was racking your brain to find the right word, then struggling to find the right word to follow it, then hammering your mind still more to find the next right word—and the next and the next and the next.

Damn, he was writing well, better than he had ever written.

The house!

The thought came to him with stunning ice-blue clarity. Tense with concentration, he'd been hunched forward at the edge of his chair but now he slouched.

The house itself was helping him. It was the source of this new self-confidence, the feeling of inevitable achievement and accomplishment.

The house was right for him. Here he would become all he wanted to be, all he was meant to be. The house was imbued with a spirit that had summoned him here to his rightful place, as the sea had once beckoned Herman Melville.

Warren smiled to himself. He was being quite ridiculous and grandiose. A house was a house was a house.

Except the typewriter on his cluttered desk was not a typewriter; it was *his* typewriter. The green portable manual, an Underwood circa 1959, noisy as hell, was the typewriter he'd used to write the very first short stories, years ago, the machine which had produced his two novels, *Fishing With Live Bait* and *The Endurance of Lynn Tomer*. Certainly he could have afforded a new electronic typewriter or, the way prices were dropping every month, even a word processing computer, but he felt emotionally and spiritually linked to the Underwood. Call it superstition, but Warren Barringer considered it gut level intuition.

And he trusted his intuition because he was a writer!

A writer, by Christ!

A Civilized Man was going to be a masterpiece. And if not? If the book got bad reviews?

Warren Barringer was prepared for the future.

He pushed back the chair and opened the right hand desk drawer.

He didn't take out the gun, a loaded .25 caliber automatic. He just wanted to make sure it was there.

The gun was his secret, unregistered, bought from a lowlife he'd met in a lowlife bar during one of his lowlife bad spells. If he were forced to, if choice no longer existed for him, then he had the gun to put a final exclamation point to an intolerable life.

But hell, he had no reason to think this way, not now, not when *A Civilized Man* was shaping up so beautifully.

Warren slammed the drawer.

He checked his watch and was surprised to see that it was 11:45. When the writing was going well, he lost all track of time. He'd done enough for tonight. It was wrong to push it.

It was time for a drink. He'd earned a reward.

Drink number three, the nightcapper, so he could shut his eyes without his eyelids vibrating like the head of a snare drum. Only drink number three tonight, never more than drink number three in a day—Uh, what about that noontime Bloody Mary? That was different. There was a reason, so it didn't count, all right? He was okay. He was doing fine. He had control.

He shut off the lights in his study and went down to the basement rec room. At the bar, he poured a shot of Johnny Walker Black into a highball glass. He plopped in two ice cubes from the freezer of the half-sized refrigerator under the counter.

He was about to add water but, three drinks a night, no harm in making the last one potent enough to not only take off the rough edge but to sand it down fine. Another full shot of Johnny Walker, then a splash of water, and he had a drink worth drinking.

It warmed his belly and immediately began to relax him, and as he drank, he seemed to feel the house—*my house*—all around him. Ten minutes later, the glass held only two melting ice pellets. He thought about another drink. One more wouldn't hurt.

Warren smiled. Uh-uh. He had will power. He was in control. He rinsed the glass and left it in the stainless steel sink.

On the main floor, he checked to see the doors were locked. The bannister guided him up the long flight of stairs to the second floor.

Passing the door of Missy's room, he thought he heard her call.

Drink of water? Nighttime tummy ache? A dream?

He opened the door.

The covers were on the floor. Close to the edge, Missy lay on her stomach, an arm hanging off the bed. Her head was turned, no longer on the pillow where her Winnie-the-Pooh bear lay alone. In the dim glow of the nightlight, her slender legs seemed made of ivory.

She was sound asleep. He didn't want to wake her, but he couldn't let her stay as she was; she could so easily fall out of bed.

He moved her gently onto her back in the

center of the bed and covered her.

He straightened. Missy sat up.

"Hi," he said.

She didn't answer. She looked at him. Her eyes were big.

She was asleep with her eyes open, Warren thought. His realization that she was beautiful came with that familiar feeling of delighted amazement that he'd so often had, and he wondered if every father felt like this about his kid. Missy was Tinker Bell and Alice-In-Wonderland and Alpine Heidi. There were times it was hard to believe this lovely little girl was his, his and Vicki's, the miraculous result of biology, blind chance and genetic patterns.

Missy's lips moved soundlessly.

"What's that, baby?"

She mumbled. He made out only two words. "Love . . . you . . ."

"Love you, too. Go back to sleep now, Missy," he said. He touched her shoulder, lightly pushing her back onto the pillow. "That's the girl."

She smiled.

"She loves you," Missy said.

She closed her eyes.

FOUR

Melissa?

Melissa . . . Melissa!

Hey, go away and leave me alone 'cause I'm asleep and anyway, nobody calls me Melissa. I told you that. Melissa is nerdy. It's Missy.

I like Melissa better. It sounds like my name, Lisettte.

Well, it is not your name, Lisette. That's cause I'm me and you're you. And besides, you're not even real.

I am real, Melissa.

No, you're just imaginary, like an imaginary friend. I knew this girl in kindergarten and she had an imaginary friend just like you that wasn't real. Everyone thought she was real loony tunes.

You can see me, Melissa. That means I'm not imaginary.

I can see you but you look real weird, kind of like you're not even really here. And your clothes are so funny. They're like old-timey, like in a movie or something.

You're being mean, Melissa. Don't be mean to me. I'm lonely. I'm always so lonely.

Phooey!

I need you, Melissa. And I'm nice to you. Didn't I teach you a funny song? And didn't I give you a present?

Yeah.

Isn't the paperweight pretty? Don't you like the rose?

I guess it's pretty neat.

I have other gifts for you. You can have them if you'll be my friend.

I don't know. Dorothy at school said she'd be my friend. I asked her. Amy Lynn, too, and she's got her own playhouse in her backyard. They're nice, and they're real. They're not imaginary like you.

Melissa, you're making me sad. I'm so lonely.

Hey, stop crying, okay? I don't want to make you cry.

Mama?

Where is your mother anyway? You're always crying for her like a big dumb baby.

Mama's not here. It's just me here, and I'm so lonely.

Will you stop crying, huh?

Mama?

Just stop it. You can be my friend. You be my friend, and I'll be yours.

Do you mean it?

Sure, I do.

Really and truly mean it?

Yeah. Cross my heart and hope to die.

I'm happy now, Melissa.

If you want, you can give me more presents. And I'll tell you what, I'll give you presents, too, 'cause you're my friend.

Yes.

Should I give you a Strawberry Shortcake sticker? I have lots of 'em. They're fun.

No.

Well, what do you want? What kind of present?

You're pretty, Melissa. I like your hair and your eyes and your ears and your nose and your mouth. I like your arms and your legs.

You're being silly. Come on, what kind of present should I give you?

Your pretty hair. Maybe one, just one hair?

Phooey! That's stupid! What a dumb present. You're just being silly!

No.

Hey, I can be silly too, you know. I know something real silly. And it's dirty, too. Want to hear?

Yes.

I'm horny. Are you horny? Isn't that funny?

Is it?

Sure, I think so. Anyhow, I guess we're friends, okay?

Yes, and now I want you to let me have one of your hairs.

Well, take it.

I will.

Hey! That hurt.

We're friends now, Melissa. You and I.

Always?

Always, Melissa, always.

FIVE

"**H**ow has it been going for you?"

At ten o'clock Tuesday morning, in an office on the eighth floor of the Hamlin Building on Michigan Avenue, Kristin Heidmann sat in a Danish modern arm chair, chewing gum and saying nothing. Her hair, bleached blonde, dyed red and black, was a spiky punk nightmare that might have been the comb of a prehistoric rooster. Her lower lip was painted blue, the upper carmine. Though she had on a light blue dress that her parents had ordered her to wear, the smirk on her face and even her posture were a defiance not of any authority in particular but of the existing order, no matter what that order might be.

"Nothing you feel like talking about today, Kris?"

Kris popped her gum.

Kristin Heidmann was 14. When she was 12, she'd run away from the Malling Academy, an exclusive boarding school where she had been on the high honor roll, and hitchhiked to Los Angeles, where she became a prostitute.

"Look," Selena Lazone said, "if we're going to get anywhere working together, you're going to have to do your part." Seated in a matching chair, angled so that her clients could look at her or not as they chose, Selena tapped her ballpoint pen on the pad of paper on the clipboard on her lap.

A tall woman, with the slender toned grace of a dancer, Selena Lazone was 28 and had two masters degrees, one in social work, the other in psychology; she planned next summer to begin working on her PhD at the University of Chicago. Until she was 15 she had been completely illiterate.

Kristin glared at her.

"Let's try it another way," Selena said. "This is our fifth visit and nothing is happening. Next week your parents are going to want a progress report, and I'll have to say 'No progress.' Then they'll do what they planned in the first place— lock you away in a private sanitarium where you'll be under 24 hour observation. You'll have to ask every time you need to go to the bathroom. How does that sound to you, Kris?"

Kristin shrugged. In a breathy monotone, she said, "So I can always run away again."

"Uh-uh." Selena shook her head. "You won't even see the outside, let alone have a chance to get there. You work with me or that's what will happen, and you know it."

"Okay, okay."

"Okay, what?"

"Okay, so you want to talk, so okay, I'll talk."

"Fine," Selena said. "Talk."

"About what?"

"You, Kris. The subject is Kristin Heidmann. What makes you happy. What makes you sad."

"You know what makes me happy? Fucking. That's why I started turning tricks, you know. I like to fuck. Is that what you want me to talk about?" She glared at Selena.

Selena frowned. With her high cheekbones, burnished gold complexion, and features that were more rightly called noble than beautiful, she seemed to be registering almost regal displeasure. Several years before, a drunken advertising account executive at a party had tried to make a move on her with, "You remind me of a wild Gypsy princess." She had told him, "I'm no princess."

She *was* a Gypsy.

"Is that what you want to talk about?" Selena said.

"I don't give a shit."

"What does matter to you?"

"Nothing," Kris said.

"Then let's talk about this. You're unhappy," Selena said. "You're miserable. You're hurting and you think you're the lowest, most worthless creature that ever got up in the morning or went to bed at night."

"Bullshit."

"No," Selena said, "the truth, and we both know it." *Tshatsimo*, she thought; the Romany word meant "truth" and a great deal more than that. Though much was lost in translation, *tshatsimo* meant "that which truly is, the Great Truth to be found even under black lies, white lies, seeming truths and little truths."

"You don't know anything about me!" Kristin raged. "What the hell do you think you know, anyway?"

"I know girls who feel good about themselves

don't run away and become prostitutes," Selena Lazone said.

"I told you I like fucking!"

"And I know girls who feel good about themselves," Selena continued evenly, "don't try this." She reached out, tightly encircled Kristin's left wrist and turned the girl's hand over. Kristin's fingers shot up like the legs of a dying spider. Running along the blue veins on the underside of her wrist were two reddish, puckered scars—a serious suicide attempt.

The child's face turned white, and a sheen of tears glazed her eyes.

And Selena Lazone froze.

She understood.

But no, not this way, she thought. She was a psychologist, a scientist, not a *cohalyi*. Not an *ababina*. Not a *gule romni*! A psychologist—not a witch or a sorceress.

"You're . . . hurting me," Kristin said in a pinched voice, as she struggled to pull free of Selena's grip.

Hurting her, Selena thought as she turned loose the girl's wrist. Nearly all of Kristin Heidmann's life had been a hurting, and if Kristin were ever to escape that all-encompassing, enveloping pain, then paradoxically there would have to be still more hurting—and it would have to begin now.

But now she could do something for Kristin; she could help her. She had the tool to crack the girl's emotional and psychic armor, and it didn't matter how that tool had been placed in her hand.

That's what Selena tried to tell her herself, but she was still afraid.

Quietly, Selena said, "Tell me about Poppy."

Kristin's jaw dropped. Beneath her teary left eye, there was a fluttery tic. "You don't know. You can't!" she whispered.

But Selena Lazone did know, of course. *Dukkeripin*, the Gypsies called it—ESP, the sixth sense, psychometry, the terms employed by investigators of psychic phenomena. She was the seventh daughter of a seventh daughter, born with a caul over her face, and so *dukkeripin*, this way of knowing that did not rely on the rational senses, was her birthright, one that she'd rejected, part of a life she had fled. But her powers of *dukkeripin* had been dormant for years and years; a talent not used, not even wanted, is a talent that atrophies and dies. That is what she had believed, what she had so fervently hoped.

"You cannot run faster than your shadow" was what old Pola Janichka had taught her. *Tshatsimo*, Romany truth.

"Poppy," Selena insisted. "Your grandfather. You loved him."

Kristin nodded. "He was always making jokes. He kept saying stuff like about how I had to eat mashed potatoes because that would put hair on my chest. He used to take me fishing . . ." Kristin fell silent.

"The first time," Selena said, "you were six years old, staying with Poppy and your grandmother."

Kris nodded, then she exploded. "No, I promised. I said I would never tell. I promised Poppy."

"It's time to break that promise, Kristin. You have to. Your grandfather was wrong, wrong to make you promise that and wrong to do what he did. You were a little girl, Kris, a baby, and you loved him and trusted him and he took advantage of that."

"Poppy wasn't a bad man."

"Maybe not, Kris, but he did bad things to you."

"But it was my fault. I made him! He told me it was my fault!"

"Wrong, Kris. You were a victim. You were the good little girl who did what her Poppy told her, what he made you do. And until we talk about it, get it out in the open so that you can start seeing it all for what it really was, you're going to keep on being a victim."

Head down, Kristin sobbed dryly.

"Kristin," Selena said gently, "trust me."

It all came out then, with explosive bursts of tears and gurgled sobs. Kristin's story of being sexually abused could have been an archetypical case study from a psychology textbook, Selena thought. "Kristin H's grandfather introduced her to 'our secret game,' sexually fondling her, having her fondle him. When she was nine, Kristin H's grandfather had intercourse with her. She recalls the experience as being painful." No, Selena thought, nothing unusual about what had happened to Kristin Heidmann, nor about the emotional toll it had taken—not unusual, only terrible.

The hour came to an end with the girl saying, "That's it, I guess, all of it." She sniffled, having run out of tears.

No, Selena thought, this was only the beginning, but it was a real beginning.

"So," Kristin said, "do you think . . . can you help me?"

"Yes," Selena said. Kristin Heidmann had to believe that she could be helped, and, for that matter, so did Selena if she were to aid the girl. "I'm sure I can help you," Selena said, "and I will."

And she wished she could be so positive that she'd be able to help herself.

A bath and two glasses of chablis had not relaxed her. In a green velour lounging robe, she stood gazing from the picture window at serene Lake Michigan, a view that boosted the Lake Shore Drive apartment's rent a hundred dollars above those on the opposite side of the building.

For the thousandth time, she wished David were here, but he wouldn't be in until late. He was working hard, taking pictures for the new collection that would be published as *The Blues In Black and White*.

Selena didn't want to be alone with the past that threatened to enfold her, to become the present.

Her stomach rumbled. She realized that she had not eaten since breakfast, and it was now nearly eight o'clock.

She'd fix something light, an omelet, and then sip wine until she could fall asleep.

In the kitchen, she cracked an egg into a mixing bowl, then another.

The yolk of the second egg plopped into the bowl and staining its center was blood, a blob of deep red the size of the nail on the little finger, a clotty, mucusy mass that was a face, a face with a piglike snout and demonic, close-set tiny eyes, and a twisted mouth.

It was a miniature face from hell, and it was an omen.

"*Diakka!*" Selena screamed.

SIX

Invisible steel arrows, the notes from King Pemberton's Gibson electric guitar shot through the smoke and alcohol redolent fog, each arrow aimed straight at your soul, each a bulls-eye. On the small stage, King Pemberton leaned away from the microphone, as though he needed no electronic amplification. He was a gut-shouter, a huge black block of a man, and maybe he was 65, or maybe 75, or maybe a few years younger than Methuselah (he'd recorded 87 albums and never offered the same year of birth for the liner notes on any two of them!), but he hadn't lost a thing. Just the same as when he cut his first sides in the mid-thirties, King Pemberton could still wail and moan and holler and come at you full force.

It was one in the morning, the final set at Big Red's Stony Island Lounge and Nightclub.

At the table directly in front of the bandstand, a man raised his Nikon and sighted through the view finder. He was the only white person in the club, likely the only one within ten square blocks. He had no sense of not belonging here because he had no sense of belonging anywhere.

It was a strange thing. When he had his eye to the camera, he often thought of himself as invisible. He disappeared, ceased to be. There was only the camera, of itself impersonally re-cording reality without even the most subtle comment or imposition of viewpoint from the man behind the lens.

When he was taking pictures, he often felt he did not exist. No less often, he felt that when he was not taking pictures.

He zoomed in tight on King Pemberton's face to catch the glittering beads of sweat rolling down that black skin. He triggered the shutter, the auto-advance, tick-tick, zipping the film along at two frames a second.

Not yet, not yet, but we're coming up to it, he thought, his photographer's gift of seeing be-coming more acute by the moment. There were preliminaries, of course; you had to shoot frame after frame, and all those pictures would go from developing tank to wastebasket, but they were an essential part of the ritual leading up to *the* picture.

Tick-tick, tick-tick, two frames a second. The glint of light off King Pemberton's gold tooth. The moment when an eyelid began its descent in a "let's share the secret" wink. The brief self-satisfied nod at an explosive flurry of treble notes.

And there it was, there it was. He had it! King Pemberton, the Blues Man, no sham, no pre-tense, nothing of the self-willed mask people create and wear to protect their most secret selves from the hurts of the world, tiny and great. This was a nakedly honest face, the face of a man who could boldly declare, "I know who I am."

That face was *The Blues in Black and White*, and it would probably be the cover photograph for the collection of pictures.

The man with the camera had no doubt. He had a photo that was *tshatsimo*, the truth.

Selena Lazone had tried to drink wine until she passed out, but long before that, she hit the stage in which her choking tears erupted, and for five straight minutes she had lain on the sofa, sobbing and moaning and hugging herself. After that came an attack of the hiccups, then a staggering rush to the bathroom to vomit her way back to near-sobriety.

It was after three in the morning, and she felt like hell and terribly alone. All the living room lights were on, as though she could defy darkness and any of its manifestations merely by flipping a switch. On the stereo, WFMT, Chicago's fine arts station, played a Bach fugue for string quartet. She'd hoped the precise, eminently rational baroque music would offer subtle comfort, a promise that the universe was structured and meticulously arranged, a puzzle, perhaps, but a puzzle with pieces you could identify and fit together until a sensible pattern could be discerned.

But the universe was mad and malign and never before had she felt so alone in it.

Where was David? She needed him.

Selena went to the window and for the thousandth time gazed out. The sliver of the moon scattered pinpoints of light that rode the peaks of Lake Michigan's waves.

Where was he? She loved him.

Not that she wanted to. She had promised David Greenfield she would not love him. That would tip the delicate balances of their sensible relationship; after all, he did not love her, could not.

But David Greenfield understood her, perhaps even better than she understood herself. He knew Gypsies and had been raised by them, growing up among the people of *tacho rat*, true blood—with them, but not one of them. His first major collection of photographs was the prize-winning study of Gypsies entitled *Rom*. David knew who she had been, what she had been, knew why she had split herself off from that person and her people to recreate herself as an entirely new individual, one who had a meaningful place in the *Gaje* world.

She did not hear his key in the door. A moment later, though, when he stepped into the living room, she sensed him and turned even before he said, "Selena?", the single word asking just what she was doing up at this hour, as he slipped the Nikon off his neck and placed it on the low coffee table.

"I need you," was her only answer. She ran to him and threw herself at him, his arms strong around her. She pressed tight against him, feeling the familiar exactness of his legs, his stomach, his chest, that made him uniquely David Greenfield, him and no one else . . .

, His lips were on hers, their mouths open, tongues touching, exploring protuberances and depressions, softness and hardness and wetness. His breath was inside her, hers within him.

Like clumsy wrestlers, they awkwardly dropped to the floor. His hands were under her green gown, peeling it from her like a banana skin. She threw herself into feeling, turning off the part of mind given to thought. There was the soft itch of the carpet beneath her buttocks and shoulder blades, his hands on her breasts, fingers forcefully scissoring her nipples.

She experienced a moment of separation and fear, long enough for him to work his trousers and shorts down, and then he was between her thighs. She reached out to guide him and he thrust hard, and she enfolded him with arms and legs, cocooning him within her flesh. Sensation overwhelmed her, and she writhed and clawed and spasmed until the blinding shock of release slammed into her.

She wept as, a few moments after, he hissed and stiffened and let out a deep groan.

They rested a while as WFMT broadcast Prokofiev's sardonic, teasing *Lt. Kije Suite*. The next time was slower. They were completely naked, skin upon skin, long caresses and bone deep shivers and, at last, peace.

In the still solemn moment before dawn, she told him what had happened. "It was an omen of *diakka*," she explained. It was *Baht*, her fate, to encounter a child's spirit, a lost soul that had not made the journey beyond the waters, *anda l thema*, a spirit so hungry for life it could suck the very life from the living. No, she did not know how or when, did not know anything more than that—except that she was afraid as she had never before been afraid.

David did not interrupt with a single question. When she was finished, he said, "I understand."

The sun rose over Lake Michigan, radiant orange and eternal. David went to the window and recited the Romany words she asked him to say, offered the incantation she could not bring herself to speak because she was *marhime*, an outcast, an unclean woman.

Great Fire, Defender and Protector,
Celestial Fire Who cleans the Earth of foulness,
Deliver us from Evil.

There were other words Selena could not speak aloud, but she said them to herself:

David, I love you.

SEVEN

"**G**ood morning," Laura Morgan said when Vicki walked into Blossom Time.

"Hi," Vicki Barringer said, for variety's sake. She'd already said, "Good morning," a half dozen times as, with the sun shining in a sky dotted with white puff clouds, she'd walked the two blocks to the flower shop. There was a greeting to Ralph Sorenson, Grove Corner's retired postmaster who'd been coming out of Milly's Family Restaurant, to Vera Pelman, the school crossing guard at Main and Lisle who stayed at her post an extra half hour for the late-to-class kids, to Chick, a bag boy at Knutsen's Certified, who was carrying Mrs. Tremont's bags to her station wagon, a greeting for each of her neighbors.

Yes, Vicki thought, definitely a good morning, and a good day—Friday, her very first pay day! Tonight they'd have to celebrate; she would take the family out to dinner.

Vicki set about watering the plants, then checking the cut flowers in the refrigerated case. Laura took a telephone order for a plant to be sent RFD to a hospitalized friend in the central Illinois town of Chenoa. At 10:15, the old gentleman with the plaid cap, Mr. Shelley, Vicki's first customer of the week, was back. "Another spat with the wife," he explained, with a sigh. "Last night at supper, 'cause she don't want me putting so much salt on my food. Can't help it. When you get old, if you don't put salt on your food, you just can't get any taste at all." He needed the usual—a single reconciliation red rose. "Married fifty-two years," he said, "so I guess the trial period is over. We do a lot of fightin', lot of making up and just keep on lovin' each other."

Time passed pleasantly. There wasn't much to do, really, except smell the flowers, watch through the plate glass window as Grove Corner's citizens walked by at a small town pace, and chat with Laura Morgan about this and that. One subject, of course, was "the kids." Laura's daughter, Dorothy, the same age as Missy, was in the same second grade class, and the girls had already taken the first tentative steps toward friendship.

Three years older than Vicki, red-haired Laura Morgan was a tall, big-boned woman with a plain face, round and freckled, that became almost pretty when she smiled. Laura's incongruously delicate hands were naturally gifted at flower arranging, and, by the end of her second day of work, Vicki had decided that Blossom Time was as much an enjoyable hobby as a financial venture for Laura. Vicki thought it possible, too, that the main reason Laura had hired her was for company in the shop and not because she needed help. Judging by this week, on a good day, business was fairly slow, and on a bad day—business wasn't!

When the hands of the antique Regulator clock on the wall pointed to one, Laura said, "Lunch time."

"Sure," Vicki said. "Go ahead." Ordinarily, one or the other took first lunch.

Today Laura said, "Uh-uh, let's both go ahead. My treat."

"But who'll take care of the store?"

"Anyone needs flowers the next hour, they can go to the forest preserve and pick their own."

With a laugh and a "Closed—Back Soon" sign on the door, they went to Milly's Family Restaurant.

The question came with the second cup of after-lunch coffee. "Where do you go to church?"

Vicki felt herself redden, the heat moving up her throat and onto her face.

"We don't. Why do you ask?" she said, disliking her brusque reply.

Laura shrugged. "For the sake of asking, I guess." She sipped her coffee. "I'm sorry. I didn't mean to bring up a touchy subject, if that's what it is."

Vicki smiled apologetically. "No, not really. My husband, well, Warren doesn't go along with organized religion. I mean, he's positively hostile toward it." That was an understatement, she thought. Warren had declared, "Television is the opiate of choice for America's many mindless. Church is a near second."

"Mark never cared about church, either," Laura said. "Oh, it wasn't a big deal with him one way or the other. It just wasn't anything he thought about. Me, I grew up in church, Presbyterian. Had a gold pin for regular Sunday school attendance and everything."

I grew up in church, too, Vicki thought, but there was no Sunday school attendance pin. It was wrong to reward children or anyone for worshipping God as He commanded; that was the teaching of the Holiness Union Church.

"You know how it is. When Mark and I were married," Laura continued, "I figured if Mark didn't want to go, okay, we wouldn't go." She smiled. "And I told myself I didn't miss it or need it and that was that. Besides, there was nothing to stop me from saying a prayer anytime I chose, was there? If I was working in my garden or putting together a casserole, God would hear me just as well as if I had an organ providing a sound track."

Vicki liked neither this topic or the memories and feelings it was dredging up. But Laura was sharing something personal, something Laura obviously considered important, and Vicki could not try to change the subject. She nodded, encouraging Laura to go on.

Laura glanced down. Her index finger traced her coffee cup handle. "Then when I lost Mark, it got pretty bad. Dorothy wasn't even two then. I mean, I was honestly happy, and then, just like that, there's a drunk driver who doesn't even know Mark or me, and Mark is dead. We were okay financially, Mark had seen to that, but, you know," Laura's eyes were thoughtful, "after he died that way, nothing made any sense to me."

Laura shrugged. "So that's when I started going to church again. It helped. I'm not sure exactly how, but it got me through that bad time,

Vicki. It was like, well, there's a special feeling when people gather together to worship God. It's reassuring. Maybe you have your own doubts, but when there are other people with you, and you're all believing there's a powerful someone who does care about each and every one of us . . ." Another shrug. "But, okay, even if I didn't understand that feeling, it was there, and somehow it kept me going when I didn't think I could."

Laura laughed lightly. "Sorry," she said, "It's hard to explain. Am I making any sense at all?"

"Yes," Vicki said. She understood that special feeling, had known it years ago.

The brothers and sisters of the Holiness Union Church believed in God, in salvation through the Blood of His Only Begotten Son, in the surety of a heavenly home for the faithful and true believers, and the endless flaming punishment of Hell for sinners. The brothers and sisters of the Holiness Union Church believed in miracles, in the power of God to heal by casting out demons of the mind and heart and body.

The brothers and sisters of the Holiness Union Church believed that women wearing make-up were guilty of the sin of vanity, that women in pants were guilty of far worse, that dancing was meant to tempt too weak flesh to greater sins, that alcohol drove God out of your mind and spirit, leaving an inviting vacuum to be filled by Satan, that movies and television glorified godless people doing godless things, that the sole godly reason for sex was to fulfill the commandment to be fruitful and multiply, and that the Devil walked the Earth, eager and alert to snatch your soul and cast it into the pit the moment your eyes were not on God and your heart was not filled with Jesus.

The Millers—Brother Robert, Sister Lou Ann and their children, Victoria and her sister, Carol Grace, younger by three years—belonged to the Holiness Union Church. The girls learned to ignore the taunts of schoolmates. "Holy roller, bible banger, crazy, goofy, nutty, batty freaks." The insults might wound, but God healed the wounds of the faithful. What could a poor lost sinner do to God's children who walked in His path, knew Him as shield and comforter?

Victoria and Carol Grace believed with a single-minded intensity which only the young can achieve. "He walks with me and He talks with me, and He tells me I am His own . . ." is what the sisters felt from moment to moment in their lives, but it was when they prayed with the congregation in the white frame Holiness Union Church that they were overwhelmed by the shining force of His wondrous love. There with the benches pushed against the walls to clear the floor for those seized by the Holy Ghost, convulsing in an ecstasy of the spirit, crying out the streams of mysterious God-inspired words, they knew and rejoiced in God's might and His magnificence beyond magnificence. And when Brother Earl or Brother Talbot or their very own father, Brother Robert, laid hands on the sick, commanding "In the name of the Lord!" that Satan's imps, demons, and devils quit the body of God's servant, the servant was cured, healed of the common cold, rheumatism, colitis, psoriasis, and they beheld a miracle.

In church, when Victoria Miller thanked God

for His grace, she often cried, sobbing at the splendor of His gift, freely given.

She was saved and Carol Grace was saved, because their blessed parents were godly people who brought up their children in the ways of the Lord. That is what Victoria Miller believed.

Victoria was 14 when her father died of a heart attack. She could have accepted that. Death was "The Lord calling his servant home."

However Brother Robert died late at night in the mobile home of a bleached blonde who had known many men. Brother Robert was naked and died in a naked woman's bed.

Victoria could not accept that. She could not accept her father's burning in hell forever, could not accept his being a hypocrite, a liar, a fornicator, an adulterer.

Mrs. Miller could not accept it, either. Within a year, she was mumbling to herself about blood sins and winged serpents and communists, and six months later, muttering prayers, she tried to burn down the house. She was committed to a mental institution; a year later, she died there.

Victoria and Carol Grace were taken in by their father's brother and his wife, Uncle Chester and Aunt Toni. It was Aunt Toni who began calling Victoria "Vicki" and kept calling her that until the time came when Victoria did feel like Vicki. Their aunt and uncle were not members of the Holiness Union Church or any church. Uncle Chester's religious philosophy would coincidentally later become a beer advertisement: "What I believe is you only go around once in life."

Vicki decided that that was what she thought, too, and in those moments when she heard a tiny voice within her mind saying, "You're cutting God out of your life," when she felt something that was not exactly loneliness or emptiness within her but a particular type of longing hurt, she found ways to refocus her attention on the here and now. There were books she had never read, had not been allowed to read. There were television shows and motion pictures, and there were high school dances. She wore make-up and high heels. "Hon, you're an attractive young lady with a cute shape to you," Aunt Toni counseled, "and there's not one thing sinful about dressing yourself up!" She giggled and gossiped and went out with boys to picnics and parties. The here and now, she learned, was quite all right. It wasn't sinful; it was just the world as it was.

The farther Vicki drifted away from her strict religious upbringing, the more Carol Grace embraced those early teachings. Vicki could not understand her sister. Carol Grace . . . well, you could not talk with Carol Grace. Carol Grace did not answer questions; she issued proclamations. She did not converse; she condemned or prose-lytized or both.

Vicki Miller grew up, went off to college and dropped out in her third year to marry Warren Barringer, a graduate student who'd just been granted admission to the prestigious University of Iowa Writer's Workshop.

Carol Grace grew up and married Evan Kyle Dean, a minister, an evangelist, a faith healer who had gone on to no little renown. Carol Grace and Vicki had not spoken in ten years.

Uncle Chester and Aunt Toni retired and bought a condo in Clearwater, Florida, where they meant to enjoy their golden years, but Aunt

Toni was dead in six months, a brain aneurism, and Uncle Chester followed her with a fatal heart attack a mere two months after.

So Vicki Barringer lived her life entwined with the lives of her husband and their child, lived her life in the here and now, occasionally taking note that God was no part of it.

And sometimes late at night, so alone, when she had no choice but to be totally honest with herself, she admitted she missed . . . Him.

"Really, you don't have to feel obligated," Laura Morgan was saying. "I just thought I'd ask if you'd like to come to church with me this Sunday. I'm not trying to convert you or anything."

She wasn't tracking and hadn't been for a while, Vicki realized; she had slipped away from the here and now, but she heard Laura's invitation.

"Yes," Vicki said, "I would like that."

EIGHT

Melissa? Melissa!

How come you always bother me when I'm sleeping? It's bedtime. I'm supposed to be asleep. You should be asleep, too, Lisette.

No, Melissa. I can't sleep.

Well, I can, so good night. Go away.

No.

I cannot hear you. I am asleep. I am snoring. Szzss . . .

Melissa, you said you were my friend. I'm lonely. Do you want to make me cry?

No! When you start crying and calling for your mama, it gets real icky, all cold and everything. Not cold like winter but cold like . . .

Talk to me, Melissa. Please.

Hi, Lisette. How are you, Lisette? How old are you? I'm seven. Do you go to school? I'm in second grade. Do you like hot dogs? I like hot dogs. Here's a joke. What's orange and throws rocks? An orange lawn. I lied about the rocks.

Hey, I thought you wanted to talk, so talk!

You are being mean to me.

So what? I could care less. You don't know how to talk right and you won't play and the only time you come is when I'm asleep. You're like you're all messed up or something, not like a real girl, so that proves it. You are too imaginary, and I don't need you.

But I need you, Melissa. I need you to be my friend. That's why I gave you my beautiful paper-weight. That's real, isn't it?

Yeah.

There's another gift I have for you, if you'll be nice to me.

Show me.

Here, Melissa. Do you like it?

Wow, that is neat! It's not junky plastic or anything. And it's for me?

Yes, Melissa, but you have to give me something first.

I thought so. Don't you know that's not the way you're supposed to act? That's being selfish. You're supposed to give somebody something just because you want to and you shouldn't ask for something back.

Isn't it lovely, Melissa? Don't you want it?

Yeah. So what do I give you this time? If you want another hair, I guess you can have it.

Blood, Melissa, one tiny drop of your blood.

Blood? Lisette, you're not just imaginary, you're crazy! What do you think you are, Dracula?

Please, Melissa, please.

I had to go to the doctor last year for a blood test, you silly dope, and it really hurt. It made me cry.

It won't hurt, Melissa.

Do you promise?

I promise.

Cross your heart and hope to . . .

I said I promise, Melissa.

Okay, okay, if it won't hurt. But I have to stick

my thumb with a needle like at the doctor's, and I don't have a needle.

You'll think of something, Melissa.

Okay . . . yeah, my Smurf button. There's a pin on the back. I can use that, I guess, but it better not hurt or you won't be my friend anymore.

Please, Melissa.

Okay, okay.

Do it, Melissa.

I don't know . . .

Do it now!

Ow! Oh, it hurts, it does so hurt! It hurts bad. You're nasty! You lied to me, Lisette. You told a lie!

NINE

Sonofabitch. Son-of-a-bitch!

What happened? What had gone wrong? He'd been blazing through the manuscript, creativity racing on automatic pilot so that he hadn't even had to think to transform vision into words.

Then forget it! After countless attempts, page 79 of his novel was pure shit. He yanked the paper out of the Underwood, wadded and tossed. Two points, right in the wastebasket, a sure sign that was where it belonged.

Warren leaned back, shoulders tight, the nape of his neck on fire with tension. His reading glasses had slipped to the tip of his nose. He took them off and laid them on the desk.

So the novel wasn't working right now, but, well, that happened. He'd been flying on the proverbial wings of inspiration, but inspiration had flapped off—meaning he had a writing problem—but that was all. Problems had solutions. So, Warren, engage the brain, think out the problem and find a solution.

Brandon Holloway Mitchell, the novel's protagonist, the civilized man of *A Civilized Man*, has just been told by his wife, Claire, that she is having an affair with Darwin Leaf, Mitchell's colleague at the university.

Question: What does Brandon Holloway Mitchell do now?

Approach it rationally, objectively.

What did *you* do when you found out Vicki was getting it on with David Greenfield?

Remember, Warren?

Christ, was there ever a day when he did not remember?

Hell, time to call it quits for this session. It was nearly one in the morning, and he'd been working and getting nowhere since nine.

It was time for a drink.

On his way down to the basement rec room, he carried on a silent conversation with himself.

(Say, when you went out for supper, Vicki's pay day celebration treat, didn't you have two cocktails before and a Heineken with your meal? Mathematically speaking, Professor, two plus one equal three—and you're watching it, aren't you, keeping it to three-and-no-more-than-three? Right, but that was yesterday. It's now past midnight, a brand new day.)

At the bar, he put three fingers of Johnny Walker into a highball glass and added two ice cubes.

He sipped. Excellent, he decided, 12 year-old, peat-flavored ambrosia.

Another taste. Very good, very good indeed, that fine, familiar spread of relaxation throughout the nervous system. He went to the sofa, slipped off his shoes and put his stockinged feet up on the coffee table. He picked up the television's remote control. A good idea. Television was a mind relaxer, sure to induce mental paralysis.

He zipped through the channels with the remote control. All right, the Three Stooges, masters of the mindless! He was grinning, chuckling to himself, as Moe, Larry, and Curly as plumbers destroyed a stuffy heiress's mansion. He raised his glass. Only ice remained.

Another drink?

Why not?

After all, he needed to unwind. He knew exactly what he was doing. He wasn't going to get shit-faced, uh-uh, just slip into some theraputic numbness.

Damn, he thought, fresh drink set up, he was feeling the liquor. He was feeling . . . not drunk and not on the way to being drunk. He was feeling okay getting back in balance with himself.

But he couldn't blot out Vicki and that sonofabitch David Greenfield. Shit, it had nearly killed him. He hadn't suspected a goddamn thing until she'd told him, flatly and unemotionally. And though he had felt like killing her, he merely said they had better talk it over. He truly loved her, so he forgave her.

He thunked the glass down on top of the bar. He loved Vicki. He did. All the love he felt for her welled up inside him, the shared years and the good times. There was the celebration when he sold a story to *Chicago Review*, cheap champagne, all they could afford, but champagne all the same; going to see *Rocky Horror*, a few years older than the cult crowd, but getting into the trashy excitement, laughing and laughing; a rainy summer night in a leaky cabin in Michigan; that one time winning lottery ticket she'd bought on a whim with that big pay off of $44.00

that she insisted he take and spend on anything he chose (naturally, he bought books); and Missy, that feeling of magical omnipotence when he rested his hand on Vicki's belly to feel the movement of the life within Vicki's life, life that they had caused to be.

Warren felt his eyes sting with a wash of tears. He loved Vicki, loved the unique totality of her that made her Vicki and nobody else. He wanted to be with her, together with her now, wanted to make love, to be inside her.

He went upstairs to make love to his wife.

TEN

Lying on her side, Vicki was asleep, but not so deeply that she wasn't aware of Warren getting into bed. He nuzzled the back of her neck, pressed his lips to the hinge of her jaw and kissed her. He put his hand on her hip. "Vicki?" He kissed her again, a light tickling touch on the ear.

A moment of panicky despair yanked her to full wakefulness as she smelled the liquor on his breath. He was drunk!

A heartbeat afterward, she realized she was, thankfully, wrong. There was neither slur nor sarcasm in his words as he said, "Vicki, I love you."

She rolled to embrace him. Holding her, he kissed her deeply, passionately, and her open-mouthed response was immediate. A rush of tingling, electric shocks raced through her.

Oh, my, she thought, surprised at her explosion of ardor, this was something! She felt like the heroine of a romance novel; she was positively melting.

Of course, a romance novel heroine wouldn't giggle at the silly instant of having to lift up her bottom to slip off the bikini panties of her shorty pajamas. And the top of those pajamas wouldn't get tangled around her head when she sat up to take it off.

But she was sure no romance novel heroine ever felt more loved than she did at this moment. Warren was touching her everywhere with his hands, his lips, his tongue. It had been a long time (years?) since he had been so wonderfully ardent. She understood, knew he had so many pressures, so much to drain him—his academic career, which had turned out so different from what they had expected or hoped for; the writing, consuming the hours of his life and filling his mind from one waking minute to the next. As for the drinking, well, in those dreadful drinking days, Warren had been married to the bottle, and he had been a faithful husband.

"I love you, Vicki."

"I love hearing you say that," she whispered. Then, knowing she had never before said anything more truthful in her life, she said, "I love you."

She marched up the front stairs. One-two-three . . . Four-five-six! She stepped onto the porch and went to the front door of the house.

Missy was dreaming, and she knew it. She was inside and outside the dream. She had had dreams like this before. Sometimes they were scary and sometimes they were fun, and sometimes even after she woke up, she kind of thought what had happened in the dream was real.

Like when she dreamed she could fly. The secret was, if you got running a special way, and you breathed a special way, and you didn't take your eyes off what was straight ahead, not even a flicker to either side, and then you held out your arms just right . . . Wow, you could fly!

That's how it was in the flying dream, anyway. When she woke up, it was so real she had to try it. What happened was she ran and ran, squinting to keep her eyes straight ahead, and she kept on running until her eyes burned and the wind stung the tears on her cheeks and her side hurt so bad she thought she was going to burst. Then she fell down and ripped her jeans.

She didn't know if she was crying because her knees hurt so much or because she would never ever fly.

But that was when she was little. She was only in kindergarten then. Now she was in second grade. She knew what was real and what was not.

And this house in her dream was real. It was the real house she lived in. "My name is Melissa Barringer, and I live at 1302 Main Street, Grove Corner, Illinois. Zip Code: 60412." That was something you had to know.

All by itself, the front door slowly opened.

She walked into the living room. This was her house—but it wasn't. That was how it worked in dreams sometimes. The living room was big, much bigger than it really was. It was gigantic. There was no furniture.

Instead, there was a tall mirror. It was the trick kind with wavy glass.

But there was something weird about the trick mirror. When you stood in front of it, you were supposed to see yourself. Sure, you'd look different, maybe all squashed down or stretched out like toothpaste squeezed out of the tube. You were supposed to see a goofy you—and not someone else.

But I don't see myself in the mirror, she thought.

Yes, you do.

"What are you doing here?" she asked Lisette-in-the-mirror. "I live here. This is my house. This is where I belong."

This is where I belong.

Was Lisette being a snot? You know, repeating what she said. Oh, it didn't matter. This was just a dream.

But now she knew it wasn't going to be a fun dream.

Then Lisette held out her hands.

Missy took them. She didn't want to, but she knew in dreams you sometimes have to do what you don't want to do. She wasn't sure if she pulled Lisette out of the mirror or if Lisette pulled her into it.

Lisette was gone.

No!

Oh, this was very scary. It was she herself who was gone. Now she just . . . wasn't.

I am

She was Lisette.

No!

Mom! Dad!

She called and called and no one came.

She was not in the living room, not anymore.

She was downstairs in the basement.

But it wasn't the basement with the sofa and the television and the paneling on the wall. This wasn't the real basement.

But, oh, this basement did feel real, awful and real, and it was cold, and it had a hard concrete floor and it smelled like wet coal.

And she had no clothes on.

Mom! Please, Mom, come get me. I don't want to be here. I'm alone. I'm so alone. Mom!

Mama can't come.

Dad! Dad!

She saw him on the wooden stairs. "I hear you, I hear you . . ."

Dad was here, and everything was okay.

But then she was scared all over again. She was scared worse. Dad's face looked so strange. Sometimes on Sunday mornings, Dad slept late and Mom sent her to wake him for breakfast. When she saw him asleep, it was hard to believe he was Dad at all. His face was all changed. He looked like a stranger. And even after his eyes opened, it seemed to take a few seconds before his face would get right.

No, this was not Dad. She knew that.

"I know what you want," he said, and it wasn't Dad's voice.

Love me.

"Whore! I'll give you just what you want. Yes, I will, whore!"

He was right by her now.

Not Dad!

He was touching her.

It made her feel crawly. It made her feel sick.

Be nice. Must be nice. Let him . . .

It was wrong. Last year, at her old school, a policewoman came to talk to the first grade. Joey Douglas asked her if she knew Cagney and Lacey. She laughed. Then she told them about adults who wanted to touch you in ways they shouldn't. They were bad to do that

Kiss him and touch him and he will love . . .

And if someone touched you the wrong way—
it didn't matter who it was—you had to tell.

No, I won't tell. I promise. I'll never tell anyone!
Don't . . .

He raised his fist. "You filthy whore. You see
what you make me do? And now you'll tell the
whole world."

And he hit her and she screamed and he hit
her and she screamed and screamed and
screamed.

They lay, tired and content, not saying anything. Then they heard the shriek.

"Jesus!"

"Missy, oh God, Missy!"

Jumping out of bed, Vicki wriggled into her
pajama tops. Warren nearly toppled over, awkwardly yanking on his shorts.

The screaming went on and on, so loud it
seemed to fill all the house and their minds. In
the hall, Vicki shook her head. She was disoriented and felt almost disembodied.

Then she knew. "Downstairs!" she shouted as
the screaming stopped.

They found Missy in the rec room. She was
huddled in the corner, arms around her knees,
eyes huge and unfocused. She was naked. Her
mouth was shaped around a gigantic silent
scream.

"Sleep walking, that's all," Warren said the
next morning as he and Vicki sat drinking coffee
in the kitchen. It was 8:30, and Missy was still
asleep. "It happens. I don't think we have any
reason to be worried."

"I hope so," Vicki said. When they'd discovered Missy in the rec room, Vicki had an instant of paralysis. "It's okay," Warren whispered, as he gently shook Missy, calling her name. In a moment, Missy came around. She was bewildered and frightened. "This isn't my room. This isn't my bed." She didn't know how she got downstairs, didn't remember taking off her clothes, didn't recall anything except a "bad dream, a real scary one," the kind of fright that needed to be assuaged by sleeping with Mom and Dad. Once she was dressed for sleep, Missy spent the remainder of a restless night sometimes moaning or sniffling and once kicking out so hard that Vicki was guaranteed what would be an ugly bruise on the thigh.

"She's never walked in her sleep before," Vicki said. "I just wonder if . . ."

"It doesn't mean she's neurotic, psychotic, or autistic," Warren interrupted. "She doesn't have epilepsy or a brain tumor or any other awful thing you've learned the symptoms of from *Reader's Digest*. She walked in her sleep, that's all, and there's a first time for everything, right?" Warren grinned. "And how's that for *Reader's Digest* wisdom?"

"I guess, but . . ."

"Lot of excitement in her life, Vicki," Warren went on. "New home, new school, new people, all kinds of things. So she's off on a nocturnal stroll." He raised an eyebrow. "Don't turn nothing much into a big deal, okay?"

"I do that sometimes," Vicki admitted. "You do, too."

"I guess neither one of us is perfect. We'll just have to live with it."

Warren pushed back the chair and stood up, a

tacit way of telling her that, as far as he was concerned, the discussion was finished. "Think I'll do something middle-class and go get the car washed." He glanced at his watch. "Back in an hour, and then we can sit down to a middle-class Saturday morning breakfast, lovingly prepared by a Super-Mom who manages to run the household while being active in her professional career."

"Don't tease."

"Can if I want to. Says so in the marriage contract. Tell you what, I won't work today. We'll drive the clean car up to Brookfield Zoo this afternoon. Think Missy will go for that?"

"I know she will," Vicki said. "Me, too."

Grinning, he pointed at her. "You got it."

When he left, Vicki poured herself another cup of coffee. That Warren had been the one to suggest a family outing greatly pleased her. When he was working on a book, he often got so wrapped up that he acted as though nothing but his battle with the blank pages was at all important.

Still, she wished there could be another family outing—tomorrow. Last evening, when they were getting ready to go out for dinner, she'd told him about Laura Morgan's invitation and suggested he accompany Missy and her to church.

Warren said he was more likely to visit Uganda than Grove Corner Presbyterian, thank you very much. Okay, if she wanted to go and thought she needed a fix of socially acceptable American voodoo, that was just fine. But for him, "Well, if God exists, then I've worked out a deal with him."

She said, "What's that?" knowing he expected her to ask.

She braced herself for what was coming, blaming herself for bringing up the subject in the first place.

Warren said, "I stay out of God's house, and He'd damned well better stay out of mine."

She wished he had not said that.

Two: *O Drom Le Vila*
THE WAY OF DARK SPIRIT

A number of years ago, a scholar of ethnology, working on his PhD dissertation, sought out the *Rawnie*, *the great lady*, Pola Janichka. He'd learned of her fame as a storyteller and wished to include a number of her *Darane Swature* in his work. He thought the swature *would illustrate archetypal themes.*

When he explained what he wanted to Pola Janichka, she told him she was sorry, but she could not provide him a single swato. He tried to convince the Rawnie *of the scholarly value of his work, but she refused.* Swature *were not meant to be written down.* A swato *must be spoken, coming from the heart so that it can reach the heart. When one heart touches another, the truth is shared.*

This is a swato *of Pola Janichka:*

"Once a boy, a chavo, *went into the deep woods to check the snares of his father. As his father had set out many snares, it would take no small time for this task, so the boy took with him food and water. He took with him three coins, since one can get along in the world with little money, but not without any money. To pass* the time, he had in his pocket his favorite toys, a lead soldier and a tiny whistle carved from the bone of a hedgehog by his uncle. This was all he had with him when he went into the deep woods.

"Late in the morning, the boy realized that he was lost, far from the kumpania. *Naxdaran*, he told himself, do not fear. He had water, he had food, he had money, he had toys, and though this was all he had, what more did a child need? He would eat now and drink, and then he would pray to O Del, the good God, to show him the way out of the woods. With this thought, he seated himself, his back against a tree.

"But before he could eat and drink, and sadly, before he could offer up any prayer to O Del, the boy felt a great tiredness, and his eyes closed, and he slept.

"And when he awoke, there were children gathered about him in a circle.

"Had the *chavo* been older and therefore wiser, he might have seen that these were not ordinary children.

"There was a sadness in their eyes that was not the sadness known by living children. But the *chavo* had known little sadness in his own life, so he could not understand. There was a paleness to their faces that was not caused by the sickness or fear known by living children, but the *chavo* had always been glowing with health and he'd seldom known fear, so he could not understand. Indeed, there was much about them that was *mulano*, ghostly, but *the* chavo *recognized none of it.*

"He did not know these were not living children, not juvindo, but detlene; they were the spirits of dead children.

"Then all together the detlene held out their hands. And then all together, they spoke. 'Help us! Share with us! Be generous! Be kind! Help us!'

"The chavo laughed. These children had come to beg, mong, from him, as he himself had often begged from others!

"Though he was not old enough to be wise, the chavo had a good heart. He said, 'I have money I will share with you.'

"All together, the detlene replied, 'We have no need for money.'

"The chavo said, 'I have water I will share with you.'

"All together, the detlene replied, 'We have no need for water.'

"The chavo said, 'I have food I will share with you.'

"All together, the detlene replied, 'We have no need for food.'

"The chavo said, 'I have toys I will share with you.'

"All together, the detlene replied, 'We have no need for toys.'

"'I am sorry, then,' said the chavo. 'There is nothing I can give you. There is nothing I can do for you. When I came into the woods, I took with me money, food, water, and toys, that is all. I have nothing else.'

"All together, the detlene replied, 'Yes, you do. There is something else.'

" 'What is it that I have?" asked the chavo, 'that I can share with you? What is it that you want? What do I have that you need?'

"All together, the detlene replied, 'You have life. That is what you can give to us. That is what we need.' "

ELEVEN

With only a touch of make-up, in a yellow dress and hat that had been chain department store fashionable a few seasons earlier, there was nothing to distinguish Emerald Farmer from other worshippers in True Witness Church. She'd not spoken to anyone, but her slight New York accent would not have attracted undue attention. True Witness Church had known visitors from all across the United States, indeed, from the entire world. They'd come with afflictions of mind, body, and soul to Mt. Franklin, Alabama, to Reverend Evan Kyle Dean's home church, so that Reverend Dean might cast out foul spirits of sickness and torment, make them healed and whole, and grant them a miracle.

There hadn't been many outsiders recently, because it had been nearly a year since Evan Kyle Dean had conducted a healing service. He had not been on a crusade for two years and, for the past three months, even his television program, *Witness to Wonder*, was in reruns. Yet every Sunday, he preached at True Witness.

Though Emerald Farmer had an incurable, fatal disease, she had not come to True Witness this Sunday to ask for healing. She already thought of herself as dead, dead like Randy, the man she had loved. She had no interest in hearing Dean preach what he called the "Word of God." If there were a God, and He allowed phony bastards like Evan Kyle Dean to speak for Him, then He was either a cruel monster or a damned fool.

Just as she had the previous two Sundays, Emerald Farmer had come to church today simply to look at Dean, to let the actuality of his existence feed her hatred so that when the time came she would not falter. She would kill him.

And when her brain issued the command, "Yes! Now!", she was ready. There was the gun in her purse. But that wasn't how she'd planned it, nor the way she wanted it. She needed to talk to him and tell him why he was going to die. What would the sanctimonious bullshit artist look like when he knew God wasn't going to miraculously turn a Colt .38 into a plowshare, when he realized it was the dust to dust route, that dead was dead and that was it? She wanted him to be afraid, as afraid as the pathetic hopefuls who'd sought his help and were deceived by their own fear and his conniving.

As Evan Kyle Dean took the pulpit for his sermon, Emerald Farmer stared at him and wondered if he could feel the boiling waves of her loathing.

"I want to talk to you about God," Evan Kyle Dean said. With a half-smile, he paused to set up the tag line. "Seems only right. After all, I am a preacher and this is the Sabbath, the day He has set aside so we might worship Him and contemplate His commandments." The words were flowing smoothly. Evan hoped this time it would be right. It had not been right for months, and, he had to admit, it was getting worse—much worse.

Six feet tall, angular as an archetypal frontiersman, Evan Kyle Dean at 40 still looked like a country boy. Five years earlier, when he'd first met with Marvin Michelson, founder and president of the Christian Communications Consortium, to discuss the program that would become *Witness to Wonder*, Michelson had told him, "You're a natural for TV, Brother Evan. You have the right image."

"How's that?" Evan wanted to know.

"You look like you could be Andy Griffith's younger brother."

Live and in person, Evan Kyle Dean seemed more craggy and rough-cut than he did on television. There were grayish circles beneath his eyes that make-up would have camouflaged were he before the camera. And he was doing something he never did on TV; he was sweating. There was a chill ring of perspiration just under his collar, a film on his upper lip and forehead.

He felt cold, felt he had to keep his muscles tight so that he didn't start shaking uncontrollably.

He was freezing and, it was grimly funny, he thought, that Marvin Michelson had called him "cool" at that initial meeting. "You see, Brother Evan, you're a cool personality, in the McLuhanesque sense of the word. Low-key and nonthreatening. That makes you well-suited to video and the electronic ministry."

"I'm sorry," Evan said. "I don't understand."

"You communicate, Brother Evan," Michelson explained. "You don't shout at people." Michelson grinned. "Just between the two of us,

Brother Evan, the CCC's somewhat overstocked with screamers, even though they give us the deep South demographics and contributions that keep our stations on the air. Let's say, though, you're a young man from a cosmopolitan city like San Francisco. You've been to college, you're married, doing well at your job, but you sense there's something missing in your life. You with me so far, Brother Evan?"

"I think so."

"So you're ready to ask God into your heart, and, then you happen to turn to a CCC station after the late night movie. Here's a man bouncing around like he's on a trampoline. He's got a plaid sport coat that can cross your eyes permanently. He's condemning everything from women's liberation to the Catholic Church. He thinks we ought to nuke the Russians to show them what the Lord thinks about godless, atheistic communism. And he's yelling at you personally like he's caught you stealing his car, having sex with his wife, and selling dope and dirty magazines to his little girl. Somehow I can't see that as the way to bring the word of God to our San Francisco yuppie, can you?"

"It's not my way," Evan said quietly.

"I know," Marvin Michelson said. "You talk to people."

Evan Kyle Dean blinked. Somehow he'd slipped away—again. Talk to people! That's why he was standing in the pulpit of True Witness Church. He said, "I want to talk to you about God." He waited a moment. "Seems only right . . ." Then he stopped altogether. There was a block of ice pressing down on his Adam's apple as he realized he was repeating himself.

He tried to recover. "Quite an echo in here, isn't there, brothers and sisters?" There were a few smiles on the faces of his brothers and sisters, all the children of God. "We are, you know," he said, "all children of God."

What was happening to him? It seemed he couldn't think, couldn't talk. He was sick. The healer was ill; physician, heal thyself. These days, he had no appetite, had to force himself to eat; everything seemed to have a burnt plastic after-taste. He couldn't sleep.

And he could not heal—not anymore.

He was shaking now. Could they see it, his brothers and sisters, or was the tremor only within him, a trembling not of the body but the soul? He had to get a grip on himself.

"God is our Father," he said, "and He's a loving Father. That's what he tells us throughout the Bible." Though it was there at the edge of his mind, the next thought eluded him. A moment's anxiety, and then he was sure he had it. "God is a God of love, you see. That's what He has told us, you see. And He is a God who cannot and will not lie. God loves the truth, you see . . ." His voice trailed off.

And what of those who lie in His name?

Did he say that aloud or to himself? Or did he say it at all? Was the Lord speaking to him?

Within his mind, Evan said to God: Lord, I need you.

"I . . . I'm sorry," he told the congregation. "I keep on . . . What I think is that my tongue's getting in the way of my eyetooth and I can't see what I'm saying, so . . ."

Lord, he prayed, be with me now. Let Your love fill my heart, let Your wisdom clear my mind, let Your words be in my mouth.

He glanced down at his notes on the lectern. There'd been a time when he never outlined sermons, when he knew what to say simply and eloquently. But you could hardly work that way on television. Taping *Witness to Wonder*, he employed a teleprompter, sometimes giving him words he'd written, sometimes the words of others—and sometimes he'd wondered if they were the words of God.

Today's text was from Malachi: "Have we not all one father? Hath not one God created us?" The handwriting was slanted and jerky; it didn't look familiar. He didn't remember writing it.

When Evan spoke, the words were a surprise to him. He was not citing Malachi but Micah, chapter six, verse eight. "What doth the Lord require of thee, but to do justly, and to love mercy, and to walk humbly with thy God?" The next words he uttered were from Proverbs. "If sinners entice thee, consent thou not. Everyone that is proud in heart is an abomination unto the Lord. Better is a little with righteousness than great revenues without right. A righteous man hateth lying . . ."

Confused and frightened as he was, Evan Kyle Dean could not doubt the Lord had spoken, but not to the brothers and sisters gathered here in True Witness.

To Evan Kyle Dean.

Everything was hazy, the faces of his brothers and his sisters floating and anonymous before his eyes. He brought Carol Grace into focus. She sat in the first pew, and he saw the concern and love on her face.

"Friends," he said, "brothers and sisters . . ."

It would be all right. He would go home with his wife, and it would be all right. "I'm tired. I am very, very tired. I . . . I need to rest."

But before he could go home, he had to conclude the sermon. He knew what to say. He knew what he believed and would never doubt.

"Brothers and sisters, God is love."

The following Sunday, in Grove Corner, Illinois, with her daughter, Vicki Barringer went to church for the first time in years.

On the same Sunday, for the first time in years, Vicki Barringer's brother-in-law, Evan Kyle Dean, did not preach to the congregation of True Witness Church in Mt. Franklin, Alabama, nor to anyone in any church. He lay in bed all day long, wishing he were dead and thinking that perhaps he, or his soul, already was.

TWELVE

Missy thought the choir sounded beautiful. It was fun to sing along when you were supposed to, trying to follow the melody and keep up with the words in the book when you had never seen them before. Mom sang real nice, too. Mom seemed to know all the words to the hymns.

The church was beautiful, too. Missy had somehow expected it to be dark and smelly, but it was all golden with polished wood, and the sun came in, lightly touching everything with a soft glow. The minister, whose name was Pastor Norton, was short and round and bald and cute, kind of like the Pillsbury Doughboy. What was cool about him was how he told silly jokes about the senior citizen group's trip to the dinner theater, the men's club next golf outing, and the women's charity auction. Pastor Norton made everyone laugh. Missy hadn't been too sure about the rules about laughing in the house of the Lord, but it had to be okay, with even the minister doing it.

"The house of the Lord." That's what Mom had called it when they were getting ready this morning. Drinking a cup of coffee, Dad said, "Not only His house, but He doesn't pay a thin dime in taxes." Mom gave Dad a real angry look.

Missy was certain you had to be on your best

behavior in church—no squirming or scratching, no whispering with her friend Dorothy.

Missy had asked, "Does the Lord punish you if you're bad in His house?"

Mom didn't say anything for a second but looked like she was thinking hard. Dad said, "You'd better believe it, kiddo. He'll smite you with a plague of locusts." Mom gave him the look again, and he said something that sounded like "Superstitious bullshit," but he said it with his mouth pretty much in the coffee cup so she couldn't be sure that was what he really said.

Mom told her, "The Lord loves everyone, Missy, and He's glad to welcome them to His house. But there's a right way and a wrong way to act, no matter where you are. You know that."

"Uh-huh," Missy said seriously. "You mean good manners. I've got 'em."

"I know you do, Missy. And I know you're going to be a real lady in church and make me proud of you."

Missy did feel like a real lady. She felt pretty and grown-up in a new white and gold dress and shiny new shoes, and she even had a purse. Usually her favorite outfit was jeans and her Rainbow Brite top, but today was special.

This was what church was meant to be, Vicki thought, what religion was all about. It was a serene time-out from commonplace day to day living, with its minor frustrations and little victories. Sitting in a pew in the middle of the church, her daughter beside her, her friend Laura Morgan and her child, Dorothy, to her right, being here now in the house of the Lord with her neighbors was good.

She couldn't help compare this dignified and

restrained service to the heavily emotional and uninhibited Holiness Union Church services of her childhood. Maybe that was right for some people, maybe it had even been right for her then, but this was right for her now.

And, she decided, it would be right for her from now on—and for her little girl. She glanced at Missy, who'd been as good as gold and was still shining! She regretted that Melissa had never been baptized.

Vicki's thoughts were interrupted when Reverend Norton began his sermon. "This past week, my wife and I took a little trip. We shipped the kids off to their grandparents and went to visit another couple we hadn't seen in years, friends from our college days." Reverend Norton smiled. "You know the definition of college, I'm sure. That's where you learn you already know everything and nobody else knows anything."

There were appreciative chuckles, but Missy wasn't so sure she liked Pastor Norton's joke, if that's what it was. Was he making fun of college? Her dad taught college. He was a professor, and a professor was probably more important than a minister—at least *as* important.

"Anyway," Reverend Norton continued, "there were those awkward minutes you always have with people you haven't seen in a long time, and then we relaxed and started talking about, what else, the good old days. In the good old days, I had hair down to my shoulders and I played guitar. I was our campus's imitation Bob Dylan." He ran a hand over his head. "Everyone agreed I look much more distinguished bald than I did hairy."

Now that was kind of funny, Missy thought. Just being bald was funny!

"Not long after that, we got into the 'whatever happened to . . .' game. You know how that goes. Whatever happened to Jim? And somehow, even though nobody's seen Jim since graduation, somebody knows what happened to Jim. Jim got married and divorced and married, and he's selling aluminum siding. Peggy, the rebel, SDS member, is in real estate. Morris is in franchise foods, Lucy got a PhD in chemistry and teaches at MIT, Hank took over the construction company when his dad died . . ."

No!

The voice was quiet, but clear in Missy's mind. Lisette! No, that was wrong! Lisette only came at night. Lisette was . . .

I am . . .

". . . and then our conversation grew more serious. It was late, and that seems to be a time to talk about serious things. Wasn't it a shame about Chuck? It was so hard to believe what happened to Chuck. He was only twenty-eight, a man who had everything going for him—looks, brains, money. You're not supposed to have a fatal coronary at twenty-eight. You're not supposed to die."

No!

As though pondering a mystery and denying its existence at the same time, Reverend Norton slowly shook his head. "Life is what we know, what we have, the dearest gift our Lord has granted us, and then, here's a monstrous, inexplicable insult to all that we, as mere mortals, understand. Death invades and overpowers life and there is an ending . . ."

Oh, no . . .

Missy's eyes stung with the promise of tears. She felt sad and afraid and angry, and she did not understand at all. It was Lisette who was sad and afraid and angry—she knew that—and she was not Lisette.

I need to live! I will live!

The scream swelled, an expanding balloon of furious sound that filled Missy's mind. She was dizzy. She felt as though she were dreaming but didn't think she was. She couldn't be sure of anything—except that Death was terrible and wrong.

I will live!

Reverend Norton solemnly said, "In the midst of life, we are in death . . ."

Missy nudged her mother. When Vicki leaned her head down, Missy whispered in her ear, "Mom, let's go home."

"Shh," Vicki whispered back, "it will be just a little while longer."

Reverend Norton's voice became less intense but no less thoughtful. "Toward the end of the evening, I took out my guitar, and we all sang the way we used to. There seemed to be only one song we could all remember the words to. 'Down in the valley, the valley so low . . .'" The minister's brow wrinkled. "Naturally enough, with my religious calling, that got me thinking about the valley we all walk through, that lonesome valley of the shadow of death."

I won't die! Mama, Mama, don't let me die!

Missy wanted to tell Lisette to shut up and quit blubbering for her mother.

But she couldn't. Her own secret voice, the one that said whatever she wanted it to inside her mind, the special voice she used to talk to Lisette, that voice was hardly even a whisper.

Then it became stronger. It changed, and it was not her voice at all.

It was Lisette's voice.

It was Lisette who jabbed Vicki Barringer's ribs hard with an elbow. It was Lisette who moved Missy Barringer's tongue and shaped the words, "Mama, please, let's go."

"You behave yourself, young lady." Vicki harshly whispered, glaring.

Reverend Norton said, "Awake or asleep, we dwell in the valley of the shadow of death . . ."

No!

"What is wrong with you?" Vicki whispered in Missy's ear. "If you don't settle down, young lady, the minute we get home, I'll give you something you'll remember."

". . . death comes for us all . . ."

Mama would not save her. Mama would not help her. She could call and call for Mama, but Mama never came. Mama died and left her. Mama never came, and she was mad at Mama for going away . . .

". . . and with the ending of life . . ."

. . . hated her, hated Mama . . .

". . . with the final breath and the final thought . . ."

Death was here! And she had to go away, had to get out of here . . .

"No!"

Startled, Vicki saw her daughter stand up, drop her purse and shout again, "No!"

She felt the stares of Grove Corner Presbyterian Church and the hot flush of embarrassment suffuse her neck and scald her cheeks.

"No, no, no . . . Noooo!"

Reverend Norton stopped speaking.

In a stammered whisper, Vicki, rising, tried to apologize, to explain to Laura Morgan. She realized she was too humiliated to find words of apology and had no explanation for her daughter's tantrum. Terribly embarrassed, she wished the floor would crack open and swallow her.

She had to get Missy outside at once.

On the concrete steps of the church, heart pounding, Vicki demanded, "What in heaven's name . . . ?"

Then she stopped, paralyzed by uncomprehending anger and shame. She glared at a red-faced little girl, eyes narrowed to furious slits. The child's mouth opened, and a new scream began.

A strange thought flashed through Vicki's mind: This is not my daughter. Then Vicki slapped the little girl's face.

THIRTEEN

I wish you would go away!

No, Melissa, I won't go away.

I can make you, Lisette! You're only an imaginary friend. You're just like a game of pretend, and when I stop pretending, then you have to leave.

I'm as real as you, Melissa.

I'm going to quit pretending right now. One, two, three! You're all gone.

I am as real as your hair, Melissa. I am as real as your blood.

I said you're all gone. That's the end of the game.

Listen to me, Melissa . . .

I won't! I don't have to!

You will listen to me, Melissa.

Please, just go. Okay? Lisette, the game's over. Lisette . . .

What, Melissa?

This isn't a game.

No.

But I don't want you here anymore. I don't like you, Lisette! You scare me! I wish you would die!

Don't say that! Don't you ever *say that!*

You're not a good friend. You're bad! You do bad things. And you make me do bad things!

I'm not bad, Melissa.

Yes, you are! It was you who made me . . . It was you who started hollering like that in church. You made Mom slap me, and she never ever slapped me before. Not that way, anyhow. Not in the face.

Mama's bad.

And I can't even tell Mom it was you. I can't tell anyone. You won't let me!

Mama hit you. She's bad.

You shut up! That's my mom!

Mamas do that. They do bad things. They don't come when you cry for them. They leave you all alone.

My mom is good!

You're mad at her now. She hit you in the face.

Yeah.

And you hate her.

That's a nasty lie.

You told her you hate her. You know you did.

Yeah, I did, but so what? That doesn't mean I don't love her, too!

She wanted to talk with you. You told her to go away.

That's because I was angry!

You wanted to hit her in the face the way she hit you. You still want to hit her in the face.

Maybe I do. I don't know.

That means you hate her.

No! I don't know. You get me all mixed up.

Mama is bad, and you hate her. It's Daddy you love. Daddy never hits you. Daddy loves you.

Sure, I love both Mom and Dad.

Daddy loves you, and you have to be nice to him so he will always love you.

I am nice to Dad. I'm always nice.

You have to be extra nice to Daddy, a special kind of nice.

I don't know what you're talking about.

I'll teach you.

FOURTEEN

He knocked. When there was no answer, he turned the knob and opened the door wide enough to slowly slip his head inside.

Missy sat cross-legged on the bed, hands on her knees, head bowed. She'd changed out of her good clothes as soon as she got home, carefully hanging the dress in the closet, and now she wore jeans, a Care Bear top, and a forlorn expression.

"Yoo-hoo." She was, Warren knew, deliberately not turning to look at him, wanting to let him see just how miserable and unhappy she was.

"I said, 'Yoo-hoo.'" He stepped into the room. "Or should that be 'Yoo-whom?'"

He'd hoped for at least a hint of a smile. She usually thought he was pretty damned funny. Maybe a touch corny, as she put it, but funny.

Well, this was serious business, after all, so serious she wasn't even seeking the furry consolation of Winnie-the-Pooh, who lay on her pillow. He sat down at the foot of the bed. Quietly, he said, "Mind if I keep you company for a while?"

The suggestion was met with a shrug.

"You're feeling pretty crummy now, I'll bet."

A slight nod affirmed it.

"I understand," he said. "That's what happens when people who love each other hurt one another's feelings."

"She hit me in the face," Missy said tonelessly.

"I know," he said. That certainly wasn't like Vicki; she must have really become totally unglued. He had been uptown buying a Sunday newspaper when Vicki brought Missy home from the church disaster. When he returned, there was Vicki at the kitchen table, brooding and looking not a great deal different than did Missy right now. She'd told him the story, blaming herself for losing control that way and hating herself for it; even a whack or two on the rear when absolutely needed was rare with Missy. Honest to God, Vicki confessed, she felt like a child abuser.

But the capper for Vicki was when Missy yelled, "I hate you!" as she ran upstairs to her room, slamming the door hard enough to register on the Richter scale.

"How about you and I talk about it?" Warren said. "After all, I'm on your side, you know."

"I thought you'd be on her side."

"Hmm, maybe a bad choice of words. Try it this way. I love you. You're my kid. I love your mom. She's my wife. We're a family. We all love each other, don't we? So, the way I see it, that means we're all on the same side. We have to help one another any way we can. Understand?"

"I guess."

He tapped her on the shoulder. Missy looked directly at him. "Sometimes listening can be a big help. I'm a good listener. Anything you want to say?"

Missy nodded emphatically. "Why did she hit me in the face?"

"Because she was super upset. She lost her temper. She acted without thinking. Of course, you gave Mom pretty good reason to be so upset."

Missy said, "I guess."

"What got into you in church to turn you into a junior wild woman, anyway?"

"Nothing."

"Nothing?" he said. Personally, he thought it quite possible that Missy's built-in bullshit detector had suffered an overload. What kid who hadn't been brainwashed into believing all that God crap would voluntarily waste time in church?

"I don't want to talk about it," Missy said. "I can't."

"That's all right. We all have things we want to keep to ourselves."

For a moment, he thought she was going to tell him something, so dark a secret that it clouded her face. Her lips actually moved.

But when she said nothing, he said, "You know, Mom did try to talk to you. She wanted to tell you how sorry she was. You think it might be a good idea to go downstairs to her and let her talk to you now, maybe work out a few things between you?"

"Maybe. I don't know."

"I'd like that, Missy," he said. "You could do it for your good old man who loves you heaps and barrels and bushels and all, couldn't you?"

"I love you, too, Daddy," Missy said. Suddenly, she scurried to plant herself on his lap and leaned against him. "I'll always love you."

"And you can be sure I'll always . . ."

She put her hand on his chest, gently petting him. Then, slowly, her hand rose, and her index finger lightly slid up his neck, tickling the flesh just beneath his chin. "I love you so much, Daddy, so very, very much, and I want to do nice things for you."

Warren's guts knotted.

Missy wriggled, as though snuggling into heavy blankets on a cold winter's night. "I have a secret to whisper in your ear."

She put her chin on his collarbone and rubbed her cheek against his. Her lips brushed his ear. She breathed, "I want you to love me. Love me, and I'll do . . . anything." Then the tip of her tongue wetly flicked into his ear.

Jesus!

Warren swung her off his lap and plopped her down on the bed as he stood up. The look of surprise instantly disappeared from Missy's face to be replaced by a teasing look, like the god-damn teen queen who knows it all, has done all of it at least three times, and wants to teach it all to you!

He fumbled for his wallet in his back pocket and fought to keep his voice even. "Here's ten dollars, Missy." He handed her the bill. "How about you take your mother out for a late lunch and—well, talk about what you have to talk about."

"Whatever you want, Daddy."

He wanted to get the hell out of there, that's what he wanted.

He grabbed the doorknob and turned it.

He wasn't quick enough not to hear her, "I love you, Daddy."

"Where have you been? You're . . . You've been drinking!"

Nodding the loose nod of drunkenness, Warren said, "Observant as hell." He smiled sloppily. "Sometimes that's one of your most endearing traits, Vicki. Other times, it's a pain in the ass."

"It's almost midnight!" Vicki shouted, rising from the living room sofa. "Without a word to me, you take off like Jack the Ripper's after you, and then you come home like this!"

Warren put a finger to his lips. "Shh, hold it down, Vick. You'll wake the kid."

"No," Vicki said, "no, I told you I wouldn't go through scenes like this again, Warren. I've had enough of it."

"Aw, poor Vicki had a real shit day." With his thumb, he tapped himself on the chest. "Maybe my day wasn't a passport to paradise, either, ever think of that? Of course not. What do you know about what it's like to be me?"

Eyes blazing, Vicki said, "I know you, all right. You're an alcoholic . . ."

"I'll drink to that!"

". . . and if that's what you've chosen to be, that's your decision. But you'll do it without me."

He couldn't stop himself—and didn't want to. "And you'll get along without me very well, right?" He smiled. "I can name that tune in three notes. You'll find some fine feller to keep you from the lonelies, a shoulder to cry on, someone to fill that empty space in your heart, and"—he winked—"and that ain't all, folks."

He made a show of scratching his head and raising an eyebrow, as though a thought had just at this moment occurred to him. "I never did ask. Was Greenfield, old Davey boy, my pal and my colleague, any good in the sack?"

Rage twisted Vicki's face. "You . . . you . . ."

"Too bad you can't swear worth a shit, Vicki," Warren said. "You'd be surprised—times like this, it helps. But you're just too goddamn nice to put dirty words into your mouth, aren't you? You know, I never did figure out how Nelly Niceness wound up doing the dirty deed with David. That wasn't nice now, was it?"

She took a step toward him and raised her hand.

Quietly, Warren said, "Going to slap my face, too?"

In slow motion, her arm dropped. Then she said, "You bastard!"

"See, sometimes it feels right to swear."

She marched out of the living room. At the foot of the stairs, hand on the bannister, she turned her head to look at him with cold detachment. With no expression in her voice, she said, "Don't come up to bed, Warren. I'd rather wake up to find a corpse alongside me than you."

"Hey, I live here too, sweetheart."

"You take one step into the bedroom, and . . ."

"You'll slap my face?"

"I'll telephone the police."

He thought about that. No sense bothering the police with a simple domestic disturbance. He was a public spirited citizen, a conscientious member of the community.

"Good night, dear," he said, as Vicki started up the stairs. "Always enjoy our marital chit-chats. And by the way, fuck you very much."

He expected to hear the bedroom door slam, but he didn't. Of course not. Vicki wouldn't want to wake . . .

Missy! Jesus!

It was Missy who'd triggered this binge.

He ran his hand down his face. Oh, Jesus, he was seriously fucked up and not just booze fucked up.

Crazy-sick-nut-case fucked up.

All right, then . . . He'd spent the day trying to drown his problems, but he was alcohol courageous now.

He went into his study, turned on the light and sat at the desk. A sheet of paper was in the Underwood. There was nothing on it.

He pulled open the right hand desk drawer and took out the pistol. The .25 caliber automatic felt small and perfect in his hand.

He didn't doubt himself at all. He felt calm, almost relieved.

It was time for the truth.

He had . . . sexual desires . . . for children.

And that was all the reason anyone needed to put a bullet in his brain.

So, big deal! Everyone fantasizes. That can't be changed. That's the way it is. But he had never *done* anything.

And shit, he had never had fantasies about Missy. Missy was his kid, and he loved her, loved the hell out of her, loved her the way a father was meant to love a kid—and that was all there was to it.

But what was with Missy?

Hell, what was with *him*, turning it into something it wasn't? Missy was a daughter with her father and that was all.

He decided he was okay—drunk as a skunk, but okay. He put the pistol back in the drawer. He didn't need it. He was okay.

He told himself that with every step he took downstairs. It was his final thought as he passed out on the rec room sofa.

FIFTEEN

It was four in the morning. Vicki Barringer was asleep, dreaming she stood before the throne of the Lord. God was not white-robed and bearded, but looked something like Walter Cronkite, only with more compassionate, less analytical eyes. Vicki had a confession to make.

"I was unfaithful to my husband."

"Yet he is still your husband, and you are yet his wife. Do what you must to earn your husband's forgiveness, but first, you will have to forgive yourself," God said in a pleasant voice that had no trace of thunder rumbling in it. God nodded, as though indicating she was to move along to the next item.

"I haven't spoken in years to Carol Grace, my own sister," Vicki said. "I've cut her out of my life. I hardly even think of her. I thought she was intolerant, but I'm being no less intolerant of her than I accused her of being of me."

"Yet she is still your sister, and you are yet her sister. Love her so that she will love you."

A deep calm settled on Vicki as she slept and dreamed and had moments of understanding. She said to God, "I turned away from You."

God said, "But here I am. And I have not turned away from you."

Four hours later, when the alarm buzzed,

GOODWILL STORE
#5238
CALL AGAIN

04-21-2003   19:00
REG   001   130722

WARES   1 $0.50
TA1 $0.50
TX1 $0.03
CASH $0.53

1 No

Vicki was not able to recall the details of her dream. However she did feel a sense of peace within her, as though everything that was wrong in her life could be set right, as though there was always something she could rely on no matter what.

The child was not dreaming. She was not asleep, but neither was she awake. She was not Melissa Barringer. She understood that. She had no choice but to accept it and do what she had to do.

She slowly got out of bed. In the ethereal glow of the night light, she took off her underwear. Naked, she left the bedroom.

In the dark hall, she paused a moment, then moved to the stairs and descended without the need of holding onto the bannister.

In the kitchen, she did not turn on the light. She went to the counter and opened the drawer by the sink. Face expressionless, she took out a steak knife and touched the blade with her thumb. She rejected it. She chose a long carving knife.

The fingers of her right hand wrapped around the knife handle, she opened the door to the basement with her left. Soundless and sure-footed, she walked down the stairs.

Warren lay snoring on the rec-room sofa.

She glided across the floor. With each step, she raised the knife a bit higher until it was right before her face, and she stood over Warren Barringer as his Adam's apple bobbed with each breath he took.

SIXTEEN

"**E**van?"

On his knees at the side of the bed, eyes red, lower lip chapped and scaly, Evan Kyle Dean did not respond to his name or the knock at the door. His hands were clasped for prayer, but he was not praying. A prayer came from the heart, but his heart was dead, a heavy black stone in his chest.

Across the room, the nine inch color television on the dresser chattered away. Two women, their faces too pink, happily compared the absorbability of paper towels. He needed the television's gibberish, since he couldn't stand the awful silence of the room and the hurricane rushing of the thousands of thoughts in his mind.

"Evan, may I come in?" Carol Grace called through the door.

"No," he said. For the past week, they had not been sleeping together. She'd moved to one of the guest rooms.

"Are you all right, Evan?"

He heard the concern in her words. "Yes," he lied. "I just need to be alone. I need to think."

"Could I fix you breakfast?"

"No." He had eaten—when was it?—yesterday? The food's melted cellophane taste had sent him staggering to the bathroom to throw up.

In the eight days since he had broken down at True Witness Church, Evan Kyle Dean had lost 20 pounds. He had slept perhaps ten hours total. He could not turn off his mind. In all that time, minute by excruciating minute, thoughts raced through his brain like tracer bullets, but when he tried to catch one and hold it long enough to make some sense of it, it turned to smoke.

And he could not pray. He simply could not pray.

"Evan, are you sure . . ."

"Please, just let me be!" he curtly called out, instantly regretting it. He suppressed a groan, as with his hands on the unmade bed, he lifted himself to his feet.

Retying the belt of the blue terry cloth robe he wore over his pajamas, he went to the door and opened it.

The sickly, frightened look on Carol Grace's face knifed into him, cutting into his own pain and adding to it. He tried to smile. "I . . . I'm sorry, dear," he said. "I don't mean to be short with you."

"Evan," Carol Grace said, "we have to . . ."

"See a doctor?" he concluded the sentence for her. "Or a psychiatrist?" He gave a snort of mirthless laughter. "No, dear, this is something I have to work out on my own."

Unlike numerous others who healed through God's power, or claimed to, Evan Kyle Dean did not disparage doctors and psychiatrists. Their minds and their talents were God-given, and in their own ways, they were as much God's workers as any preacher who cast out unclean spirits by the power of the Holy Name. But a doctor's task was to heal afflictions of the body, and a psychiatrist's, afflictions of the mind.

His affliction was of the soul.

"Carol Grace," Evan said softly, "my own wife, good and true." He gently took her face in his hands. "Our union is based on trust, our trust in one another"—his mouth was dry—"and our trust in God. What's happened . . . what is happening to me is part of the Lord's plan. I know that. I don't understand it yet, but I trust Him. I beg you to trust me now. And to remember that I love you."

The smile she tried did not quite work. "All right, then," she said, "I'm going to the store. While I'm out, I think it would be good for you to get cleaned up and dressed."

"Yes." He nodded. "I've been brooding. I need to get on with the business of living."

"Good," Carol Grace said, "and when I come home, I'll put together a nice breakfast for us."

"Yes," he said, although bile rose in his throat.

He sat in the chair by the bedroom window, watching Carol Grace take the Lincoln out of the garage and carefully back down the long, winding, tree-lined driveway. The Lincoln, this year's model, was one of their three cars—three cars for the two of them. He often found himself missing the old Chevrolet Impala, even with its 112,000 miles, most of them tallied up in taking the message "God is love" from one small town to another back in the old days. The Chevy had performed beautifully. It was a faithful servant.

But a beat-up Chevrolet was not suitable for an evangelist with his own weekly television show, a minister whose message was slanted toward yuppies. In his rational, easygoing way, Marvin Michelson, head of the Christian Communications Consortium, had explained it to him. And please, Michelson wasn't suggesting by any means that Evan drive a Jaguar or a Mercedes or a Rolls! Heavens, no! That would be ostentatious, a potential turn-off rather than a turn-on to those people who needed to hear God's word. But a good, solid American car was needed, a car that subtly reminded people Evan Kyle Dean could relate.

Evan had been persuaded of that by Marvin Michelson, just as he had been persuaded about the need for a fitting house. The Deans simply could not go on living in that mobile home. Why, if nothing else, his wife deserved better. Nor could he very well live in a six-room, tract house. Nothing gaudy, but a good solid piece of real estate. Why $300,000 for a home and three wooded acres was reasonable in this day and age, with the average cost of a single-family dwelling being $117,000!

What hadn't Marvin Michelson persuaded him of? No, that was not fair to Michelson—or the truth. He had allowed himself to be persuaded, allowed himself to be convinced, to be talked into, to be gently pressured to be flexible in his thinking about about so many issues.

He ran a hand over his chin. He badly needed a shave. He would shave and shower—in a minute. He didn't feel like getting out of the chair, didn't feel like moving just yet.

He turned his weary eyes to the television set and saw a Mighty Mouse cartoon, with the Mouse of Steel rescuing the Mouseville Symphony Orchestra from the music-hating cats. Mighty

Mouse whirled two hapless cats overhead by their tails, then sent them crashing into the kettle drums. He ran another through the strings of a harp, bloodless cartoon slices of cat emerging. He stuffed a cat down the bell of a tuba, then the Mouse's lungs of steel blasted, and the cat went zooming off to the moon.

Wasn't that what people wanted God to be, expected Him to be? God was Mighty Mouse who always arrived in the nick of time to save the good little mice and to beat the stuffings out of those wicked cats.

Mighty Mouse hates cats—and so do we.

And maybe people did envision God as an abstract but infinitely more powerful Mighty Mouse in the sky, but that was not the God whose love once had filled Evan Kyle Dean, not the God of compassion, mercy, forgiveness and healing. That was not the God Evan Kyle Dean had served before he became a servant of the television camera.

The inhuman television camera saw everything, recorded everything and felt nothing. Evan Kyle Dean preached to the camera, acted for the camera, even lived for the camera.

And so he had forgotten people.

He had forgotten their Father and his Father.

Weeping, he pushed himself out of the chair and dropped to his knees. Keenly aware of the painful hammering of his heart, he folded his hands in prayer.

"Father," he said simply, "forgive me."

SEVENTEEN

She got a wake-up call at eight o'clock Monday morning. Yawning, she propped herself up on the pillows and with the remote control on the nightstand turned on the television. She watched a brief *Today* show interview with Gore Vidal. Vidal was cosmopolitan, witty, sarcastic, and bitchy—his usual self. She had a sense of displacement, as though she were back in New York. Then there was a break for a local commercial. In fluorescent red pants and a pullover blue shirt that vainly battled a beer belly, a horse-faced man urged, "Y'all come awn down to Joe Billy Keeler's for once in a lifetime deals on R-V's. Keeler the Dealer will do ya like yore own daddy would . . ."

She was centered again. She was in Mt. Franklin, Alabama. She belonged here. She had a purpose. She was going to kill a man.

Today!

The waiting was ended. She knew all she needed to know. She'd done her homework these past several weeks, never trying to ingratiate herself with the locals but staying on the periphery at the stores and the restaurants, so she could hear things and pick up messages from the grapevine without actually being plugged into it.

With Evan Kyle Dean's not appearing yesterday at True Witness Church, there were already
rumors circulating that something was wrong
with Mt. Franklin's own big-time miracle man.
That was vehemently disputed by true believers.
Nothing could be wrong with Brother Evan, no
way. He had not preached because . . . Well, he
had his reasons, and so did the Lord.

Emerald Farmer had her reasons, too.

She didn't get out of bed until 8:30. She felt no
need for haste, showering leisurely. She smiled
to herself as she selected her clothing for the
day. What was the proper attire for murder?
Blue jeans and a too large, badly faded, plaid
flannel shirt.

It was Randy's shirt. Wearing it made her feel
as though he were with her.

Damn, she was calm about it, utterly nerve-
less. She understood that. The trick was to think
of yourself not as dying, which she was, but as
already dead. Dead, you had total license, complete freedom of action. Nothing was forbidden.

"We belong dead." The line, spoken by the
enduring monster in the classic film, *The Bride
of Frankenstein*, had become her philosophy, her
mantra, her motivation. Randy was dead. She
was dead. Evan Kyle Dean was dead. He did not
know it yet, but he was dead.

Sitting on the bed, she took her gun out of her
purse. It was a Colt .38 caliber, two inch barrel,
with a grooved, nonslip trigger and a custom
hammer shroud to prevent hang-ups when
drawn from pocket or purse.

She'd bought the pistol when she enrolled in a
defensive shooting course after she'd been
mugged on the subway. It had boiled down to a

choice between the Colt and an automatic, the Smith and Wesson M61, a five-shot. With hollow point ammunition, the Smith and Wesson's man-stopping capability was about equal to that of the Colt, and it was a much more easily concealed weapon, but she didn't trust automatics. An automatic could jam. The precisely engineered Colt revolver, with its fewer working parts, had no temperament. The cylinder turned, a bullet was chambered, the firing pin struck, and the bullet flew.

She swung out the cylinder and checked it; it revolved easily. The ejector mechanism worked smoothly, unloading the six shells. The gun was clean and ready, Emerald Farmer thought.

She stood at the foot of the bed, seeing herself in the mirror above the vanity at the end of the tiny hall by the bathroom. She casually raised the weapon. She didn't aim; she pointed. The pistol was not a thing separate from her but an extension of her hand, a stunted index finger. She dry-fired. A hit, she was sure. At 25 feet, she could group six shots in the kill zone every time.

She had practiced and practiced and practiced. In the defensive shooting course she had learned, "If you reach for your gun, you have to be ready to use it for what it was made for. There's only one reason for pulling a handgun, and that's because you need to kill somebody. Not frighten him. Not wound him. You need to kill him."

She needed to kill Evan Kyle Dean.

She dry-fired five more times, then loaded the Colt without a suggestion of a tremor in her fingers. Deathly calm, she thought.

She put on her trench coat. It was inappropriate for the weather, but it was the coat she had to wear.

She stepped out of the motel room into the sun. The door, metallic and heavy, clunked shut behind her.

It was time.

She should get home as soon as possible, Carol Grace told herself, as she rolled the cart down the paper goods aisle at Cor-Mar's Supermarket. Evan might need her.

But she could not force herself to hurry. It was a relief to be away from home, out in the everyday world, doing something as commonplace as shopping. She picked up a six pack of toilet tissue, a sale item, noting she was saving 22 cents.

Not that there was any need to practice economy. They had plenty of money now. For that matter, there was no need for her to do the shopping, the housecleaning, or the cooking; they could easily afford domestic help. When they had first moved into the new place, Evan had suggested just that. He even thought it the right thing to do, providing employment for people who . . .

No, thank you, she had insisted. In their house, she was the housekeeper. Evan had laughingly agreed with that.

Evan, she thought, as she turned the cart into the next lane. He was so tormented, so depressed and despairing.

Trust in God, she told herself. God's eye was on Evan, as it was on the sparrow and every living thing in His vast and wondrous creation.

God kept His gaze on all his children. She had no doubt He knew her worries, saw her now as she played whatever part in His plans He had ordained.

As Carol Grace Dean reminded herself that God watched over her, the narrowed eyes of an armed woman followed her around the store.

Emerald Farmer put a bottle of soy sauce in her cart. Four products down, Carol Grace Dean took a yellow plastic container of mustard from the shelf. In the breakfast cereals section, Carol Grace selected a box of Bran Flakes; Emerald Farmer got Sugar Pops.

Emerald was certain the evangelist's wife had no idea she was being followed. Why would she? Who expected to be followed in a supermarket in Hicksville, USA?

She needed Mrs. Preacher.

Carol Grace Dean completed her shopping and went to the checkout lanes. Emerald tracked her, abandoning the cart and regretting the extra work she'd cause the stock boy who'd have to return her items to the shelves.

With Carol Grace Dean at the cash register, Emerald stepped outside and waited. The day was hot and humid, promising to become hotter still as it progressed. In her trench coat, she was sweating and uncomfortable, but the coat had the right kind of pockets. Wasn't that why motion picture private eyes wore trench coats? They needed a place to stash their gats, their heat, their pieces.

Damn, she felt oily and dirty. In the small shopping center lot, the sun snapped off the few parked cars in brittle diamond reflections. She was nauseated. Her breath was rancid; she could taste it.

She had to remind herself this was all real. It all felt too much like a play, as though she were now awaiting her cue to say words that were not her own, to do things the real Emerald Farmer would never do. Yes, only a play, and what she was feeling was nothing but stage fright.

There was her cue. Carol Grace Dean, carrying two sacks of groceries, walked out of Cor-Mar, and Emerald followed her.

Carol Grace set the grocery bags in the trunk of the Lincoln and closed the lid.

Emerald came up on the right. "Mrs. Dean," Emerald said quietly.

"You startled me," Carol Grace Dean said, turning to Emerald. Carol Grace's expression was puzzled. "I'm sorry, I don't remember . . . Do I know you?"

For an instant, Emerald wanted to say, "No, sorry to bother you," and for a simultaneous instant, she wanted to scream every filthy word she knew in the preacher's wife's face. Instead, she did what she had countless times watched herself do on her mind's eye. She moved in closer. A number of individual motions blended into one split-second's movement. She swung the left side of her trench coat out far enough to shield the sight of what she was doing from any casual observer. She pulled the pistol from the right hand pocket and pressed it to Carol Grace Dean's belly.

She said. "Unless you do exactly what I say, I'll kill you."

Like a stubby divining rod, the barrel of the

gun quivered. It was the retreat of Carol Grace Dean's flesh from the threat of death. The preacher's wife's mouth was open in her pallid face.

"No," Emerald said, "don't scream." Her voice was a hypnotic monotone. "Don't scream, don't faint, don't do a damned thing except what I say."

Carol Grace Dean closed her mouth.

"Mrs. Dean," Emerald said, "look at me." The look they exchanged and shared seemed to stretch infinitely. You're looking into the eyes of a dead woman, Emerald thought. This is Death, Mrs. Carol Grace Dean. See it and understand it. You must!

Emerald said. "I'll kill you if you don't do just what I tell you. You believe me, don't you?"

"Yes," Carol Grace Dean said. She nodded slightly. "I believe you."

EIGHTEEN

She braked at the stop sign, too cautiously checking left, then right, then left before turning east on the two lane blacktop. "Are you kidnapping me?"

"No questions. No answers. Do what you're told." Emerald Farmer sat with the passenger door's armrest uncomfortably punching into the small of her back. From time to time, she touched Carol Grace just above the hip with the end of the pistol barrel, a reminder of what was what and who was in charge.

"I . . . I'm sorry," Carol Grace said. "It's that I'm frightened, you see, so I guess I talk. Oh, I am scared."

Emerald Farmer could smell the woman's fear, almost as strong as her own sick odor of perspiration that clung to her like a sticky film. She couldn't open the windows. That might make Mrs. Dean do something stupid, like try to yell to a passing motorist for help. She didn't want the air-conditioning on; its whooshing roar might muffle her own voice and make Dean's wife mess up.

She wished this were over and done. "It's okay. Talk if you want," Emerald said. "Just don't do anything stupid."

"No, I won't," Carol Grace said, then improbably added, "Thank you."

"It's funny," Carol Grace said.

"What's that?"

"Evan was advised he ought to . . . to take security precautions. He always refused."

"I'm sure he figured God would protect him," Emerald Farmer said. She knew the preacher had no security guards at his home, although the Mt. Franklin police cruised by several times a day. She had thoroughly observed the house, and she had decided the simplest way to get to Evan Kyle Dean was his wife. She learned that Mrs. Dean always did the weekly shopping at the Cor-Mar store on Monday morning, and then . . .

"Not that," Carol Grace was saying. "Evan thought if someone truly wanted to harm us, then they'd try no matter what we did. But there could be people hurt, or even killed, who'd never have been part of it if we hadn't brought them into it."

"What about his own safety?" Emerald asked. "What about yours? Wasn't that a concern of your ever so thoughtful husband?"

Although her grip on the steering wheel was white-knuckled, Carol Grace shrugged almost casually, as though her husband's and her own well-being were a matter of small account.

"The Lord's will," she said. "What happens to Evan or me is what God wants."

"The Lord's will." Emerald sneered. "That covers all bases, doesn't it? One guy gets saved from a sinking ship. Praise God for the miracle. Two thousand people drown. The Lord works in mysterious ways, and let's hear it for God!"

"I wish I could explain it to you."

"You can't," Emerald said, "so don't even try." Damn, she was sweating like the interior of the Lincoln was a sauna. Her stomach cramped painfully; she kept swallowing, forcing down foul, explosive belches. She wanted to take off the trench coat, maybe even pull over to the side, get out and vomit.

No, Emerald said to herself. Nothing can stop me. Nothing will stop me. I can do what I must do.

She said it aloud, explaining it to herself. "I am dead."

"Please . . ." Carol Grace said.

"Shut up now. No more talking. Just drive. Take us home, Mrs. Dean."

When they got there, Evan came out to the car. He'd showered and shaved and put on a knit shirt and blue cotton trousers. He was smiling. He wanted to help with the grocery bags.

It was so crazy. Here was a high-ceilinged living room, delicate French provincial furniture, and Monet, Pizzaro, and Renoir prints on the walls. What had she expected? A Scotch Guard plaid love seat with a clear plastic cover and a life-sized picture of Jesus or Elvis painted on black velvet? She was sitting on a chair that would have looked lovely in her own apartment, still sweltering in the damned trench coat, holding the gun, and, ten feet away on the sofa, there sat Evan Kyle Dean. On his lap, arm around his shoulder, was his wife.

They looked, Emerald thought, as though they were posing for a photo for *Us* magazine. Christ, maybe she should have put them both in the bathtub in bubbles up to their necks; that was the standard celebrity pose.

Damn it, she'd thought she had it planned so well, but she hadn't considered anything with which to tie them up. She had to have them together to keep them covered and maintain control of the situation. All right, there was no way would Dean try anything with wifey on his lap.

"I don't know what this is all about," Evan Kyle Dean was saying, "but you seem to be troubled."

"No," she said. She was dead, and the dead had no troubles. There was something she needed to say to him, had yearned to say to him, and now seemed the time to say it. She smiled. "Fuck you, you lying bastard. Just fuck you."

Quietly, Carol Grace said, "My husband is not . . ."

"Hush, Carol Grace," Evan said. "Let her talk."

Not just "her." She was a person, and she wanted Evan Kyle Dean to know just who she was. It was all that mattered. He had to know who was going to kill him—and why. Otherwise, there would be no justice in what she was doing.

"My name is Emerald Farmer," she said. "There's somebody else here with me. You can't see him. He's dead, but he's here." She laughed softly. "His name is Randy."

Just as though she were making perfect sense, Evan Kyle Dean nodded.

Damn him! She felt as though she were back in high school, trying to talk to a guidance counselor who'd been programmed for receptivity but couldn't conceal that he'd heard it all before. To add to the impression, the minister said, "Do you want to tell me about Randy?"

"I loved him," she said. "He died."

Randy's death, the reality of it, gripped her as if for the first time. Her eyes burned, and her strength ebbed. The pistol was so heavy.

Through a thickening film of tears, she forced herself to focus on Dean's face. If he said one word, she would kill him right now.

"Randy was a dancer," she said, forcing the words out as quickly as possible. "I'm an actress. I was. We both had show business dreams. Randy . . . he was beautiful. He was so beautiful." The vision of him, lean and strong and smiling and graceful, filled her mind.

"But he was one of those horrible people. That's what you Bible weirdos would say. He was bisexual. You know what that means? He loved women and he loved men."

And he loved me, she thought.

She snickered. "Abomination unto the Lord, right, preacher? Isn't that what you'd say?"

"It is not my place to judge," Evan Kyle Dean replied.

"Oh, right, right," Emerald said. "You're not like the rest of them. Not you. You're liberal. The golden rule applies to everyone, even queers. Love your neighbor. That was your line, and that's a beautiful line. You suckered Randy with it. For a while there, you nearly suckered me."

It was all falling into place for her now. There was no longer anything unreal about this moment. It was intensely real.

Keeping her voice flat, she said, "What happened was Randy got it. The scourge. The plague. AIDS. God's punishment for gays. AIDS, that's a death sentence."

"I'm sorry."

"Shut up, Dean. I'm talking."

Emerald went on. "Randy was scared. He didn't want to die, couldn't accept he would die because he was what he was. I think it was that it was just so damned . . . unfair. Sentenced to death because he made love! And you know what else scared him? He worried he might have given it to me." She laughed. "Well, guess what? He did. Of course, he didn't live long enough to find that out."

I have AIDS. I am dead. I am already dead.

Evan Kyle Dean nodded, and in that instant, she hated him more than ever.

"Randy was desperate. When he realized there wasn't a thing the doctors could do, that's when he turned to you, Preacher Dean. He honest to God believed you were the real thing. So sincere with your 'God is love' spiel, all forgiveness and compassion and folksy bullshit.

"I don't suppose you remember Randy. He was at your healing service in Buffalo, New York. That was just about three years ago. You put your hands on his shoulders. You told him God loved him. You told him God wanted him to be well. You told him God had cured him.

"And what makes it all the worse, you lying bastard, is that Randy believed you. He honestly thought he was cured. He could feel it. That's what he thought.

"Then about two months later, Randy got a paper cut, one of those little nicks that hurts like hell and heals in about two days. But Randy's didn't heal. It got infected. His whole finger turned black, and blood poisoning shot up his arm, and his fever ran up to a hundred and four. They amputated his finger."

That was it, she remembered, the start of Randy's dying. What came after that was horror —the weight loss, the flesh melting off him, the pneumonia that made his every breath a phlegm-crackling battle for air, and the purple-red lesions running with pus and plasma. Then his kidneys failed.

She could not doubt that something similar or perhaps even more agonizing awaited her, but she was not afraid. The dead do not fear.

"You're not a minister, Evan Kyle Dean," she said. "You're a monster. You gave hope to the hopeless. You lied."

It was then the minister said what she never expected to hear. "Yes, I did."

It rocked her like a kick to the solar plexus, but it set everything perfectly right.

She stood up and took a step. "Mrs. Dean," she said, "get up. Put your hands behind your head. Then sit down at the end of the couch."

"No! I won't!"

"Do what she says, Carol Grace," Evan Kyle Dean said, as though urging a reluctant child to listen to the babysitter.

"Now you, Dean. Get up. I'm going to kill you."

He stood with his arms at his sides. She'd expected him, wanted him to look terrified, but instead he seemed only terribly thoughtful.

Kill him now! She heard the command within her mind. Let his wife watch him die the way you watched Randy die.

"Do you want to pray?"

"I've been praying," Evan Kyle Dean said, "but I want to tell you something."

"Say it."

"I'm sorry, Emerald Farmer."

She thumbed back the hammer of the Colt. It clicked.

"No!" Carol Grace screamed.

Emerald pulled the trigger.

NINETEEN

He gradually drifted up from one level of sleep to the next, until his eyes opened and he was awake and surprised. He had expected the iron claws of a horrible hangover to be digging into his brain, but there was no headache, no cotton mouth, no nausea, no shakes.

He felt good, damned good, better rested than in quite some time.

He raised his arm and glanced at his wristwatch. 9:50. He'd be late for his class. No, he wouldn't. The hell with his class, the hell with teaching today.

Slowly, he sat up on the rec room sofa, still marveling at the way he felt.

No hangover, but damn it to hell, no blackout either. Last night replayed itself clearly—the fight with Vicki, then dragging his ultra-intoxicated ass down here and zonking out.

That was all of it, he was sure, but he double-checked, searching through his memory. Nothing else, he was certain, but what was there was pretty bad.

The fight had been a gem. He remembered every rotten, slashing word of it. Last night a long time festering boil went "pop," spewing its poison all over his wife and his marriage.

He had to set things right, and he would.

Not only last night, but everything that was wrong, everything that had ever been wrong between Vicki and himself could be straightened out. He was confident of that. They had to . . . *he* had to make it work for Missy's sake.

She needed him.

When he stood up, he felt something unusual —not unusual, but strange. He had the fleeting impression he was no longer himself.

He was . . . different. It was a subtle change, but somehow there'd been a delicate alteration in his perspective, in the way he viewed the world. There was a similar change, too, in the way he looked at himself.

Warren Barringer was neither pessimistic nor optimistic. He had a vague feeling of acceptance, as though from this point on, things would take care of themselves.

He scratched his head. Something had happened to him. A thought that seemed completely irrational flashed in his mind: Something was taken from me, something was cut out of me.

The idea disappeared like a bug snatched off a pond's surface by a hungry fish.

Warren went to the bar and picked up the bottle of Johnny Walker Scotch. He unscrewed the top. "Johnny, we've had some good times together and some bad times, but I don't need you. Not anymore. So long, pal." He tipped the bottle, and a brown stream gurgled into the stainless steel sink to swirl down the drain. He ceremoniously emptied each bottle, bidding farewell to Smirnoff, to Seagram's, to Gilby's.

He went upstairs. In the kitchen, he opened the telephone directory and jotted down a number on the top sheet of a pad. Then he called North Central University. He wouldn't be in today. No, he wasn't sick. It was personal.

He had things to do.

It was all right, Laura Morgan assured her when Vicki had come in. No need to apologize for Missy's misbehavior in church. Kids, who could figure them? After all, her own Dorothy wasn't exactly "sugar and spice and everything nice."

Vicki was grateful that was all there was to it. She didn't feel up to talking, not about anything that had happened yesterday, her personal Black Sunday. Sitting on the stool behind the counter, she flipped through the pages of *Flower News*, a trade magazine for florists. Every brightly colored photograph seemed drab, and she didn't care to read about new styles in funeral arrangements.

Last night, the rug had been yanked away to reveal the huge mound of dirt that had been swept under it—Warren's long repressed anger and her usually repressed guilt. Warren's drunken tirade hurt, of course, but he had not said anything she'd not expected to hear years ago when she had confessed her affair with David Greenfield. It was, she thought, just about what she deserved. She'd kept Warren from their bed last night, but she had not slept alone. Her guilt had been with her.

"It's not the church thing bothering you, is it?" Laura Morgan called from the back of the shop, where she worked on a wicker basket centerpiece.

"No, not really."

Laura came over and put a hand on Vicki's shoulder. "Sometimes it helps to share problems."

"Thanks," Vicki said. "I don't think it's that kind of problem." Maybe her problem couldn't be solved, she thought. Maybe the only solution, partial at that, would be to wear a scarlet "A" and proclaim her guilt to the public, as well as herself every time she looked in the mirror.

"Whatever you say, but remember, I'm around." Laura went back to her arranging.

The bell above Blossom Time's front door tinkled as Warren walked in. The late morning sunlight followed him, silhouetting him and blurring his outline. Of course Vicki recognized the familiar figure, but she had an incomprehensible feeling that sent chills shooting down her spine, as though Warren had cast off a disguise to reveal himself as a menacing phantom.

"Vicki," he said, "we have to talk."

He didn't look the way she would have expected. His eyes were clear and not bloodshot; no trace of aches and pains was evident on his face.

"Not here," Vicki said. "Not now." Maybe never, she thought.

She'd been into the heaviest guilt trip she'd experienced in years, but, no matter what, she would not stay married to a drunk. She would not spend the rest of her life fearful of a drunk's unpredictable rages. She would not allow Missy to grow up with a drunken father; better no father at all. She would not be a willing witness to the slow suicide of alcoholism, would not sit by the bed of a man dying of cirrhosis of the liver, a man who'd embalmed himself before his death.

Warren said, "Please," and reached for her hand.

She pulled her hand back. "You ought to be at the university. I don't want you here."

Laura Morgan came to the counter. Standing alongside Vicki, she nodded, introducing herself. "You're Warren."

He said, "Vicki's told me about you, Laura. You're her good friend."

"Yes, I am." After a lengthy pause, Laura said, "Sometimes good friends butt into each other's business. I guess that's what I'm doing. I think you and your wife have something to talk over."

"We do."

Laura looked at Vicki. "I'm not trying to tell you what to do, but if you want to take off the rest of the day, I'm sure I'll be able to manage."

"No," Vicki said, eyes down, "that's all right."

"Vicki, please." It was how he said "please" that got to her. She peered at him, studied him, and saw or thought she saw desperation, an emotion which he'd never shown—at least not to her. "I'm asking you to come with me. We can work it out, Vicki. Talk with me."

She made up her mind. "I'll be in Saturday then, Laura," she said.

"That'll be fine."

She walked home with her husband. Work it out? she thought. No, she feared that was impossible, not this time. It was over. All they might have had together, all that they once might have been, was no more.

It's time for an ending, she said to herself, even as she hoped she was wrong.

TWENTY

"**Y**ou're angry and you're hurt," Warren said.

They sat on the living room sofa, the middle cushion separating them. Looking at her folded hands in her lap, Vicki said, "Go on."

"It's a hell of a thing," Warren said. "I'm a writer. I teach English. Words are important to me. Sometimes you can say it all with words, but other times, words are so damned inadequate." He got up, stood before her, head hanging. "Vicki, I'm so sorry."

The corner of her mouth twitched up in what was not a smile. "I've heard that before, Warren. I've believed it before."

"I know. But this time is different."

"I've heard that before, too."

"No, I mean it. Liquor *is* a problem for me. I've never admitted it, not to you, not to myself, but now it's time. Drinking is a real problem, and there's only one way I can handle it. No more alcohol, period." He smiled hopefully. "That's something I haven't said before."

"No, you haven't, but now I have to ask if you mean it."

He told her he'd dumped all the liquor, and that was that. He thought he'd be able to stay sober on his own. He meant to try, anyway. He reached into his wallet. "If not," he said, flourishing a scrap of paper as if it were a winning lottery ticket, "this is the telephone number of Alcoholics Anonymous. This goes with me from now on."

Then he did the last thing on earth she could have predicted. Warren was proud, sometimes proud to the point of arrogance, but he slowly sank to his knees. It was so flamboyantly melodramatic that she questioned the act's sincerity even as she was touched by it.

But she couldn't question his tears or the sobs that choked his words as he said, "I am sorry, so sorry. Forgive me for hurting you. Forgive me for hurting our marriage and our life together. Love me, Vicki, and let's start again."

Her own tears blinded her. She didn't know if she was convinced because she wanted to be convinced, but she could not doubt Warren was definitely trying to change.

She loved him. That's what she told him, crying, on her knees, too, holding him, their hot, wet faces touching. A new start, that's what she wanted, what they needed. But she had to talk to him, really talk to him at long, long last.

". . . about what happened with David Greenfield."

"No, there's no need," Warren said.

"It's something I have to explain, if we're to make a new start."

"All right, then, but let's move to the couch. My knees are getting calloused." Warren said.

Vicki gave the feeble joke a louder laugh than it merited, a laugh of release. She needed to confess so Warren would understand and forgive her. No, not only Warren. She had to get it all out if she was ever to pardon herself.

She fetched a box of tissues from the bathroom, and they both blew their noses. It was funny, she thought. Life's most serious, heartfelt moments summon up tears—and the rudely comic noise of blowing noses!

She sat down, and when Warren put his arm around her, she leaned against him, assuringly aware of the gently shifting solidity of his body as he breathed.

"It was a bad time for me," she began, then corrected herself. "It was a bad time for us."

"Yes," Warren said.

Missy had been 18 months-old, but plunging into the discover-touch-break everything "terrible twos" without regard for the calendar. Warren, teaching at Laurel Valley College, a small school in southern Indiana, had been directly told not to plan on being a member of Laurel Valley's faculty in the future.

That was, Warren maintained, because he had been asked to read the manuscript of a novel. The English department chairman, the book's author, sought Warren's advice because, "Ah, uhm, it's possible there are some minor flaws in the work that are preventing its publication," the book having been rejected by 43 publishers in nine years. Warren found only one flaw—the book was garbage. He could have been more diplomatic in rendering that verdict, but he was still young enough to believe writers were obliged to be honest.

Warren was working on his new novel, the book that eventually became *The Endurance of Lyn Tomer*. It was not going well. How could he write? Jesus, here he was on a frantic job hunt, sending out resumes and coming up zilch. And here was the kid, always screaming when he needed peace and quiet. And here was Vicki, always getting on his case with her pathetic bleating. "I'm your wife. I'm alive, I'm here. Will you please pay attention to me?"

Goddamnit, didn't she understand? He needed to write the book. The book would save their asses. It would take care of money. Universities would come courting him, wanting him as a status symbol writer-in-residence. Granted, his first novel, *Fishing with Live Bait*, hadn't made it big. There were reviews calling him "promising" and all that shit, but no sales. The first printing was 5,000 copies and only 312 sold.

But that was how it worked in the American literary game! It was your second book that established your reputation.

Was she too damned insensitive to realize his writing, his art, was a monumental concern in his life? With her religious upbringing, it was a weird irony she turned out to be a goddamned Philistine! Christ, she was enough to drive a man to drink, which Warren did often. He just wanted to be left alone.

He certainly left her alone—all alone.

Vicki reached for the tissues as fresh tears began rolling. "Warren, I missed you. I wanted you."

"I'm sorry, Vick . . ."

"Please, it's my turn to be sorry. And please, just let me get on with it. This is hard for me." She shook her head. "I was childish. I dreamed up crazy fantasies, but I wasn't too original. There was the old stand-by—suicide. 'Then he'll be sorry for the way he treated me.' But that was too scary. What if the razor blade did too good a job or I took one pill too many? Only way I was willing to commit suicide was if I had a guarantee I wouldn't die."

She dabbed at her eyes. "I put together a corny scene, right out of a 1940's Technicolor movie, complete with violins. I'd be holding Missy in one arm and waving your manuscript in the other hand. 'You must choose between your wife and child and your precious art!' Every time I projected that on my mental movie screen, I could just about hear myself using a British accent. But you know, I almost worked up the courage to try it."

"You didn't," Warren said. "I'd remember something like that."

"I was afraid you'd laugh at me."

"I probably would have."

"So," Vicki said, her tone detached, "that's when it happened. David Greenfield." Her shoulders rose and fell in a shrug. "Nothing original there, either. A classic stupid strategy. 'This will make him pay attention to me!' "

Not yet the renowned photographer, but obviously on his way, David Greenfield had been awarded a state arts council grant to teach at Laurel Valley College for a year. Greenfield was no academic. He had never even graduated high school. That was part of the charisma that established him as a very big deal on the Laurel Valley campus. He wasn't ivory tower isolated, but real. He was also strikingly good-looking. He projected a cool competence that held particular attraction for confused people in an indecisive era. It didn't take long before there were faculty jokes, some envious, about the photographer's harem; not numbered among the jokers were the men whose wives had joined the harem.

"Most women found him appealing," Vicki said, "but it wasn't like that for me, Warren. I knew you liked David. The stupid way I was thinking, I decided an affair with your friend would be sure to . . ." She paused, searching for words.

"Get my attention?" Warren said flatly.

Vicki put a hand on his knee. She suddenly wished she could take back everything she'd said, but she had to forge ahead. It all had to come out now, because it hadn't been dealt with then.

Warren thought a great deal of David Greenfield, respected his work and considered him a comrade in arts. Several times, they'd had lunch in the student union cafeteria. They'd discussed the goals of art and the struggles faced by American artists. They'd gone drinking together, and David Greenfield had been a supper guest.

"But there was another reason," Vicki said. "I didn't want to get seriously involved with another man. That sounds ridiculous, I know, but I loved *you*, Warren. No matter what I did, I never stopped loving you. I couldn't run the risk of falling in love with anyone else. The way my mind was working, or maybe wasn't working, David seemed perfect."

David Greenfield was bright, intense, talented and witty when he chose to be, but he was not quite complete. There was something lacking in him. He could not give or accept love; you could sense that. Totally independent, he needed no one. "And no one should need me," was the message he subtly telegraphed in a myriad of ways.

She approached him, awkwardly flirting and turning red-faced with embarrassment. David told her, "If you want to go to bed with me, say it. But mean it if you say it."

She said it.

Naive in such matters, she didn't know exactly how many trysts constituted an affair. She kept count. She went to bed with David Greenfield nine times over a six week period.

Vicki's attempt to emotionally remove herself from what she was doing was unsuccessful. Her moods swung wildly between rage and guilt.

But Warren never even seemed to notice, not a thing.

She ended it then and told Warren.

"Not long ago, you told me I was angry and hurt," Vicki said. "You kept it hidden inside, but you were angry and hurt by what I did."

"Yes."

"And you still carry that anger and hurt inside you, Warren." She took a deep breath, deliberately not looking at him. "Last night, when you were drunk, it came out."

"Yes."

She leaned forward, slipping away from his arm and turning to look directly at him. "Warren, I want your forgiveness. I need it. But can you really forgive me?"

He nodded, but she couldn't accept it. "No, I want you to think about it. Now that you know why, that as stupid as I was all I wanted was your love, can you forgive me?"

He took her shoulders. "Let me ask you a

question, Vicki." His eyes were piercing. She felt as though a lie detector within him would instantly register even her slightest falsehood.

"Do you love me, Vicki?"

"Yes." Her heart felt like a stone frantically skipping across a pond.

"And do you know I love you?"

"Yes."

"Then that's all that matters now—and forever."

"I . . . I'm going to cry again."

"Maybe me too. It's a time for tears, I guess. It's a time for something else, too." His voice dropped. "Let's make love. That's what I want now, Vicki."

It was what she wanted, too. But upstairs in the bedroom, with the sun slipping around the edges of the lowered window shades, she wondered if it was a mistake. They were distant and silent, undressing slowly without looking at each other.

Then it all changed. In bed, Warren was forceful in a way she had never known him to be. He held her as though challenging her to try to push him away. His lips attacked her mouth, and it was hard for her to breath. Vicki twisted her head. "Warren, please . . ."

"Be quiet." His voice was soft, but there was no question it was a command. It surprised her. In a way she could never have articulated, she realized what this was all about.

This was a ceremony, a covenant of the flesh, a living symbolic act, as he claimed her as his and only his.

It was what she wanted, what they needed.

She yielded to his demanding mouth and hands. He moved and positioned himself between her thighs.

She braced herself, not yet ready, but willingly surrendering. On his knees, Warren slipped his hands under her buttocks, lifting her up and curling her back onto her shoulders, as his mouth voraciously fell on her womanhood, his tongue a spearing wet shaft.

She became only feeling, all heat and tightenings and tremblings. He was doing what he wanted. He was forcing her, taking her. He was doing what she wanted him to do—taking her! The climax he forced upon her was so intense she screamed, and only the quivering totality of her body kept her from losing consciousness.

Warren moved, turning her over, his arm under her heaving, damp belly, lifting her to her knees, buttocks high. She was utterly vulnerable to him.

He thrust into her. His hands on her hips, he lunged against her again and again.

She climaxed in a blinding rush. A moment later, he pounded hard against her, pouring himself within her. Then, gasping, he was curled over her back, arms tightly wrapping her to him.

That was when he said something that made her feel loved and protected, cared for and looked after, something that made her know she was his. That was when he called her by a dear name he had never used in their years together.

He said, "Everything is all right, and everything will be all right . . ."

And he called her, ". . . my little girl."

TWENTY-ONE

Behold, God is my salvation; I will trust and not be afraid. Those were the words of the Prophet Isaiah. They also had been the words of affirmation in the mind of Evan Kyle Dean as he watched Emerald Farmer cock her revolver.

I trust in God. I am not afraid.

He stood before a woman who meant to kill him, yet he was at peace. The peace of God which passeth all understanding, a blessed radiance, filled him. The Lord's will be done.

"No!"

He heard Carol Grace scream. He wanted to reassure his wife, to remind her of God's eternal promise to His children, but he could no longer speak. The Holy Spirit had seized him and taken over his mind and body.

Emerald Farmer pulled the trigger.

The Colt's hammer fell. The firing pin struck the casehead of the .38 caliber bullet. There was no explosion, no discharge.

"No! Oh, no . . ." Emerald Farmer's face screwed up in horrified surprise. Then she thumbed back the hammer and again pulled the trigger. The gun clicked harmlessly, and she pulled the trigger and pulled the trigger and pulled the trigger.

Head canted to the side, Emerald stared dazedly at the pistol she held. With awe and misery in her voice, she said, "Something is wrong. I don't understand."

Evan Kyle Dean took the pistol from Emerald, and Carol Grace ran to him. "Praise God for deliverance!" she whispered, tears streaming down her face.

Emerald Farmer staggered back, moving like a short-circuited robot. She dropped to the chair behind her. In slow motion, she put her face in her hands, and then a ululating wail burst from her.

An arm around her husband, Carol Grace whispered, "I'll phone the police."

"No, the police aren't needed."

"But Evan . . ."

He patted her shoulder. "It's all right. Please, could you make some coffee, Carol Grace? Yes, coffee. That would be nice."

In slow motion, Emerald Farmer tumbled to the floor, curled on her side in a catatonic fetal position. Her eyes glazed over. Her tongue protruded wetly from her mouth.

"Coffee," Evan said, softly nudging his wife in the direction of the kitchen. "And a prayer, too."

His wife out of the room, Evan knelt beside Emerald Farmer. So much anger and hatred, he thought, so much hurt. And so much of it his fault.

"You lied." That had been the woman's accusation—and the truth. There *had* been lies to those who'd come to him seeking God's healing. Not at first. But when it became "heal on cue and we'll go with camera three," when he became a performer and charlatan because God had withdrawn His favor and His gifts, yes,

Evan Kyle Dean had lied. No less had he lied to himself, rationalizing he was still doing God's work. After all, so many of the afflicted suffered strictly from psychosomatic illnesses, you could say they were cured, or rather, as good as cured, by the power of their belief in him.

He had put himself before the Lord. He'd been handing out popular positive thinking disguised as God's grace. But eventually he was no longer able to justify the charade. He'd ended his healing crusade services. Abandoned by God, he had despaired—and repented.

Now, once more, the countenance of the Lord shone upon Evan Kyle Dean, so that he might do God's will and heal Emerald Farmer.

"Bless the Lord . . ." Evan whispered, reciting the opening verses of the 103rd Psalm of David, ". . . bless His Holy Name and forget not all His benefits."

He touched Emerald Farmer's cheek. She whimpered and then relaxed. Her limbs straightened as the shock-induced rigidity left her. She turned onto her back, trenchcoat puddling on either side of her. She licked her lips, squinted at him.

"I . . ."

"Shh," Evan said, "God is with you now. God is with us." He prayed, "Bless the Lord, O my soul, Who forgiveth all thine iniquities, Who healeth all thy diseases . . ."

The power of God burned inside him.

It was in his soul and his heart and his mind.

He was uplifted. He was transfigured.

His eyes were as the eyes of the prophets of old, and as he gazed at Emerald Farmer, he beheld a vision.

There was illness in this woman's body, dark, insidious, and amorphous, but the disease lacked consciousness; a mindless thing, it meant her neither good nor ill. It simply existed.

In the secret voice of the heart, Evan called upon the Lord to heal this woman of her sickness of the flesh.

In a measureless instant of time, the woman's illness ceased to exist at the command of God who heard the plea of His servant, Evan Kyle Dean.

Emerald Farmer no longer had AIDS.

But Emerald Farmer was not yet cured. The eyes of Evan Kyle Dean, opened by the Lord, saw that, and for an instant, he was afraid for her— and for himself.

Not within her body but within her soul resided an evil, one of the limitless manifestations of The Great Evil. With a dark sentience not akin to human thought, it yearned for Emerald Farmer's destruction, as it desired the destruction of all that is human and all that is good. It was a spirit of hatred. It was a spirit of murder. It was a spirit of dissolution and decay, of fury and madness, of catastrophe and cataclysm.

"The Lord is my shepherd." Evan put fear behind him, placing his soul in the hands of The Lord.

God lifted him from the temporal world of three dimensions and surfaces and substances. Evan experienced a vision, not seeing it but within it.

He stood on a desolate, colorless plane, a vast expanse of nothingness. A black cyclonic cloud whirled toward him across the limitless reaches.

Then, close, so close to him, the frenetic advance ended, and Evan discerned the form of the spirit.

It was a too angular, layered shadow, a shape meant to mock the form of Man who was made in God's image. Its face gleamed leprous silver, neither male nor female. Its eyes were bottomless red vacancies.

Calmly, Evan spoke. "Leave the woman."

"Evan Kyle Dean." When the spirit spoke, its voice was a cacophony of inhuman sounds—locusts devouring a wheat field; a derailed train careening off the tracks; the hiss of high tension wires and the thunder of erupting volcanoes. Then the voice changed. Though the spirit was not bound by the constraints of time as mortals reckon time, it chose to speak in the language of today. It had a distinctly twentieth-century voice, well-modulated, thoughtful, and even seemingly compassionate. It was a contemporary, cool, calm, and wicked voice, the very voice of sweet reason.

"Evan Kyle Dean," the spirit repeated. "Let's talk."

"Back to the pit!" Evan roared.

"Shh," counseled the spirit. "No reason to boost the blood pressure, Evan. We can work this out. Compromise, so that we can both have what we want."

"Compromise? Never! I mean to free this woman's soul from your pernicious grip!"

"Evan, Evan," came a chuckling reproof. "You're being a bit stiff-necked about this, if you don't mind my saying so. After all, this woman, Emerald Farmer, virtually sent me an engraved invitation, asking me to take up permanent residence in her soul. That is the way it works, you know."

"It was her grief, her pain, that gave you entry into her soul."

"Perhaps, Evan," the spirit interrupted, "but it was still her choice."

"And it's God Who loves her and Who will free her of you!"

It seemed to Evan that the spirit shriveled, as though its angles were softening and compacting. But when it spoke, its voice was stronger and, if anything, more confident. "Why, Evan? Why involve yourself this way? The woman did not come to you for help."

"No." Evan smiled. "But I am a child of God, and she is a child of God. It is our duty to the Father and to each other to help one another. I will bring God's miracles to her because she is my sister, and Our Father commands us to love one another."

"I understand, Evan. You say that even better live than you do on television. Is that it, Evan? Are we being filmed? Is it like a *cinema verité* documentary?"

"I serve God Almighty, our Eternal Father . . ."

"But you have served the Nielsens and the Arbitrons, and you have served yourself rather well, too, isn't that so?"

The spirit laughed lightly. "Evan, let's cut to the chase. A deal. I do have valuable connections that could be of aid to you. You can be big, my friend, the biggest. The times are right for someone like you; you've got credibility. Evan, this is not nickel and dime stuff we're talking. Think mega-ministry! I'm seeing the future, and it's a Billy Graham scene, Preacher to the Presidents. And, Evan, you like it. You know you crave that kind of power and celebrity."

"No."

"Evan!"

"Yes!" Evan admitted. "Yes, I sought to magnify myself and to glorify myself, but I have changed. I am humbled and I am humble."

"There's pride in your saying that, Evan," chided the spirit.

"Offer what you will, tempt me as you shall," Evan continued, "I answer you in one way only. 'For what is a man profited, if he shall gain the whole world and lose his own soul?'"

The spirit no longer spoke in the diplomatic voice of a business manager. The spirit screeched, and its screech was the roar of nuclear wind. "Only two choices, Evan! Two! You can sell your soul, or you can lose it. Those are the options your loving God has so thoughtfully provided Mankind."

Evan laughed. "One other. Salvation. A gift. An offering of love. His love!"

A crooked black finger pointed at him. "Salvation? We'll see if that is your fate. Another spirit awaits you, Evan Kyle Dean, far more powerful and devious than I. And when you confront that spirit, it just could be that the soul you prize so highly will be thrown down and lost, eternally lost."

Evan said, "I don't fear you or the future." God was with him. "It is ended," he said. "Leave the woman."

"No!"

"God is love, and he that dwelleth in love

dwelleth in God . . ." Evan recited from John, Chapter Four, ". . . and this is the confidence that we have in Him, that if we ask anything according to His will, He heareth us . . ."

"NO!"

"And in His name, according to His will, I pray God to send His love to the woman, His all-powerful, healing love to drive you and all unclean spirits that have sought her undoing back to your lonely, devastated and loveless realm!"

With a single lipless snarl of defeat and disgust, the dark spirit yielded before the indomitable force of God's love and vanished.

It no longer dwelled within the woman.

In his living room, Evan Kyle Dean, on his knees, gazed down on Emerald Farmer and knew she was whole once again.

And so was he.

TWENTY-TWO

On Thursday, Vicki Barringer sat at the kitchen table, pen in hand. Autumn's afternoon sunlight poured through the window above the sink, as though promising there would never be a winter.

In the past 15 minutes, all Vicki had managed to put on paper was "Dear Carol Grace." She'd considered telephoning, but feared the silences that might plague the conversation; there'd already been too many years of silence between her sister and herself.

So she decided on a letter, asking if they could renew their relationship—no, begin a new relationship.

This was something she had to do.

Strange, she thought, but one day everything is chaos and craziness, and the next it's all so normal that you're almost convinced that nothing will ever be wrong again. Thank you, God. The phrase was in Vicki's mind, and it felt as though it belonged there. The future somehow seemed to promise no crisis that could prove more than an annoyance. The furnace's thermostat might need replacement, but its heat exchanger wouldn't crack and fill the house with deadly carbon monoxide. Missy might trip on an uneven sidewalk and split her lip, maybe even require two or three stitches and gain an interesting scar, but she would not fracture her skull and slip into a coma from which she'd never awaken. A customer at Blossom Time, thinking he was overcharged, might get surly, but he wouldn't be out of his mind on cocaine or angel dust and burst in blasting away with a shotgun.

And Warren was and always would be all right. She really felt that. Warren and she together were all right.

And things would be even more all right once she and Carol Grace were reconciled.

When Missy got home from school, Vicki had written three lines to her sister and crossed them out.

After Missy hurriedly changed out of her school clothes, she asked if she could go play at Amy Lynn Elliot's. The Elliots lived only a block and a half away. There was only the one street, and Missy reminded her mother that she was always real careful crossing streets. Dorothy was going to Amy Lynn's, and they'd just be in the backyard at the Elliot's in the playhouse, and it wasn't cold or anything, but in case it did get cold, she would take her jacket.

"Sure," Vicki said. "No problem."

Missy blinked in surprise and didn't get a chance to use the rest of the persuasive arguments she'd prepared.

"I want you home in time for supper."

"Sure, Mom."

"And one other thing."

"What?" Missy frowned with suspicion.

"Before you go, I want a real big hug. You know why?"

"Uh-uh!"

"Because I love you very, very much."

Missy giggled, hugged her mother, added a bonus kiss and an "I love you very, very much, too!" assurance, and raced out.

"Let's be the Brady Bunch," Dorothy Morgan said. Like her mother, Dorothy was red-haired and tall, the tallest girl in the second grade.

"I don't want to," Amy Lynn Elliot said. "The Brady Bunch is stupid." "Stupid" came out "thtoopid"; twice a week, Amy Lynn was taken out of class to work with the speech therapist. "And they're all old reruns, too. Let's play school."

"Oh, sure," Dorothy said. "That's what you'd want to do. You love school!"

That was true. Dark-haired, petite Amy Lynn had been teacher's pet in kindergarten, first grade and now second grade. Teachers seemed to think her lisp was charming, an extra cute touch on a totally cute little girl.

"We have to play what I want to," Amy Lynn said, with a possessive wave of her hand, "because this is my playhouse. And if you don't like it, you can go home, Dorothy Morgan."

Maybe Dorothy didn't like it, but she did like the playhouse. It was ten by ten with a pitched shingled roof and windows all the way around and a battery operated doorbell that really rang. It was excellent! Amy Lynn had just about everything in the world in it, too—toy kitchen appliances, a table and chair set, and a canvas camp cot in the corner for a bedroom.

"Missy," Dorothy appealed to her friend, "you don't want to play school, do you?"

Sitting on the cot, Missy shrugged.

"Come on, Missy."

"Maybe we could do The Cosby Show," Missy suggested.

"That is really ignorant!" Amy Lynn declared. "I want to play school and we've got all the stuff, and it is my playhouse, so there!"

"Okay, okay." Dorothy sighed, then she brightened. "Come here, Missy," she said, and when Missy came over to her, Dorothy whispered in her ear.

"It's not nice to have secrets," Amy Lynn whined. "You guys stop it or I'll go tell my mom right now!"

"It was not either a secret," Dorothy said. "It was only something I wanted to tell Missy."

"Well . . ."

"Come on, let's play school!" Dorothy said.

School began, but not the way Amy Lynn had planned. Not more than ten seconds after the morning bell—a long ring of the playhouse doorbell—started the pretend day, an outraged Amy Lynn Elliot was being taken to the principal's office by her teacher, Miss Barringer.

"She was bad," Miss Barringer announced.

"I see, I see," the principal, Miss Dorothy Morgan, said. Looking stern, she folded her hands on her desk, the playhouse table. "What did she do?"

"She didn't do her homework."

"I always do my homework. And I always get it all right. And I always get a gold star!"

Dorothy wagged a threatening finger at Amy Lynn. "Don't you dare interrupt your teacher, little girl!"

"You guys aren't playing right!"

"That does it!" Dorothy pushed back the chair

and rose. She glowered. "Now you're going to get punished."

"You're dumb and mean!"

Dorothy came round the table and gripped Amy Lynn's elbow. "You need a good spanking, young lady!"

"No!" Amy Lynn jerked free and backed away from the advancing Dorothy. "Principals can't spank kids. It's against the law!"

Shooting Missy a look, Dorothy said, "Let's get her and spank her!"

"I'll tell!" Amy Lynn squealed, blinking back tears. "I'll tell my mom and then you'll be sorry."

"I . . . I was only kidding." Dorothy retreated from the potent "I'll tell" threat. "We were only teasing you, weren't we, Missy?"

"Yeah, we were just kidding. That's all. Don't tell. Okay, Amy Lynn?"

"Well, will you guys play school right?"

"Sure we will," Dorothy said.

"Uh-huh."

For the next ten minutes, the children played school Amy Lynn's way. Amy Lynn was the teacher. Missy and Dorothy were the pupils. According to the teacher, the pupils passed notes when they should have been working on their arithmetic. They shouted out answers without raising their hands. They were naughty and had to be punished—the right way. The misbehaving students had to write "I will attempt to improve my shameful conduct" 20 times.

Placated, Amy Lynn agreed when Dorothy asked, "Could we play something else now?"

"I've got an idea," Missy said quietly. "I know a special game."

"Well, what is it?"

"It's like a secret game, just for us and nobody else. Do you promise you won't tell anyone about it?"

"Sure!" Dorothy's eyes sparkled with enthusiastic curiosity; she was ready to try anything once—and most things twice.

"I guess so," Amy Lynn said.

"Okay." Missy dipped her head and sucked at her lower lip as though having second thoughts.

"Come on," Dorothy said. "How does it go?"

"You're the little girl, Amy Lynn, and Dorothy, you're her mama."

"What's my name?" Amy Lynn asked.

Dorothy giggled at the silly way Amy Lynn pronounced the name Missy gave her: "Lithette."

"What about you, Missy?"

"I'm the uncle, see, and Lisette comes to my house to live."

"So what do I get to do?" Dorothy demanded.

"You just go over there"—Missy gestured at the corner—"and that's all you have to do. And if Lisette calls you, you never come for her. Not ever." Missy's voice was dreamy and faraway.

Dorothy sneered. "Wow! Some fun for me!"

"It's the way we have to do it," Missy said. "This is the real way. Later, you can be the uncle."

"And you'll be Lisette?"

"Yes," Missy said, and she held the final hissing sound of the word a long time. "That is who I will be."

"Okay," Dorothy said, "just as long as I get to really play later, too." She took up her position in the corner as the mama who could not come to her daughter.

Missy sat down on the chair. "Come here, Lisette," she called, making her voice so deep she had to whisper. "Sit on your uncle's lap."

Amy Lynn did, even though she commented, "This is kinda silly."

"Do you like your old uncle?"

"I guess."

"I know you like me, sweet baby girl. You like all the men, don't you?"

"I don't either like boys!"

"Shh, play our game, Lisette."

"Huh, some game!" called Dorothy from her corner exile. "For me, it's boring!"

"You have to be nice to Uncle, Lisette."

"Hey, you're tickling me. Quit it."

"You like when I tickle you, Lisette. Sure you do. You want me to touch you, touch you all over."

Amy Lynn tried to squirm away, but Missy's arms tightly held her. "I don't like this. This is—funny. It's creepy."

"You *do* like it," Missy whispered, her mouth brushing Amy Lynn's cheek. "You're a whore, a whore the way your mama was a whore. And this is what whores like."

Amy Lynn was afraid in a way she had never before been afraid. She sagged against Missy. She couldn't move or do anything but whimper.

Then Amy Lynn felt Missy's hand inside her clothes, beneath her undershirt, resting on her stomach.

"Don't . . ." Amy Lynn bleated thinly.

"Hey, what are you guys doing?" Dorothy left

the corner and came nearer, just as Missy kissed Amy Lynn on the lips.

Amy Lynn catapulted off Missy's lap as though she'd been propelled by a trampoline. She hit the floor on her knees and scrambled to her feet, gasping.

"That's sick! That's dirty! You stuck your tongue . . . in my mouth! You . . . You queer!"

With each word, Amy Lynn backed up a step. "I'm telling my mom!" she vowed. "I'm telling her right now!"

Then she burst into tears and ran into her house.

TWENTY-THREE

"Mom!"

Missy raced into the kitchen. Vicki wasn't expecting her back so soon. Uh-oh, Vicki thought, setting down the pen that still had not managed to write a full line to Carol Grace. One look at Missy's flushed face and Vicki intuitively decided there'd been some sort of falling out between the little girls at Amy Lynn's house.

Just as Vicki was about to ask what was wrong, the telephone rang, and she got an answer—more or less.

A furious Willa Elliot informed her, "I do not care at all for your daughter's dirty games." Mrs. Elliot proceeded to briefly describe those games, based on what her none too coherent daughter had told her. And Mrs. Barringer had better keep an eye on that child of hers. There was something wrong with her, something positively sick.

"Mom!" Missy protested, shaking her head, in regard to Vicki's worried look, "I didn't do anything bad! I didn't. We were only playing."

Pressing the yammering phone between shoulder and ear, Vicki put a silencing finger to her lips.

". . . and in the future, Missy Barringer and her . . . lesbian tendencies had better stay away from my Amy Lynn, who is a nice, normal, little girl . . ."

Willa Elliot declared it would be a good idea for the Barringers to consult a psychiatrist about their child's deep-seated, serious mental problems. And then she hung up.

Vicki put down the receiver. Striving for a reasonable tone of voice, she asked, "What did you do to Amy Lynn?"

"Nothing!" Missy shook her head. "We played school in Amy Lynn's playhouse. She got mad 'cause she didn't want Dorothy to be principal . . ."

Vicki interrupted, "I am not talking about that and you know it."

"Then I don't know what you are talking about," Missy said, eyes down as though her shoes were suddenly fascinating.

"Go to your room, Missy," Vicki said. "We'll talk about this . . . soon."

Without looking up, Missy said, "Are you angry at me, Mom?"

"I'm not sure. I don't know if I should be."

"Are you going to punish me?"

"I don't know that, either," Vicki said.

"Mom . . ."

"Your room. Now!"

Missy slunk out of the kitchen.

Vicki picked up the telephone and dialed Blossom Time. The line was busy. She could bet Willa Elliot was talking to Laura Morgan, giving her an earful.

More likely than not, Vicki thought, this was one of those "much ado about nothing" episodes, innocent childish foolishness that gets magnified, amplified, and blown totally out of proportion by greater adult foolishness. It was the kind of thing that served as the shaky premise for so many situation comedies in the early days of TV, the parents making utter nincompoops of themselves and the kids settling everything with a shared ice cream cone!

But why did she feel so nervous, so downright twitchy, if she truly thought this wasn't anything worth getting all worked up over?

She had to calm down.

The telephone rang. It was Laura Morgan who had indeed heard from Willa Elliot. But Laura was not, she assured Vicki, terribly worried, and she thought Willa would cool off once she had time to think about it.

"But what did Missy do?" Vicki asked. "I'm still not clear on that."

"She kissed Amy Lynn," Laura said. "That's pretty much what I got from Willa's ranting and raving. I guess it was kind of a French kiss or something . . ."

"Oh," Vicki said. "Oh, my."

"Hey," Laura said, "don't make more of it than it is."

"Are you saying it's nothing?"

"I'm saying it's the kind of things kids do."

"Is it?"

Laura Morgan laughed lightly, and Vicki was a touch annoyed at her casual attitude. "Come on now, Vicki, kids play all sorts of games. 'You show me yours, I'll show you mine.' Hey, I remember giving my cousin Marty all my Halloween trick or treat candy so he'd let me look at his wee-wee."

"You did?"

Laura laughed again. "Sure did, but he didn't

let me touch it until I gave him a dollar besides."

"But that was . . ."

"Vicki, children are curious. If every kid who played doctor had a real problem, there wouldn't be a soul who didn't wind up in the looney bin."

"Maybe you're right," Vicki said.

"I have been every once in a while," Laura said.

"I probably ought to talk with Missy and explain that I can understand what happened, but that you just can't . . . touch people . . ."

". . . in certain ways," Laura completed the thought for her. "Okay, every month the women's magazines tell you how the ideal mother talks about stuff like this to her kids, but it never seems to have much to do with talking to your very own kid, does it?"

"No," Vicki said. Though confused about what she'd do next, she was considerably relieved. She didn't know exactly what she would say to Missy, but whoever said it was easy being a mother?

"I'm sorry to bother you, Warren."

"No, no, that's all right." Vicki's knock on his study door hadn't disturbed him. Ordinarily, he hated being interrupted when he was writing, but he wasn't writing. The sheet of paper in the Underwood was blank, and Warren Barringer's mind was just as blank.

He pushed the chair away from the desk and turned to look at his wife.

"Missy's finishing her bath," Vicki said. "If you could, she wants a bedtime story from you tonight."

Missy's bedtime already? He glanced at the clock on his desk. It was 7:45. He'd been sitting at the typewriter since 6:30, writing nothing.

"Story from me?" he said. Vicki usually read to Missy before bed.

Vicki nodded and smiled thinly. "I think she's had enough of me for one day."

What did she mean by that? Warren wondered. Oh, right, right. Vicki had filled him in as soon as he'd got home. A hassle with Missy's friend. No big deal.

"How's your novel going, Warren?" Vicki asked.

"Hmm, what's that?"

"Your writing. I haven't been hearing the typewriter for a while."

He held up his hands, palms out. "Sometimes you've got the words, sometimes you don't. It'll be okay."

He said, "Tell Missy I'll be right with her."

"Sure."

For five minutes after Vicki left, he sat looking at the empty piece of paper in the typewriter. He did not stare. Staring is an act of intensity, of concentration. He only looked at it.

Then he went upstairs to Missy's room. "So you want a story, kiddo?"

"A good one," Missy said. "Not from a book. I want you to make up a story." Missy, sleepy-eyed, lay beneath the covers, her head next to Winnie the Pooh's on the pillow. Alongside the bed, the nightstand lamp glowed and, in the outlet by the closet, the Mickey Mouse nightlight shone its pinkish, happily retarded smile.

"A made-up story?" Warren said, sitting down on the side of the bed. "That's hard to do." He scratched his head. "Help me. Get me started."

"Once upon . . ." Missy said.

"Once upon . . . What comes next?"

"You know!"

"Once upon a dog biscuit!"

"Dad!" Missy giggled.

"Once upon a midnight dreary, let's watch a movie with Wallace Beery."

"Do it right, Dad. Be for real."

"Okay, okay." Once upon a time . . . what? His mind seemed not unpleasantly filled with cotton, but he couldn't think of a thing.

Ah, he had it.

"Once upon a time, there was a rat. He was a big rat and a strong rat . . ." His throat tightened.

"Was he a mean rat, Dad?"

"I . . . I don't know. The thing was, he didn't want to be a rat." A rat? What in the hell was he saying? And why in the hell was he saying it?

"You see, Missy, he didn't want to be a rat, didn't want to ever do anything wrong. And he never, never ever, wanted to do anything to hurt anyone he loved. But"—he looked at his daughter—"he couldn't help it. He just couldn't help it."

"Dad," Missy said quietly, "you're crying."

He was. Goddamn, he didn't understand it any more than he understood what he was saying, but there were the slow tears rippling down his face.

Missy sat up. She touched a fingertip to the tip of the tear trail on his left cheek, then his right. "Don't cry, Dad. It's all right. Let me tell you a story, Dad."

He nodded. He needed her story. He needed her love.

"Once upon a time there was a little girl who loved her dad very much."

Warren nodded again. He loved his little girl very much. He needed her.

"And she wanted to make sure her dad would always love her forever and ever and ever. So she learned how to do magic."

Missy's eyes became dreamy. "It was a special magic. One night, she took off all her clothes. Then she took a big sharp knife. Her dad was asleep. The little girl went up to him then, and with the big sharp knife, she cut a hair off his head, and that was the magic. After that, no matter what, her dad would always love her."

Missy smiled. Warren felt a warmth within his chest, an assurance.

"I'll always love you, Dad, and you will always love me."

"Yes," Warren said. Slowly, he stood up. He felt detached from the present moment, from the whole world, even from himself. But he knew and understood that everything was okay.

"Dad," Missy said, "there's something I want to give you. It's a present."

It was a gift for him—a secret gift.

He told Vicki he'd be working late, but he got no writing done. He sat at his desk in his study, trying to think and unable to.

Every few minutes, he picked up the round glass paperweight, tracing the swirls and folds of the rose within it, the rose inside her gift.

Three: *O Drom Le Beng*
THE WAY OF EVIL

Paramitsha *are stories the* Rom *tell their children and grandchildren, fairy tales of wonder and mystery, of delight and dark fear—a dancing frog and a weeping violin made of flowers; the flying* vurdon *which travels from one cloud to the next;* saliya machka, *the laughing cat, whose mouth drips silver coins. This is the light-hearted imagination we find in* paramitsha.

But the Darane Swature *are not stories for children, nor are they stories for all adults. The* darane swature *are to be heard by those who wish* tshatsimo, *the truth, those who not only seek the truth, but who have the courage to confront it.*

This is a swato *of the* Rawnie, *the Great Lady, Pola Janichka:*

"Once there was a young man, a shav, *no longer a child but not yet ready to be a* Romoro, *a married man. He was a serious youth, too serious by far, for he did not dance, and he did not sing, and he did not joke, and he did not say flattering and foolishly endearing things to the girls, as you might expect of one his age.*

"A pity, then, but the shav's *time was*

spent in thinking, thinking of the most serious kind, and, as we know, too much thinking must lead to profound unhappiness. It makes us realize that there is ever so much evil in the world, and that one must constantly be wary of Beng in all its many forms.

"And this is exactly what the shav did realize! Beng was everywhere! Evil was in the earth and evil was in the water and evil was in the air. The shav was terribly afraid. He feared being lelled, overcome by evil, and so, he sought the counsel and guidance of an ababina, a sorceress skilled in the practice of the old ways.

"'Kako, Puri Dai,' he said with deep respect, 'Please, Old Mother, I am so afraid of the evil of this world. Can you sell me drabas, charms and enchantments, so that I might be safe against all the wicked spirits, the puvushi vilas of the earth and the nivashi vilas of the water and the zracnae vilas of the air?'

"The ababina nodded. 'Indeed, there is draba to keep you safe from the puvushi vilas in the earth, and this is it.' The draba was exceedingly powerful, employing as it did a silver knife, a tshuri, and three lungs and three livers of frogs. More than this, I cannot tell you, as the draba is not mine to share.

"And when the draba had been worked, the shav said, 'Now I need not fear the puvushi vilas.'

"'You are safe from the earth's evil,' said the ababina.

" 'Now, please, Puri Dai, a draba against nivashi vilas.'

" 'There is draba to keep you safe from the water's evil and this is it.' The draba was most potent, making use of 13 playing cards, a glass of plum brandy and the tail of a pig.

" 'And now I need not fear the nivashi vilas,' said the shav.

" 'You are safe from the water's evil,' said the ababina.

" 'Then, please, Puri Dai, a draba against zracnae vilas.'

" 'There is draba to keep you safe from the air's evil and this is it.' The draba was complicated, requiring black garlic, the tail feather of a raven, a seashell, and a crucifix, but such a charm had marvelous strength.

" 'And now I need not fear the zracnae vilas,' said the shav.

" 'You are safe from the air's evil,' said the ababina.

"For the first time in many years, the shav was happy. 'I need not fear the puvushi vilas, the nivashi vilas, or the zracnae vilas. I am safe against the evils of the earth, the water and the air. No beng can touch me!'

"At this, the ababina smiled, but her smile was mocking and knowing and more than a little sad. 'Oh, but there is yet one more evil, my little shav, and it is the most cunning and fearsome evil. Yes, it is the greatest of all evil spirits.'

" 'Kako, Puri Dai,' the shav said, a

black cloud in his head and a roiling emptiness in his middle. 'Please, Old Mother . . .'

"The *ababina* shook her head. 'No, my dear little shav, there can be no *draba* against this evil spirit.'

" 'Then I am lost!'

" 'No, no,' the *ababina* consoled him. 'You can be aware of this evil spirit and thus always be on guard against it. Though you cannot rely on charms and spells, you can use your own mind and your own heart and your own soul to combat this wickedness, to resist both its attacks and its even more dangerous enticements. And now I will show you this evil.'

"And the *ababina* did.

"She held a mirror before the young man's face."

TWENTY-FOUR

"I hate him. I hate his fucking guts."

"But you don't want to hate him?" Selena Lazone deliberately kept her tone neutral. But she was pleased to hear Kristin Heidmann vent her rage against Poppy. Anger directed against others was not anger that was directed against self, and it was self-anger and self-hate that had turned Kristin into a suicidal prostitute.

Kris had come a long way since the breakthrough, Selena reflected. In just under two weeks, you could see the change. The 14 year-old's hair was now a single color, no longer a multicolored symbolic defiance. Kris spoke instead of snapped, replied to questions with words rather than a popping of gum or a bored, irritated sigh. Once or twice, Selena had caught the girl smiling instead of sneering.

"I guess I'm a shit for feeling like that. Hell, you shouldn't hate your own grandfather."

"Let's not worry about 'shouldn't' right now, Kris. Don't worry about right and wrong. What do you feel?"

Kristin did not look at Selena. Her fingers were white-knuckled on the arms of the Danish modern chair. "Selena, I . . . I'm sorry he's dead, you know, because if Poppy were here right now, I think I could kill him. Yeah, I know I could . . ."

Her voice trailed off.

"You're that angry?" Selena said. She sat in her usual place, chair set so that with a slight turn of the head her clients could talk to themselves, to the wall or to their therapist, as they wished.

It was 9:25, halfway through Kristin Heidmann's appointment. They'd changed Kristin's time to Saturday mornings. Over half of Selena's practice consisted of children and young adults; she reserved midweek evenings and Saturday mornings for the kids. They typically needed order and stability in their lives, had to feel like everybody else, and certainly did not need to miss school for an appointment with the shrink.

"Yeah, I'm mad," Kristin said. She rocked forward, twisting to face Selena. "I've got a right to be, don't I?"

"Why?" Selena challenged. "Didn't you tell me Poppy told you that you were the one responsible?"

"Yeah, that's what he kept telling me, but I wasn't."

"You were the one who led him on?"

"I didn't! I was only a kid!"

"A rotten kid," Selena said, her voice flatly condemning. "A no-good, wicked, born-evil kid. Six years old and hot to trot. You were a sexy, seductive, luring slut of a kid who turned a white-haired, pipe-smoking, mild-mannered, lemonade-drinking sweet old Grampa into a dirty rotten child molester!"

"Bullshit!"

"Bullshit?" Selena's eyes met Kristin's and demanded a response.

"Yeah!" Kristin said. "Bullshit!"

Selena smiled. Quietly she said, "That is absolutely right, Kris. Bullshit."

Kristin rubbed the knuckle of her thumb on her lower lip, perhaps to hide the twitch of a smile. She dipped her head and gazed at Selena through her eyelashes. "I see what you're up to."

"Tell me. Then we'll both know."

"You're making me look at things, well, the way I ought to look at things."

Out of the mouths of babes, Selena thought.

"Oh?" was Selena's noncommittal response, the classic psychologist's answer.

"It's hard," Kristin said.

"What's that?"

"Seeing things the way they really are."

Kristin abruptly rose and walked to the office window. With her back to Selena, she ran a finger along a slat of the Venetian blind. Then she too casually said, "I don't know if I'll ever see things the right way."

"Hmm?" Selena sensed this was it. Once rapport with a client had been established, there was typically a center to each appointment, something the client wanted to say, needed to bring out, a specific psychic hurt or trauma to lay before the psychologist for healing.

It was just the way people bring their trouble and pain to a *cohalyi*, a Romany wise woman; they come in sick in their minds and souls and all they want is magic.

"So the other day," Kristin was saying, "my dad tries to give me a surprise hug. He just reaches out and grabs me. It was kinda sweet, you know, because Dad, well, he's not that way, never was a real huggy person. He was trying so hard! And as soon as he touched me, I couldn't help it, I started screaming and just couldn't stop. It was funny, even though it wasn't. My poor dad jumped back and hit his elbow on the sideboard. And he said 'Jesus Christ, are you crazy?', and I was still screaming and I kept saying, 'You scared me! I'm sorry! You scared me!' but I think I was really crying because he's a man and I just felt dirty like shit when he touched me."

Kristin fell silent. Her shoulders moved, and Selena wondered if she were weeping. But when Kris turned there were no tears on her face. "Will I ever stop feeling dirty, Selena?"

"Yes," Selena said without hesitation.

"You promise?"

"I promise."

It was a promise Selena Lazone could not keep.

She spotted it—a space! She turned off Ellis Avenue into the "C" lot by the Court Theater. Parking at the University of Chicago was often impossible, so you took what you could get. Anything under ten miles away from where you wanted to be was a perfect parking spot.

Selena was outlandishly pleased at her good fortune, parking without hours of driving up, down and around. This was one of life's little victories that keep us all going.

With the temperature in the low 60s, the day was beautifully sunny. The soft breeze carried not even a thin promise of forthcoming chilly weather, but autumn had arrived, the leaves turning early and the campus exploding with color.

It was an invigorating walk to the bookstore. In jeans and a flapping long sleeve, frayed collar shirt, one of David's castoffs that he wasn't quite ready to cast off, she felt very young, girlish almost, as though she'd shed her "mature adult responsibility" guise with her tailored suit.

Yet Selena felt something else, too—disquieting, out-of-place feeling. This time it hit her as she zigzagged around a hand-holding couple, giving them a quick glance. Both of them had book-laden knapsacks. Yuppies? Not hardly. The young man wore unfashionable wire rim glasses; with his shock of unruly hair, he looked like a 1930s socialist labor organizer. The woman was strikingly plain. Her thin lips were pursed as if that was their natural expression. She had the look of a film critic who hadn't seen a worthwhile movie since Cocteau's *Beauty and the Beast*.

What was the young couple discussing on such a fine day?

University of Chicago students belonged here. They had been bred for the U of C, growing up in homes where Miros and Chagalls hung on walls, where bookcases held signed copies of Dos Passos, Sinclair and Wilder, where the radio was incapable of playing rock and roll or country and western but broadcast only Studs Terkel's retrospective on the music and politics of Paul Robeson.

As an undergraduate, Selena had often thought herself a fraud, an impostor. It was still the feeling she could never quite shake whenever she was at the U of C.

Self-hate? she asked herself, knowing she was thinking like this because of the morning's session with Kristin Heidmann. But yes, it was indeed self-hate. She despised what she had been—an illiterate nomad and outcast skulking on the edge of civilized society.

But she had not let herself remain a slave to unthinking genes or tradition. She'd had a vision of what she could be, and she worked to turn her vision into reality.

And she had.

And that was that.

"Enough bullshit," she quietly scolded herself.

An hour and a half later, she stepped out of the bookstore. She had purchased three psychology texts, including a new translation of an early Binzwanger, and a reprint of a collection of short stories by John Updike. Now she felt all right. Buying books was always reassuring, reminding her that she was free to acquire any knowledge she sought.

Chances are David would be in now. She'd call and lure him away from the *Blues in Black and White* project that seemed to be his 24 plus hours a day obsession. She'd have him meet her at The Woodlawn Tap for a drink or two, and then maybe they'd go somewhere and catch a bite, and then this evening, maybe hear some jazz, and then, late, a little drunk and laughing easily, they could go back home and fuck like crazy. When they'd totally had it, totally, didn't dare give it another go because their butts would just plain fall off, then they could peer out the living room window and see the moon drifting high and cool and eternal over Lake Michigan, and they would sigh and she would nuzzle his ear and whisper about needs and desires, and maybe, just maybe, he would say for the first time ever, "I love you."

Her thoughts were romantic and erotic and silly and nice, so Selena giggled to herself. Then she stopped giggling and stopped walking and stared with eyes she could actually feel straining in their sockets.

Not more than three yards in front of her, it perched immobile on the lowest limb of an elm tree. Its huge yellow eyes were wise and cruel, horrible and hypnotic.

Selena stared, and the great horned owl stared back.

Mulesko chiriklo.

The owl should not have been out in the daylight hours; it was a nocturnal hunter. The owl should not have been in a crowded urban center; it belonged far to the north, deep in the woods, in the quiet, in the dark.

But the owl was here because it was not a bird but an omen.

It was *mulesko chiriklo*, Selena Lazone thought, the bird of death, and it was a warning sign of death to come, a portent to be seen and understood by the *Romany cohalyi*, the Gypsy sorceress, Selena Lazone.

The *mulesko chiriklo* rose from the limb on its silent pinions and like a feathered nightmare shot straight at her face.

Then at the very last possible instant, when Selena knew she did not have the control to protect her eyes with even a reflexive blink, the owl shot straight up. It zoomed into the sky and disappeared.

But not before she heard, or thought she heard, the owl make a sound that was not quite sharp enough to be a screech but that had the perfect cutting edge to be a warning.

Her plastic bag of books fell, and her knees slammed into the concrete sidewalk. It hurt, but it was a normal hurt, what anyone would feel, and she savored it, kneeling on the walk, laughing and crying, nose running, tears blinding. She ignored the gathering passers-by, even as she hysterically laughed at the crazy show she was putting on for them.

Selena tried to fill her mind with the pulsing pain in her knees. And she tried hard but unsuccessfully not to think about the warning of the *mulesko chiriklo.*

Of revenge. Of wickedness. Of death.

Of fate and futility.

And of the *diakka.*

TWENTY-FIVE

Saturday evening, while Missy was taking her bath, Laura Morgan called to see if Vicki would care to join her tomorrow.

"No, afraid not," Vicki said. For a while, at least, church would have to be off-limits. Oh, in her heart of hearts she did want to attend services tomorrow, but she couldn't—not until she thought she could enter Grove Corner Presbyterian without being embarrassingly tagged as "that woman whose kid had that tantrum." Then Vicki reminded herself that she was also "that woman who slapped her kid's face." She would only feel guilty about that for the rest of her life.

Sure, Laura understood. Well, how about they get together after church, lunch then, at Laura's?

"Fine," Vicki said, "but we'll make it my house. The kids can play and we can visit."

Visit? Warren interrupted in a Ralph Kramden inflected bellow, loud enough so that he was sure Laura heard. He had been getting something to drink from the refrigerator and was eavesdropping on her end of the telephone conversation. Didn't the two of them get in enough visiting at the flower shop, or was business just so pressing that they had no time for chit or chat?

Laughing, Vicki told Laura she had to hang up.

Of course, Warren was welcome to join them tomorrow.

"Oh, wow! Hey! Yippee! Some fun," Warren said. "Two women and two little girls. Cackle, cackle."

Warren started singing, off-key and loud. Just then, Missy, in her bathrobe, popped into the kitchen. "Dad, why are you singing so goofy?"

Warren scooped her up, twirled around and around. "Because this is the real me! I am just a goo-goo-goofy guy!"

Missy laughed. "Dad"—she put her head on his shoulder—"this is not either the real you."

Warren stopped his graceless pirouetting and stood still. For the merest fraction of a moment, Vicki thought she saw something distant and strange and frightened on his face.

Then it was gone. Cradling Missy to him with his left arm, Warren held out the right. Vicki went to him, and, sighing, happily molded into his embrace.

It was a moment Vicki would remember the rest of her life.

There was an overnight change in the weather, a common occurrence in the Midwest. The temperature dropped to the low 40s, and a penetratingly damp wind gusted from the north. The sky held the weighty, dismal promise of rain, and gray seemed to permeate the very air.

After a long spell of splendid days, it was a depressing Sunday.

But it didn't depress him, he thought, as he stepped out of the back door. Not Warren Barringer. He felt great.

Since his farewell to liquor, he had been aware of subtle changes in his psyche.

The changes had taken place. The metamorphosis of Warren Barringer was *fait accompli*. Right at this very instant, as he walked toward the Volvo, he knew he was exactly who he was supposed to be.

He had it all together! It came to him just like that, a jolt of pure understanding—and he for damned sure knew he was all right.

Zero problems for Warren Barringer. No booze problems. No problems in the hallowed halls of academe. No artistically agonizing writer's block. No marital hangups or hassles.

There was nothing now that could thwart him or block him, nothing that would not bow to the indomitable will of Warren Barringer. Warren Barringer was totally in control of his own life.

The feeling was heady.

But it was cold out, and his short sleeve shirt didn't make it. He needed something warmer.

"A jacket," he told Vicki when he went back into the house. She agreed it was probably a good idea. But he couldn't find the jacket he wanted in the hall closet or upstairs in the massive walk-in closet in their bedroom. Funny, because he remembered seeing it just the other day.

"Vicki! Hey, Vick! Can't find it," he told her. "Where'd you put it?"

With a smile she asked him which jacket he was after.

"Aw, you know. My all-time favorite."

Vicki gave him the weirdest look. Then she said, "You're kidding."

"Kidding?"

"We threw it out," Vicki said.

"That jacket?"

"It was pretty ratty-looking."

"Yeah," Warren said. "Ratty."

"Warren, that jacket went into the garbage five years ago."

He scratched his head. Vicki put her hands on her hips. "I think I like it better when you just act kind of dippy. When you tease with a straight face like this or act like you're getting Alzheimer's or something, I don't know what to think." Her voice grew quieter. "It frightens me."

Yeah, he did remember the jacket getting pitched. He hadn't really forgotten—not really.

Five minutes later, carrying the Sears all-weather car coat they'd bought him last spring, he got into the Volvo and drove off.

He was no more than a mile away when a light drizzle began. The windshield misted, but he didn't turn on the wipers right away. He waited, noticing how his view of reality could be altered by motion and water on glass. It was fascinating, seeing the ordinarily sharply angled eight sides of a stop sign seem to soften.

A stop sign!

Calmly, he braked. He was in perfect control of the car, the situation, himself. Soft stop signs. He understood how Dali had come to see soft watches, how Scriabin played an F-sharp on the organ and saw green tongues of fire, how poet Edgar Lee Masters could write of a "stone in the sun / trying to turn into jelly."

Everything was mutable, capable of transformation. The entire world was alchemy, transmutations occurring each moment.

A horn blared behind him.

He stepped on the gas and turned on the wipers. The worn rubber blades smeared the windshield. There were 100,000 different, plastic views of the world with each sweep of the wipers!

The grayish light faded. The dark day grew darker still—and he marveled. Changes, all is changes. Without a thought about where he was going, Warren Barringer drove on into the rain and the dark.

Far off, thunder rumbled.

Up in Missy's room, Dorothy Morgan asked, "You want to play something?" She'd been to church, so she was wearing an almost new, dark green, long sleeved dress. She had a purse, too, that she'd set down on Missy's table.

Standing at the window, in a North Central U sweatshirt and corduroy jeans, Missy watched countless, fat drops of rain ponderously run down the pane. She said, "I don't know."

Dorothy didn't much feel like playing either. It was weird, nothing she could explain, but all dressed up on a rainy day, a day so wet and dark it felt heavy, it was as though she was supposed to be an adult. Playing was fun, and no way could she see that adults ever had fun, even when they told you they did! Fun just wasn't what grownups did.

Like her mom and Missy's mom, downstairs. Right now, you knew they were sitting and talking and drinking coffee and maybe looking at catalogs or magazines or something, and if you checked on them two hours from now, they'd be doing the same thing. How could you call that fun?

She moved alongside Missy by the window. "I

wish it would stop raining. I get scared when it rains."

Missy didn't pick up on it, so Dorothy had to push. "You want to know why?"

"I guess."

"See, each raindrop is a soul. It's the soul of a person who died and who's up in heaven with God."

No!

"But when it starts to rain, then all the souls come down. They become raindrops. You know, it's really creepy to think about all those souls falling on everything."

"Don't say any more, okay?" Missy said.

"But the soul can only stay for a little visit," Dorothy continued. "Just until the sun comes out. Then the raindrops dry up and all the souls down here have to fly right back up where they belong."

No! I will stay here! I belong here! I need to have life. I need . . . to live!

Missy turned her head sharply to glare at Dorothy. "That's ignorant. It's a stupid lie."

"Well, that's what Betty Summerfield told me."

"She doesn't know anything," Missy said. "And she's fat as a cow, and she smells like cheese!"

Dorothy couldn't argue with that, but she said, "Betty Summerfield goes to church everyday, just about. And in her church they pray real loud and jump around, and Betty says they know more about God and heaven and hell and everything than anyone who goes to some other church."

"They don't know anything. Neither does smelly Betty. And you don't either!"

Dorothy made a nasty face. Then she pointed an accusing, interrogatory finger. "And what do you know, Missy-Sissy? You're dumb about church and God. *I* go to church and *I* listen and *I* act right. *You* don't even know how to behave in church. And you don't know anything about God. And I'll bet when you die, Missy Barringer . . ."

No!

"You shut up, Dorothy Morgan!"

". . . you will go right to hell and that will teach you!"

Missy's face was sickly white, but in her eyes was a sudden pinpoint flash—and Dorothy Morgan was afraid.

Years later, out of nowhere, Dorothy Morgan would find herself thinking about this moment of intense and chilling fear, about what had been there in Missy's eyes. She would remember this moment, not what happened a few minutes later. Pain can be forgotten, but terror is always remembered.

Dorothy Morgan expected Missy to hit her or kick her. She really did. But in that instant of paralytic fright, Dorothy almost hoped it would be a fist or a foot and not something unimaginable and ever so much worse.

Oh, no, no, no . . .

Missy's lower lip trembled. The menacing spark in her eyes blinked out, washed away by tears. "Dorothy, don't say things like that. Please don't . . ." And then, Missy bleated, "Oh, I don't want to die."

"Aw, Missy, c'mon now . . ."

"It's terrible to die!"

Yeah, Dorothy agreed, but it wasn't that thought that made her feel like crying, too. She felt just about as bad as Missy, because she had made Missy feel so awful by saying all that nasty stuff.

If you did something bad to someone else, then you felt like you were a bad person. That was how it worked. That was because of your conscience. It wasn't like they showed it on TV cartoons, a joking around, funny-looking tiny dude on your shoulder, but there really was a voice inside you that you could hear.

And Dorothy Morgan's voice was telling her: You were mean. You made her cry. You are bad.

It wasn't right. Missy was her friend, her very best friend. You don't hurt friends!

"I'm sorry," Dorothy said. "Don't cry, huh?" She awkwardly touched Missy's shoulder. Then, feeling really dumb and weird doing it, she hugged Missy. It was what she figured a grown-up would do, but, maybe it was wrong to hug if you were all alone with your best friend.

"There, there, Missy," Dorothy said, patting her back. "I am sorry, and I won't say mean things to you again."

"Okay." Missy pulled away. She sniffled a final tear and formally held out a hand. "I forgive you."

Dorothy solemnly shook with her.

"You are my best friend for always, Dorothy. I don't need any other friends. I don't want anyone else."

Dorothy frowned, not quite sure what Missy meant.

Missy said, "If someone was picking on you,

I'd be on your side. And if someone was against me, then you'd help me. I know you would."

"Yeah," Dorothy said. Missy was saying things that made sense, but that at the same time somehow didn't make sense.

"I'll be right back," Missy said, walking toward the door.

"Where you going?" Dorothy asked. She had a moment's panic, fearing that Missy was on the way to tattle.

"I just have to go to the bathroom."

Dorothy didn't have to worry. Missy was her real and true friend, and a friend wouldn't do anything rotten like tattle to your mother.

Your friend was on your side, you were on your friend's side, and even if sometimes you got in fights with your friend, it didn't really mean anything.

Friends were friends forever.

And a friend would never do anything to really hurt you.

After she'd gone to the toilet and washed her hands, Missy decided to rinse her face when a glance in the mirror showed her she had that look that always prompted Mom to ask, "Have you been crying?" Then she brushed her teeth, trying to wash the gunky crying taste from her mouth.

She slipped her toothbrush back in the holder.

She stood, cold sluicing down her spine, staring into the mirror over the vanity, staring at herself, staring at a face that no longer seemed to be her face.

Don't you understand? I am you! Now I am the only you that there is!

No! I am Missy! You are Lisette! I am real! You are not real! I am alive!

Don't . . .

I am alive and you are not alive! And if you are not alive, then you've got to be dead. That's what you are, Lisette!

Don't say it!

There was a burst of empty silence in her mind that went on and on.

Lisette?

Missy smiled. She had done—something. She wasn't quite sure what. There was no more Lisette. Imaginary Lisette, Pretend Lisette, Lisette Who Made Trouble, Lisette Who Cannot Be was gone.

And she, Melissa Barringer, called Missy, was herself, just herself and nobody else!

Missy took a deep breath. That was that.

She'd just stepped back into her room when she heard the voice like scratchy smoke.

No more Missy.

She hated Dorothy Morgan. Dorothy Morgan was Missy's best friend. Dorothy Morgan would want to help Missy. She would be on Missy's side, wouldn't she? Maybe Dorothy Morgan could be fooled. Maybe it was better to fool her, yes, and to fool her in a way that would get rid of her.

"Dorothy!"

That was Missy's scream—a scream that could be heard only by Lisette who was now Missy. Melissa Barringer? She was here—and not here. She could watch and wish, but do nothing.

It was Lisette who was alive and smiling a fake

smile at Dorothy Morgan *I will trick her.*

Lisette was alive and . . .

Oh, it feels so lovely to smile. Your upper lip curls wet on the smooth hardness of your teeth . . .

And it's lovely the way everything you see is swollen with color when you see with real eyes, my eyes . . .

And it's lovely the way the air feels buzzing and tickly when you breathe in . . .

And it's lovely the way my feet feel in these socks, inside the warm pinch of these shoes, and I love to hear that scritchy-scratchy sound when I walk in my corduroy pants . . .

It is beautiful to be alive.

"Hey, Missy?" Dorothy said. "Is something wrong with you?"

"Hmm?"

"You're doing something, you know, freaky-like with your face. Like in that movie, *Carrie*, when she burned up the prom and everything."

"I don't know what you mean, Dorothy."

"It was on cable."

"Oh." She had no idea what Dorothy Morgan was talking about.

But she did know she wanted to get Dorothy Morgan out of here, Missy's room—*no, my room.*

"Dorothy! Help me!"

The cry made Lisette grind her teeth. *No, you fool! You gave me your hair, your blood. You gave me your life! No one can help you. No one will!*

And Dorothy wouldn't help. No, Dorothy wouldn't be around long because . . .

"Want to see something?"

"What?" Dorothy asked.

"Something secret." She smiled. "I've got lots of secrets."

"I guess I want to," said Dorothy Morgan. "Yeah. Okay."

"It's in here," she said, and she opened the dresser's top drawer. "Look."

"Huh?" Dorothy said, staring quizzically at neatly arranged underpants and undershirts. "What are you talking about, Missy?"

"It's a surprise. Look under the underpants."

Cautiously, as though expecting to find a live worm, or worse, a dead one, Dorothy reached inside the drawer. "I think you're just kidding, Missy."

"It's big. You'll need both hands."

"Okay." With both hands, Dorothy dug beneath the stack of underwear. "I don't feel anything."

"No! Dorothy! Oh, Please don't do that!"

Missy's outcry came from somewhere else, from someplace ever so faraway, a warning that Dorothy could not hear.

And a plea that Lisette-who-was-Missy ignored.

As she put the palms of her hands against the drawer and slammed it shut.

TWENTY-SEVEN

The Volvo's rear speakers hissed static. A weak FM station broadcast a nostalgia show, *When Radio Was Radio*, ". . . those well remembered, best loved shows from the good old days when we were all so very young." The wipers dragged sluggishly over the windshield, working hard. The heavy rain seemed timeless. He could not doubt that it would go on forever. It seemed he'd always been driving like this, in the constant rain.

There was the moody intro music, and then, "There he goes . . ."

There he goes, Warren thought, and he knew who he was. The radio character was a private detective named Brad Runyon. The Fat Man. Warren wondered how he knew that. After all, when radio was radio, Warren Barringer had been too young to know it. His was the first generation to grow up with television as an electronic babysitter. He was an alumnus of Howdy Doody's Peanut Gallery, not Tom Mix's Ralston Straight Shooters.

Still, the announcer and Warren said it together:

". . . into that drugstore . . ."

It was time for him to go somewhere, too.

It was . . . time.

He clearly understood that now that he was in control.

"Sure, Vicki, I'll leave you womenfolk to your-selves, and I'll go rustle myself up a bit of grub. Be back later, not quite sure when I'll mosey in . . ." That's what he had told her.

He had stopped for lunch about an hour ago, but what he was really going to do was nothing he could have told Vicki, nothing he could have explained to her. He couldn't have told her he was off to do battle with demons.

And he was ready.

This was the day that everything would be forever set right by Warren Barringer's will-power.

In control, in control. I am the master of my fate. I am the captain of my soul. He repeated it in his mind, a ritual chant perfectly synchro-nized to the cadence of the windshield wipers.

Far out to the west, three-pronged lightning lanced from the sky and stabbed the earth. He thought about symbols and coincidences. The rear speakers responded with a crackling rush of static, almost, but not quite, drowning out the announcer's words.

Bursting thundershocks followed, echoing weighty crashes of sound.

Warren turned off the radio. Then he heard a voice, taunting and familiar—and expected. It was the voice of The Rat within him. *I'm here, Warren, I'm still with you, you know.*

Warren smiled and felt the tightness at the edges of his mouth.

You will never be rid of me, said The Rat.

Warren gripped the steering wheel harder. A mile or so ahead, through the momentarily clear screen of the windshield, he saw the shopping center.

I am you! I am! said The Rat.

He pressed down on the accelerator, speeding to the battleground.

Tolando Park was a middle-class suburb some 50 miles northwest of Grove Corner. Although he'd never been here before, the Tolando Park Magna-Mall was exactly what he knew he would find—a standard issue 20th century shopping center, open seven days a week, 52 weeks a year. Tolando Park, Illinois, Lebanon, Missouri, Horseshoe Bend, Arkansas—it didn't matter where you went, you had two or three levels and the same basic layout under one roof. The three major department stores had only different names, not the merchandise. The not so special specialty stores had discount records and discount shoes and discount eyeglasses and discount jeans.

He was alert, all senses fully engaged, watching. With his hands in the pockets of his car coat, he ambled along in what seemed an aimless manner. Anyone paying attention to him would have thought: Here's a guy killing time while his wife takes the Visa card to the limit, or, maybe he's here to pick up his kid and the kid's friends . . .

Here to pick up a kid, said The Rat.

A few steps ahead, an ancient woman with parakeet legs stopped abruptly. He stopped just in time to avoid impaling himself on her shoulder blades, as she turned a smart right angle into the Hi-Standard Uniform Center.

At the entrance to the video arcade, snippets

of strobe light and sirens shooting out, a punky girl (teen? pre-teen?) broke away from her loitering friends.

"Spare change?" She held her hand out, palm up. She wore mirrored sunglasses and an ancient, baggy pin-striped, man's suit jacket; he could smell the damp wool. "Got any spare change?"

"No."

She didn't move. The palm stayed where it was. She smiled. Her plump lips were adorned with fluorescent purple. She had braces.

"Hey, come on, okay?" she said. "I wanna play some games."

She wants to play games, said The Rat.

"Come on, lemme have something. Don't be a shit." Her friends were laughing and egging her on. "Give me some spare change."

"No," he said, "get away from me."

Too old for you? said The Rat.

He walked on, hearing her call him a shithead.

An old guy was licking an ice cream cone with a reptilian tongue. Those too-goddamn-garish-to-be-true plaid pants! What was there about old men and hideous plaid pants? Hope to hell I remember so I don't one day wind up an old man in ugly plaid pants . . .

A dirty old man in plaid pants? said The Rat.

Though he knew he was in charge of the situation, Warren felt a trill of impatience. It was time.

Are you certain, Warren Barringer? You sure you want to meet The Rat? Let's not forget, I am you, the worst of you and the real you.

No, not anymore. I'm the master of my fate, captain of my soul.

Spare me the melodramatics. Take a look over . . .

There! Across the way, in front of The Pay-Lo Shoe Store, he saw her. For an instant, his heart stopped, and then jumped to a rapid thudding in his chest.

She was lost. He could see that by the panicky way her eyes darted up and down and all around, by the way she slipped inside the shoe store, then popped right back out again.

People walked past her, ignoring her as if she were invisible. She turned her head with the stiff precision of a bird, hoping to bring a familiar face into focus.

Then it was his face she focused on, as he stooped down in front of her. Her eyes were so big and frightened they were almost cartoony. She was a perfect towhead, but her hair had been clipped roughly and amateurishly. She was missing a tooth on the bottom, and her lips were full and pink.

And she was a beautiful child, he thought. Five years old? Six?

She was a beautiful little girl who needed him.

"You're lost, aren't you?"

A nod and a sniffle.

Lost and more than that. In weather like this, she was wearing skimpy shorts and a filthy T-shirt. And her feet were dirty and her knees were bruised and it looked like infected bug bites on her arm.

She took a small step back, as if perhaps recalling warnings about talking to strangers.

"What's your name, honey?"

"Angie." Her voice was small and sweet and Southern. "My mama went in there"—she turned to point back into the shoe store—"an' I was with her, and then she was gone, and I came out to find her." More sniffles, and then, bright teary diamonds rolling down her cheeks.

"Angie," he said. "I think you ought to come with me."

That's just what you think, isn't it, Warren? That's just what you need, what you've wanted all your life! The Rat was laughing.

"I dunno . . ."

"I'll help you, Angie. I'll take care of you."

Take care of her, be sweet to her, and touch her and feel her sweetness and her softness, feel her all warm and trusting and yours . . .

He stood up and held out his hand. He waited. She looked up at him.

He saw it, then, knew that she would do whatever he wanted, knew that she wanted him to take her, that she desired him, wanted his touch, his caress, his love . . .

No more pretense! said The Rat. *You are what you are. You cannot fight me. You cannot fight yourself.*

He took her hand. He walked slowly so that she would have no difficulty keeping up with him.

In front of Sears, he found a green uniformed security guard.

"This is Angie," Warren said. "I'm afraid her mother's lost."

"Happens," said the security man. "We'll get her found."

Angie looked scared as he transferred her hand to the guard's. She said, "Oh . . ."

Warren did not permit himself to think about what she meant. Quietly, he said, "It will be okay, Angie. Don't worry, little girl. Nobody is going to hurt you. Nobody."

Then, still more quietly, he spoke to her and to himself, "You are all right now."

A few minutes later, he was driving south on Route 83. The rain had eased up. The radio was playing Brahms's "Concerto in A for Violin and Cello."

He listened appreciatively to the intricate in-terplay of stringed instruments and did not hear the voice of The Rat.

TWENTY-EIGHT

The rainy Sunday afternoon sucked. That was 15 year-old Bobby Smith's verdict. It sucked the big suck because he was totally bored.

Sometimes Bobby Smith blamed his name for his blah life. Bobby Smith! Wasn't that about the same as naming your kid "Zero Nobody"? Maybe that was the reason the old man divorced his mom. His father probably wanted to name him something cool, something like D'artagnan or even Spuds, but Mom was Mary Smith, nee, ready for this, Mary Nelson!

No way with a name like Bobby Smith could he be a jock or a nerd. He wasn't a party animal or a class clown or a brainchild or an airhead or a Trekkie or a preppy. He wasn't a punker. He wasn't a stoner or a head-banger; no one ever bothered to approach him about trying or buying dope, so he never even had a chance to say no to drugs.

When Bobby Smith wasn't daydreaming about who he would like to be—kind of a cross between Chuck Norris and any male porn star with eleven-plus inches—he saw himself as he was, and that was uncool. He was the goddamned Invisible Man, or, if you want to be technical, the Invisible Sophomore. He was totally anonymous, the guy that nobody notices.

And nobody noticed his absence when he wasn't there, either.

Yeah, so Sunday was boring and Sunday sucked, but a lot of days were just about the same.

So, what to do, what to do? Might as well jack-off. He hadn't done that for about an hour and a half. He wouldn't go into the john this time. The old lady was out doing who knows what. And what if she did walk in on him while he was choking the chicken? Probably wouldn't even notice!

Time for some serious pud-pounding. Definitely.

He got ready. Sitting on the floor in the hallway, spine curved against the wall, he took out his penis. Three facial tissues were ready and waiting.

He picked up the phone and he pushed the touchtone buttons. He put the receiver to his ear, holding it with his shoulder.

He heard one ring. If it was a woman's voice on the other end, it was A-OK. If it was a guy, click!—and try again until you get lucky.

The digits Bobby Smith had dialed were chosen at random.

You might say it was luck as well as the fiberoptic technology of AT & T that brought him a young-sounding, definitely female "Hello?" You might say it was coincidence.

You might say that—but that's not what a Gypsy would say. A Gypsy would say that the sequence of numbers beneath Bobby Smith's fingertip had been dictated by *Baht*.

For a Gypsy, there is no coincidence.

There is no chance. All things are as they must

be. All events happen as they must happen.

That is the working of fate.

That is *Baht*.

In the exact moments before Bobby Smith invaded her life, she was happy—not only happy but, as happens once in a great while, aware that she was happy.

She lay on her bed, lazily gazing at the ceiling. She had on one of her father's old L. L. Bean chamois shirts, about eight times too big and cuddly and nice, and a pair of blue jeans that were washed out enough to be really comfortable.

There was the murmur of rain on the roof and William Ackerman's "It Takes a Year" album on the turntable. Ackerman's solo acoustic guitar sounded like a wispy dream. She'd never really been into the high decibel anger and defiance of Punk music, even though that had been all she played when she had first come—been brought back—home.

William Ackerman's music was all so mellow, that's what it was.

And that's what she was. I am mellow and happy and I'm glad to be me.

Then the telephone on her nightstand rang and she picked it up, wondering if somebody from school had to ask her about the homework.

"Hello?" she said.

There was a moment's silence. Wrong number, she thought.

And then she knew it was no wrong number. It wasn't a voice she recognized, but she subliminally identified the tone of it, and she somehow knew what was coming.

"Hi, baby. Been waiting for me to call? Been waiting for me to give you a nice hot fuck?"

There was a flashback to who she really was!

A feeling of damp and musky rottenness filled her, bubbling up from within her. It seeped out her pores, a slimy, sick sweat on her forehead and in the hollow of throat.

And there was that disgusting, buzzing, warmth between her thighs.

She could smell herself, that stink aura that never vanished, the stench of the rot inside her.

She was dirty.

And he knew. Whoever he was and what did it matter, he knew she was dirty or he would not have called her.

". . . my cock. Want to suck my big hard thing? That what you want?"

"Yes." She couldn't keep from answering. "Yes." It was a hiss. That was the way you talked to men, the way you lured them on, made them come on to you. That was the way you talked when you were never clean but always dirty.

"Cunt. You're one drippy hot cunt, huh! You're a real whore. Sucking and fucking. Whore cunt pussy! You want my hard cock in your . . ."

Whore! That's what she was—a dirty whore.

Dirty whore! The two words defined her. They were her. Kristin Heidmann, her name, was meaningless. She was wicked, born wicked.

She was the wicked whore cunt evil thing who'd forced her own grandfather, to fuck her, fuck her, dirty whore cunt, whore . . .

"Hey, you listenin'? Hey, cunt . . ."

She let the phone drop to the bed and sat up. She put her hand over her mouth. She wanted to throw up, to let everything rotten and vile and dirty come spilling out of her. But she couldn't vomit and she couldn't cry, so she simply hung up the receiver and then stood up.

"I am tired of being dirty," she said aloud. That was it. She no longer felt happy, of course, but nor did she feel bad. There was only a great tiredness, a deep weariness, and a powerful and overpowering desire to be clean at last.

And she would be.

There was no one to stop her. Her mother and father were away. She was alone.

She turned off her stereo. She had a moment of near-laughing anger, wanting to snap William Ackerman's tranquil guitar record. It was just such a goddamned lie!

Then Kristin Heidmann went into the bathroom. She adjusted the water carefully—warm but not hot. She undressed and got ready while the bath ran.

When she sank into the warm water, it felt good. It promised cleanliness.

She held her left arm up out of the water. The blood gracefully spiraled down.

She let her arm slide into the water. It stung a bit, but only a bit. She had split the vein lengthwise with a razor blade she'd pried from her mother's disposable Bic with a nail file. Red curlicues swirled against her hip. The dirt is spilling out of me, she thought.

After awhile, she opened the drain, letting bloody water out, and adjusted the tap to a steady tepid flow. It seemed to be in balance, the water level remaining just about the same. This way, when they found her, there wouldn't be that much of a mess. It would have been wrong to have Mom find her in a blood bath.

Blood bath. Was that a joke? Would it be Mom who found her? What if Dad were the one and he came in and there she was, not only dead but naked? That would be embarrassing.

Would they understand? Would they know she had to do it?

She wished there were a way to tell them, to explain, at least to say, "I am sorry."

Oh, she was sorry about everything. She didn't want to hurt anyone, certainly not Mom and Dad. All she wanted was an end to being dirty.

And she was sorry, Selena. You tried, Selena. We both tried, but this is the only way because I am what I am.

Kristin Heidmann grew dizzy, as though there were a gyroscope whirling faster and faster inside her skull. She leaned her head back against the ledge of the tub. There was a butter-fly fluttering within her, and she thought she was asleep and dreaming, although she had no idea what she dreamed.

Then she felt it, sweet and warm and final.

I am clean.

And Kristin Heidmann died.

TWENTY-NINE

With a silent prayer, Vicki Barringer snatched up the telephone a heartbeat into the first ring. She'd been waiting only about 45 minutes, but she could not have been more tense had she been a Death Row prisoner hoping for the governor's last moment stay of execution.

Thank God, everything was much less bad than it could have been.

"Cuts and bad bruises, but no broken bones. The one knuckle, well, once they were able to stop the bleeding, it was okay," Laura Morgan reported from Lawn Crest Hospital, six miles away. "Of course, they can't be certain there won't be nerve damage . . ."

With the wet weather that morning, Laura had driven to church instead of walking as she usually did, so her Toyota had been at the Barringers' house for the unexpected trip to the hospital.

The hospital. Lord!

It all came back to Vicki, just as it had been coming back over and over ever since Laura and her sobbing child had sped off.

That shriek! The entire house shook. A howl of shock and pain that scarcely seemed human, while at the same time it could have come only from a child.

"Dorothy!" Jumping up, Laura identified the screamer.

Later, Vicki would feel guilt among the myriad of emotions washing over her, but right then, she had to admit what she'd experienced was relief. It was not Missy! Missy was okay!

Getting upstairs seemed to take about two days longer than forever. Then they burst into Missy's bedroom.

Dorothy staggered spastically around the room. Tears and pain wetly twisted her face. No longer howling, she punctuated a constant moan with a gasping, "Uh-uh . . ." Arms thrust woodenly before her, she looked like an oafish child doing an impression of the Frankenstein monster.

Dorothy's right wrist was braceleted by swollen black and blue flesh that seemed to be growing and rippling in pain right before their eyes. The left hand was worse still, center knuckle of each finger a purple mound of ripped flesh and gleaming blood. The middle finger showed the too clean white of bone.

Everything became sheer pandemonium, Laura trying to comfort Dorothy and assess the damage and Dorothy whimpering and groaning like a grievously wounded animal.

Vicki was gaping at Missy, her kid, who looked as though she'd just beamed down to Earth from a faraway and completely alien world.

Missy's face was utterly placid. She sat at her little table, tapping her fingers on its top. Even her posture seemed to declare none of this was her least concern.

Though she could not explain why, seeing Missy like that infuriated Vicki.

"She . . . She . . ." was Dorothy's accusatory sob as her mother held her.

"What happened?" Vicki asked Missy.

Missy shrugged an indifferent "I don't know."

"She did it!" Dorothy cried. "She hurt me!"

"I didn't do anything," Missy said.

Dorothy was crying, "I hate her! She did, she did it."

More confused now, but knowing she should do something, Vicki said to Laura, "Maybe we ought to run cold water on it."

"Really, it doesn't seem too bad," Laura said, "but I guess we need to have a doctor take a look." Vicki could hear that Laura was deliberately trying to sound casual for Dorothy's sake.

"No, not a doctor! I don't want a shot!" Dorothy blubbered.

"Hey, it'll be okay." Laura exchanged a glance with Vicki. "It just looks worse than it is."

Vicki wondered for whose benefit Laura said that. Dorothy's fingers could be broken.

"Missy! You did it! You did it! I hate you!" Dorothy pulled free of her mother. Her head shot forward like a striking snake's. The words spewed out, twisted and poisonous. "I hate your guts!"

Laura said she was taking her daughter to Lawn Crest Hospital. Vicki said they—she and Missy—would go along.

"No," Laura said, "I don't think that's a good idea."

"Vicki, you still there?" Laura Morgan's voice buzzed in the telephone.

Vicki jumped back to the present. "Yes, I'm here, and I want you to know, you and Dorothy, how sorry I am that . . . I wish I . . ."

"I know what you're saying, Vicki. I know you're sorry."

"Missy is . . ."

"Vicki," Laura interrupted, "Missy hurt Dorothy, okay? I know kids are kids. Sometimes they do things that work out a lot worse than anything they might have really intended. That's what might have happened with Missy and Dorothy. That's what I'd prefer to think, anyway."

Vicki took a deep breath. "But what is it that you do think, Laura?"

"I think we'd better keep the kids apart for awhile, if you know what I mean."

"I think I do know what you mean, Laura," Vicki said. The hand holding the telephone had gone numb. She felt numb all over. She felt rotten and angry and sad.

"If it's all right with you," Vicki said, "I won't come to work tomorrow. Maybe we all ought to have some time away from each other."

"Maybe," Laura said.

"Laura," Vicki said.

"What is it?"

It came out of her in an honest rush. "I like you, Laura. I like being your friend. I don't want to lose your friendship."

There was a lengthy pause at the other end of the line before Laura said, "And I want your friendship, too, Vicki, but you can't always get what you want."

With a final apology for her daughter, Vicki hung up.

She took another deep breath. She thought of three dozen top-priority household chores she could assign herself right now. Anything, including toilet bowl cleaning, would be better than confronting Missy—and confronting her own angry feelings.

But she was Mom, and Mother had better find out exactly what had happened.

And why.

And Mother had better find out right now.

Missy ran the tip of her tongue over her upper lip. She ran the tip of her tongue over her bottom lip. She did it again. She wondered if you could wear out your lips by licking them. She wondered if she'd been sitting in the corner of her room for an hour or two hours or a week.

She was in trouble, bad trouble, for sure. As soon as Mrs. Morgan and Dorothy left, Mom was yelling, "Young lady, you are to sit right here"—Mom swung one of the chairs from her table and chair set into the corner and pointed—"and you are not to move even an eyelash until I tell you otherwise."

But it was not fair! It was not right!

I didn't hurt Dorothy, Missy Barringer thought. I wouldn't do that.

Dorothy was her friend.

Lisette!

You did it. You're the one, Lisette. You always get me in trouble. You smashed Dorothy's hands! You did it!

I am you!

You're mean, Lisette. You're bad and you're wicked!

No.

You've got to stop it! You've got to leave me

alone. You have to let me be me!

No, I am you. I have your hair. I have your blood. You gave them to me.

Oh, but you gave me stuff, too! I understand now. It was kinda like magic, but it was a real trade! That is what it was, Lisette, wasn't it?

Yes, Melissa, it was a trade. I gave you what I loved, and you gave me what I need.

The paperweight that I gave my Dad, and the doll . . .

Yes, my pretty doll.

No trades! I'll give them back, Lisette! You've got to take them back, both of them, and then you have to give me . . . Lisette, you have to give me back my life!

No, Melissa!

Yes! Yes!

Melissa stood up. Then, as though attached to the chair by rubber bands, she snapped back down. Mom had told her to stay in the corner, and the way Mom said it, she meant it.

The rose paperweight was downstairs in Dad's study, but the doll was here. She would make Lisette take back the doll, and then she would make Lisette take back the glass paperweight. She would make Lisette go away, go back to wherever it was she had come from.

You cannot. You can't.

Yes, I can!

Expecting her mother to surprise her any moment, Missy stood up. She felt sneaky and naughty and frightened. She tiptoed to the closet. Reaching for the doorknob, she stopped to listen carefully. Was that Mom on the stairs? Was it only the sound the roof sometimes made on a rainy day? There were so many sounds in an old house, you were better off not to listen to any of them.

Melissa . . .

She felt her heart jump so hard it hurt.

You shut up, Lisette! You shut up now!

She opened the closet door.

Then she stepped into the closet that was so big she sometimes thought of it as her special secret room, a place where you kept secret things, things made magical because you were absolutely the only one in the whole world who knew about them. On the rods, clothes hung like lonely invisible people. The lower half of one wall was all shelves for her folded sweaters and shoes, and on the top shelf, there it was! The shoe box. Her collection. Private. Personal. Secret.

I am the secret. You cannot tell. You will not tell.

On the shoe box's top, in the very best crayoned letters she could do last year, it read: MELISSA BARRINGER.

That is who I am.

I am . . .

The shoe box contained her secret collection—a pretty stamp from a letter some professor in Belgium had sent her father, a rock from her old school's playground so that she would never forget, a pair of huge earrings glittering with rhinestones.

There it was. The doll.

My doll. Your blood. My life, Melissa. Now it is my life. Mine!

The precisely crafted china image of the little girl with the bonnet, basket of eggs on her lap, felt scratchy and cold. It feels dead, Missy thought, not knowing how she knew what dead felt like but not doubting that this was it. The doll's face, she thought, might have been her face—or Lisette's face. Or it might have been her face *and* Lisette's face.

Missy stepped out of the walk-in closet. Eyes half-closed, she held out the doll. She swallowed a hot, excited sob down to her racing heart. "Take it, Lisette. Take it and go away and leave me alone," she begged.

No.

"Then I'll smash it! I'll break it into a million pieces!"

Eyes wide now, she squeezed the doll as though to crush it in her hands. She wanted not to shatter it, not to destroy it—but to kill it.

But its lifeless eyes caught hers for a long moment, a moment in which she could not feel her heart and thought it had stopped beating.

And she knew she could not kill the doll. It wasn't alive. It had never been alive, and so it would never die.

It was and it always would be.

Carefully, she set the china doll on the top of her play table.

She looked at it—and she felt lost.

Then she spun around as her mother came in.

THIRTY

"**D**idn't I tell you to sit in that corner and stay there until I said otherwise, young lady?" When Vicki had thrown open the bedroom door, Missy froze.

Moments ago, as she'd started up the stairs, Vicki was convinced she had cooled down and could deal with the situation. Had she found Missy in the corner, penitent, guilty, perhaps a tear or two, then everything would have been okay, she was certain of that.

But Missy's defiance was a blazing patch on each of her cheeks and a squint so tight it was painful.

Vicki curbed her fury and saw that her daughter was terrified! It was time for Mom to have a discussion with Missy to learn what had happened with Dorothy and to learn why Missy was acting so strange lately, so unusual.

"Are you mad, Mom?" Missy backed up, her retreat halted by her play table.

"No," Vicki said. She was upset, but she was not angry. She was . . . concerned. Yes, that's what she told Missy. ⟍

Mom needed to know what happened and why it happened. They had to talk about it so that nothing like this would ever happen again.

She had to know why Missy had hurt Dorothy like that.

"I didn't," Missy said softly and seriously.

Vicki did not raise her voice, nor did she acknowledge Missy's words. She continued the interrogation. Was it something that had been meant as a joke, a trick played on a friend? Was it just an accident? Vicki persisted. Accidents do happen; she could understand that.

"It was not an accident," Missy said, "but I didn't do it."

Vicki drew a resigned breath. "Missy, your friend, Dorothy, was really hurt. She was hurt badly, and she could have been hurt even worse. Do you understand? You cannot . . ."

"I didn't do it."

Missy's not quite innocent but definitely not guilty look and her repeated denial of wrongdoing got to Vicki. She folded her arms. Goodbye, cool, she thought, as she severely demanded, "Then who did?"

Missy's face screwed up. Her mouth worked wetly. Her lips soundlessly shaped words as though each one was too momentously weighty and awful to be said aloud.

Then in a rough-edged rasping whisper that hurt to listen to, Missy said, "She did."

What the hell was Missy saying? What the hell kind of game was this?

And who the hell did Missy think she could fool?

Three strikes and out, Vicki thought. I will not get angry, Vicki told herself, but how about a good, old-fashioned, bottom-whacking, administered by a non-angry, totally in control Mom who has rationally decided that a spanking will benefit her daughter's behavior? Yes, Vicki decided, a paddling was a definite option.

She was about to warn Missy of that, but she didn't, because, just then, an expression flickered across the child's features.

And what Vicki saw on Missy's face was hideously wrong, a look that should not have been on her child's face, on any child's face.

Vicki's mind flashed back to the past summer, a day in Chicago.

It was early August, temperature 91 degrees, no lake breeze, no chance of rain, the kind of humid heat that makes you feel you are melting and the city is melting around you. Warren had Missy on an educational jaunt—Adler Planetarium, the Shedd Aquarium, The Field Museum. Vicki had been shopping at Water Tower.

Then she stepped out of the air-conditioned rationality and civilization, and madness accosted her. He was albino, crossed eyes blazing pink and wild, frenzied tangles of white hair exploding around the feral face. He was as tall as a pro basketball player. A woolen coat, stained and stinking of body odor and urine, flapped around him.

"Spare change?" He jabbed a hand toward her, and she managed not to scream. "I need help, lady!" Then he thrust his face at her, and he was the only reality she saw as he whispered, "I need help, lady. I got seven demons in me and they're eatin' my soul!"

For that one, awful, unforgettable moment, she did not doubt that it was so, that his inner demons were devouring him, because on his face was unimaginable torment.

That was what Vicki Barringer thought she

had just seen on the face of her little girl.

Or she had a new, invasive thought, one perhaps more credible but no less awful: Missy was crazy!

Missy was mentally ill, blaming someone else for Dorothy. It was like Sybil! The Three Faces Of Missy!

It was crazy, all right, and the craziness was totally on the part of good old Mom, because this was Missy, no one else, with her Winnie-the-Pooh bear and Mickey Mouse night light. This was a good kid, her very own good kid—and that was that.

Not crazy.

She sat on the foot of Missy's bed. "Come here," she said. Missy tentatively walked to her and no less tentatively settled on her lap. Vicki felt the child's slim warmth against her as Missy leaned back. She wrapped her in a loose hug.

"Mom?"

"Hmm-mm?"

"There's . . . I want to tell you, I really do."

"You can. I'm your mom. You can tell me anything. Missy, I love you. I love you more than anything in the whole world, and there's nothing that can ever change that."

A silence.

"Mom?"

"What is it, honey?"

A silence, only a silence. Vicki couldn't hear Missy's breathing nor her own.

"Mom, sometimes . . ."

Missy stopped talking.

"You can say it," Vicki said.

Missy did. "Sometimes I am not me."

Even as Melissa Barringer said that, she wasn't. She was Lisette.

It was Lisette who heard Vicki say with a worried sigh, "I don't understand."

The child who was not then Melissa Barringer understood.

Lisette understood completely.

She pressed against Vicki Barringer and hated her. She knew this woman loved Missy. She would do anything for her daughter, her little girl, her Missy . . .

But I am Lisette and I am alive!

She could not share a life, a body, with Melissa. Melissa and Lisette could not both be here in this beautifully real world. So Melissa had to go away, go away forever! And the woman, Melissa's mother, would do everything she could to keep Melissa here, to keep Melissa from going away.

Though she might not have used that precise term, Lisette knew her mortal enemy, this woman who would deny her need and right to be alive.

With a voice that was Missy's voice, she said, "Give me a kiss."

The little girl twisted on Vicki's lap, offering a cheek. She turned her head before Vicki's lips touched her face.

In the next wild instant, Vicki's rational mind knew exactly what was happening, but could give no commands to her body because of the fiery, tearing pain, a pain ballooning inside her head, so intense and awful in its sheer surprise that it literally could not be believed.

She bit me! She is biting me!

The child ground her teeth into Vicki's lower

lip, gnawing at wet and bloody pulp, and Vicki felt the blood flowing, coating her teeth and running down her throat. She tried to scream but could only moan as pain mingled with the child's hot breath invading her mouth.

Then came another pain. There were hands on her throat, small but with animal strength, strangling hands.

Insane! It was beyond belief, but Vicki Barringer did not doubt that her little girl meant to kill her. How can this be?

A heated and weighty blackness rushed from her lungs.

Within the pain, Vicki felt her mind melt to liquid. There were things like thoughts swimming there, but nothing seemed to have meaning or to be of any importance.

Finally it was outrage that brought Vicki around. If I do not do something, she is going to kill me.

With awkward determination, Vicki wedged her arms in between herself and the girl. She forced her hands between the thin, straining forearms and levered against them with all her strength, strength that was rapidly slipping away, until the fingers left her neck.

Then Vicki's right hand shot up beneath the child's chin. Index, middle, ring fingers sank into the hinge at the jawbone, while her thumb found the same spot on the other side. Vicki squeezed, pushing the girl's head back, prying open her jaws until the awful grip of teeth was broken and the little girl thumped off her lap to the floor.

Vicki tried to think, tried to understand what was incomprehensible, as she drew a breath that corkscrewed painfully into her. She snuffled blood and spit and snot, trying not to throw up.

Then, as though launched from a spring-board, there was Missy!

Face twisted and smeared with blood, she bounded up, landing hard, right knee punching into Vicki's thigh, left stabbing just above the pelvis, arms reaching to . . .

No! Vicki did not think. No, damn it! Before the child could secure a grip, Vicki, as hard as she could, slammed her fists against the slender shoulders, thrusting as she snapped forward.

It was ludicrously graceful, a perfect slow-motion backward somersault the child per-formed as she rolled across the floor, the back of her head heavily thunking the base of the dresser.

Vicki heard that sound. She saw the little girl lying there, still, head twisted at an unnatural angle. With a shining lucidity that she realized meant she was, right now, out of her mind, she thought, I have killed Missy. Missy tried to kill me. I killed her instead.

"Missy?" she said, as she stood up and the child on the floor did not move. I am not going to start screaming, Vicki said, not sure if she spoke aloud or only with her mind. If I start screaming now, I will never stop. "Missy?"

She stepped closer. Then Vicki halted, as from the corner of her eye, she saw something unfa-miliar, too cold and calm, in the craziness that swirled all about her.

The white porcelain doll sat on Missy's table, the basket of eggs on her lap. The doll seemed to be observing with detached irony. No, it was just a doll, a strange doll that did not belong here.

Not a Barbie or a Cabbage Patch, this doll belonged to that long ago time when kids might have toys but were not expected to play with toys. It was an antique, probably worth a good deal of money to a collector.

It was not Missy's doll.

That mattered somehow, she thought. It mattered a great deal. It . . .

No, she wasn't making sense.

The hell with the doll.

Then she was kneeling, holding a wrist, patting a cheek, calling, "Missy!"

A flutter of eyelids.

"Missy?"

The little girl sprang up, and the top of her head butted into the soft vulnerable angle of Vicki's neck and jaw, and Vicki gagged and thought she felt her heart stop. The blow was so solid and unexpected that, for a sliver of time, she must have blacked out, because when she next knew what was happening, she was on her back, and the child was on top of her, on her knees, bouncing up and down and punching her in the face.

And Vicki screamed and felt a thud vibrate through the floor beneath her back, a sound that she thought was the convulsive shaking of this unfathomable, insane universe. Then a thud-thud-thud, and she understood then—the stairs.

Warren Barringer stood staring in the doorway. He was winded from the run to the second floor that had been prompted by the sounds he heard the moment he'd stepped into the house. "What in the goddamned hell?" he wanted to know.

The little girl who was not Melissa toppled off

Vicki Barringer, and Vicki struggled up to get to a sitting position.

The child started to run to Warren. After two steps, she stopped dead. The words were a garbled and agonized crescendo. "It's *my* dad!"

Then the child pitched backward. Her body angled into a quaking bow between heels and back of head, and then she went all loose and thrashing for perhaps five seconds before, twitching, she lay unconscious.

THIRTY-ONE

Warren Barringer's life was in perfect arrangement. Each individual object, event and instant that made up the sum of Warren Barringer's existence was in precise and inviolate order. Warren could feel that.

Oh, yes, all of it was so right! Warren could see the patterns, the sometimes complex but always sensible connections, and when he could not actually discern such synchronization he could sense it.

It was simple, really: A place for everything, and everything in its place.

A place for everyone, and everyone in his or her place.

Melissa was in the hospital, where she had been since that crazy Sunday, because that was where Melissa belonged. Missy had gone bonkers, whomping the shit out of his wife, and Vicki had done some whomping back. Now they had to find out what was wrong with the kid. Can do, thanks to modern, high tech medical science, and all of it paid for by the university's family plan medical coverage. Not to worry, not to worry. Missy would get the very best care and diagnostic examination—and he was *not* worried.

Vicki was in bed, somewhat banged up still, not a real black eye but light purple and yellow, a puffy lip, a rib that pained when she breathed too deeply, but, all in all, no major damage. Vicki was exhausted, utterly spent, what with the tension and all the running to the hospital everyday. Now Vicki slept, really resting for the first night since that crazy Sunday.

Sleep, Vicki, he thought, it's okay. It really is. It will work out the way it's all supposed to work out. So, sleep, like the rest of the world right now. It was 2:45 on Wednesday morning, and people slept.

But Warren Barringer could not sleep. Of course, lately, with his blood chemistry unaltered by booze, he felt wide awake all the time.

It was not his place to be lying unconscious next to his wife. Warren Barringer was a writer, and a writer belonged at the typewriter. It was that compulsion and knowledge that had drawn him to his desk in his study. He was going to write. He would write a great book.

But first, he had to check to make sure he had a place for everything and that everything was in its place. This was preparation, the sacred rituals of Warren Barringer. Before his fingertips touched the enchanted keys of the magical Underwood, there were private and personal and secret ceremonies to be performed.

Check the first drawer of the desk to the right. Uh-huh. The-just-in-case pistol, ready and waiting and secret. Interesting to hold it, to feel death lying smooth in his living palm.

In the same drawer, a new secret, Missy's secret.

At Lawn Crest hospital last Sunday night, when he and Vicki had been about to leave her, Missy cried out, "I'm sorry I was bad!" She honestly did not remember what she had done, didn't remember the attack or the seizure that followed it. "Don't make me stay here!"

"But we have to find out what the problem is so the doctors can help . . ."

They'd got her settled down to sporadic sniffles, and then she asked for a private moment or two with her dad.

Then she told him what to do.

Later, on the way home, Vicki asked what Missy had wanted. He told her something, a lie. He did not tell his wife that the little girl expected him to get . . .

" . . . the doll. Keep it for me. And don't let *her* get it."

He'd smuggled the doll to his study. Now, his fingers found it in its place in the first drawer, along with the pistol. They belonged together, somehow. Yes, he decided, it seemed that was so. It was part of the pattern of the life of Warren Barringer.

So was the rose paperweight alongside his typewriter. Cold glass and cold flower, unchanging.

All right, then, a place for everything and everything in its . . . No, not quite. He slipped on his reading glasses. There! He felt authorish!

Now it was time to write.

Just how long had it been since he last sat down to fill the white space with black words? The sudden thought disoriented him, rather frightened him; it made him feel as though a block of time had been mysteriously excised from memory and cut out of his life.

His last writing session seemed so long ago it could have been in a previous lifetime.

And what had he written then? He could not remember.

He had written, had been writing . . . something. A book. It had to be here, in the second drawer on the left side of the desk. That was the manuscript drawer.

He opened the drawer. There it was. He picked it up and looked at the title page: *A Civilized Man*. He remembered now—didn't he? —or was he merely pretending that he remembered?

He began to read the story of Brandon Holloway Mitchell, a civilized man. At the end of the first chapter, 13 pages, he took off his glasses and placed them on the desk next to the manuscript. He picked up the rose paperweight, sliding his thumb back and forth on the smooth roundness.

A Civilized Man was well-written, he decided. There were a number of commendable passages and some lyrical prose, but the story was uninvolving. The protagonist, Mitchell, struck him as curiously bloodless and bland. Mitchell was a static neurotic who did nothing but cringe and reflect.

Worse, Brandon Holloway Mitchell was what no main character in any novel should ever be. He was dull. He was boring.

Warren Barringer did not give a damn about Brandon Holloway Mitchell.

He had certainly written these 98 pages of *A Civilized Man*, and, if he dug into his memory, he recalled writing them, but he had wasted his time with this project.

Suddenly he had it.

A Civilized Man was the work he had been obliged to write—then. It was the writing of the Warren who used to be, but that Warren was long gone.

Farewell to Warren Barringer, the man who was and who can never be again, the man who had been given the guise of the fictional, but ever so autobiographical Brandon Holloway Mitchell.

It was the end of Brandon Holloway Mitchell, and the end of hard-drinking, Rat-battling Warren Barringer.

Warren felt a sudden salty sting of tears. You didn't say a meaningful goodbye to anyone, much less yourself, without it getting to you, one of those poignant, bittersweet moments that you will never forget. Then his tears became a wash as, one page at a time, in slow-motion, he ripped each sheet of the manuscript of *A Civilized Man* to bits and consigned the pieces to the wastebasket.

The tie was severed between the weak, dependent, neurotic Brandon Holloway Mitchell and the capable, dynamic, self-reliant Warren Barringer.

When he was finished, Warren Barringer sobbed, not bothering to wipe away the tears rushing down his face. He wept and felt grand.

He felt . . . new.

It was time to begin.

He cranked a sheet of paper into his Under-wood.

And he began to type.

Although he did not know it, nor did anyone else yet, Warren Barringer was crazy. But it was Warren Barringer's daughter, Melissa, who needed psychotherapy.

Or at least, that was the diagnostic verdict of the doctors and the sophisticated equipment at Lawn Crest Hospital at the end of the week. X-Ray, CAT-scan, ultra-sound, EKG, blood tests, urine tests, etc. detected no sign of brain tumor or lesion or hemorrhage or epilepsy or brain dysfunction. In short, there was nothing physically wrong with Melissa Barringer, but there was something mentally wrong with Melissa Barringer.

That is, there might be. It was a possible explanation for what they called a psychotic episode. Actually, the psychological data was inconclusive. The child seemed somewhat evasive during the psychiatric evaluations. The projective tests somehow wound up not projecting but concealing.

The Barringers had to understand that psychology was not an exact science. That's what a neurologist with a badly fitting toupee told them. Irked at what he thought was the doctor's haughty attitude, Warren said he had so thought psychology was an exact science. Live and learn. Of course, what did he know? Hell, he was only a college professor, an author with several important novels to his credit.

Vicki gave him a tired, sidelong look.

The neurologist wanted to refer them to a

psychotherapist who specialized in working with children. The woman had an outstanding reputation. It wasn't going too far to say she'd positively worked magic with a number of profoundly disturbed young people.

Vicki suppressed a shudder.

The psychologist had an office in the city. Her name was Selena Lazone.

THIRTY-TWO

It was Monday morning, an hour before the alarm and sunrise. Not able to gauge when she'd left sleep and had become so wide awake she thought she could see through her eyelids, Selena Lazone felt a foreboding, heavy sense of the future weighing down on her. Next to her, David lay on his stomach, body subtly moving with the loose inhalations and exhalations of deep slumber. David's naked body radiated warmth that failed to warm her.

The hour before dawn, Selena thought, and I am afraid. There had been the omens and portents invading her life, signs of her own past and the supernatural, ripping at the façade of normalcy she had created for herself. She couldn't discount it or dismiss it or try to avoid reality by filling in her moments with the bits and business of day-to-day living. She had seen and recognized the threat that was always the ultimate threat—Death.

Selena thought of Kris Heidmann, as she had thought of her and thought of her and thought of her. Dead Kris Heidmann! Kris had lived 14 years and had been dead eight days, dead by her own despairing hand. I could have helped her, Selena thought, if only, if only . . .

Thinking of a child's death and thinking of my

own death, and in the hour before dawn, Selena thought, I am afraid. And I am so alone. She touched David's shoulder.

"David?"

"Hmm?"

"I want . . . to be with you." She hated saying it that way.

She looked into the darkness overhead. We are born alone and we die alone and in between there are so many hours in which we are condemned to our aloneness. That was it—the human condition.

And without someone else, without love, life was too empty to endure.

Then because she felt so damned bad, she said it aloud as she had never before permitted herself to say it. "David, I want you to hold me. David, I want you to love me."

She felt him stir and felt his breath on her face. He'd propped himself up on an elbow. His hand moved to her belly, patting and petting. It wasn't foreplay, not yet; it was foreplay to foreplay. Then there would be sex.

"No," she said. "Not that."

"What is it you want?" he said. "Tell me."

I don't want to be alone and afraid in the dark. I want to be held and loved and touched by you.

She said none of that. She answered David Greenfield's question with a question, the one she had promised never to ask.

"Do you love me, David?"

The reply took awhile, but it came, exactly as she feared it would. "No."

He moved away from her and lay back heavily. The distance between them felt wide and cold. "I love you, David," she said. "You have to know that. Doesn't it mean anything?"

"Why are you doing this, Selena?"

"I love you, goddamn you, and I want you to love me!"

He sighed. "You're asking the impossible, Selena. I do not love you. I cannot love you. Or anyone."

"That is bullshit, David Greenfield! You are a human being. Your mother and father gave you life. That makes you a person! And people want love and need love. They want and need to give love. David, it's love that makes us human."

In a voice so calm and detached it could have been termed clinical, David Greenfield said, "Why me, Selena? What made you decide to share an apartment and a bed with me? You know the way I am. You know what I am."

"Maybe," she said. "Maybe I know you better than you know yourself."

David's tone remained flat. He could have been politely conducting a telephone consumer survey. "Did you choose me as your live-in punishment, Selena? I'm Selena Lazone's cross-in-residence. Is that what I am? Or maybe I'm your case study in abnormal psychology."

She did not answer.

David said nothing more, and then, after a little while, he got out of bed. She heard the whisper of his clothing as he dressed.

"Where are you going?"

"Out," he said and paused. "Do you want me to come back?"

She thought about it. "Yes."

"Things go back to what they've been?" he asked. "You can live with that?"

She shuddered. "Yes," she said, wishing for

that much or that little, even as she realized it would not, could not be.

There would be changes soon. That was *Baht*, momentous turnings and twistings of lives.

And there would be endings.

It had the feeling of *deja vu*, even though it was not precisely that. She knew the Barringers, felt she had met them before. That kept popping into Selena Lazone's mind as she conducted the initial interview with the parents of her prospective new client.

It was one o'clock in the afternoon. The Barringers had the Danish modern armchairs in Selena's Michigan Avenue office, Melissa on her mother's lap. In a blue dress, knee socks and shiny black shoes, two ribbons in her hair, the little girl might have stepped out of the pages of a catalog offering "Fashion for Bored Children." She exhibited none of the agitation or curiosity one might expect in such a situation. She hardly even blinked.

Facing them in a straight-backed chair, the window behind her to turn her into a more or less anonymous silhouette, Selena had a clipboard on her knee, a pen in her hand and questions to ask. She'd already thoroughly reviewed the preliminary evaluations from Lawn Crest, and, frankly, she didn't see much validity in most of the standard tests administered as a matter of course by the hospital. Once in a while, a projective test might reveal a psychotic, perhaps a paranoid schizophrenic, but the majority of tests were valuable in confirming only what a psychotherapist already suspected.

Actually, the questions in this introductory

interview were not all that important for informational purposes. Later, if it was agreed to proceed with psychotherapy, there would be more meaningful, even painful questions for Vicki and Warren Barringer. For the present, Selena wanted simply to observe the Barringers to form initial assessments of the family's dynamics.

Warren Barringer: Brusque but articulate responses. Seems to think this is all a waste of time. Amusing, maybe, possibly interesting—but a waste. Obviously a bright man. No less obviously a man who thinks himself bright. Seems relaxed, self-confident. Too relaxed, too self-confident?

Had she read something of his? He does seem so familiar—they both do—but she didn't recognize the titles of the novels he mentioned. She asked him what he was writing currently. He explained he didn't like to dissipate creative energies talking about projects until they were well along. She noted unease and thin hostility in that response.

Somewhat sensitive and secretive about your writing, Professor? Selena wondered. Do you have other secrets to hide? Well, who doesn't?

Vicki Barringer: So straight-forward, albeit on the shy side, that you can read her not like a book but a child's primer. The kind of woman that you think of as Midwestern. Not plain and not really pretty and fairly comfortable with that reality as shown by natural hair color and a style to suit her face and not fashion. She's worn down now, really worn, but discovering strength of character she probably didn't know she had. A deep rooted and powerful spirituality.

Selena frowned. Spirituality? Where did I get that? Selena asked herself. No, what makes me feel that?

Dukkeripin? Second sight? A little flash of Gypsy-style ESP?

Suddenly a picture exploded in her mind of David. Somehow, David was a link!

David was the connection.

Other connections were tenuous and strong, dark and light, subtle, dangerous, good and evil and spiritual, all working together in inexplicable, inevitable consort.

It was *Baht*. It was fate.

It was not happenstance that had led the Barringers to her office. Mother and father and daughter were here, right this minute, because here was where they had to be. And David, too, his presence was here.

But why? What was the will of *Baht*? What did Fate hold for the Barringers?

And David?

And me?

There was a way to find out.

Selena rose, putting the clipboard on her desk and smoothing her skirt. "Well, now I think it's time Melissa and I had a talk."

"Missy," Vicki Barringer said.

"What's that?"

"Missy, that's what we call her."

"Yes," Selena said. She held out her hand. "Would you like to come with me, Missy?"

The little girl smiled. She slipped off Vicki Barringer's lap. Her long fingers reached out.

Selena felt the chill and the challenge in the little girl's grasp. And she knew that *Baht*, fate itself, held her by the hand.

THIRTY-THREE

The three foot tall teddy bear on the top shelf had dark brown fur, a small, friendly smile, and a nasty-looking raw patch where its left eye had been. A year before, a four year-old girl had gouged out Mr. Bear's eye. She was explaining, "This is how my aunty hurt my eye." That wasn't exactly correct, since the child was missing her right eye, not the left.

The playroom, shared with another psychologist, was just down the hall from Selena's office. At first glance, it could have been a classroom in a day care center or kindergarten. There were the shelves loaded with toys, a blackboard, two felt bulletin boards and bright posters. There were huggy blankets and bean bag chairs large enough for adults and kids.

There were, however, a number of differences between this room and what you might find in a school. Instead of cold tile marked with circles, squares and the classic hopscotch design, the floor was thick, soft, beige carpeting, suitable for crawling, rolling or pitching a fit. In a locked cabinet were such items as whiffle bats ("You want to hit something really hard? You can use this") and anatomically correct dolls so that, for example, a three year-old child whose vocabulary didn't equal the horror of his experience, might reveal the homosexual rape performed on him by Daddy's friend. The mirrored east wall was one way glass; there were concealed microphones and a video camera so that the playroom could be monitored and recorded from the small adjoining room.

Releasing the little girl's hand and glad of it, Selena said, "Now we can talk and get to know each other."

She had no response. The child walked to the toy shelves.

Selena settled herself into one of the bean bag chairs. "Is there a toy you'd like to play with?"

No reply. A silent little girl, with her back to Selena, picked up a green-faced Oscar the Grouch puppet and put it down, picked up a G.I. Joe doll and put it down, picked up a Skipper doll and put it down.

"If you could be any one of the toys on that shelf, which would you be?" Selena asked.

The child didn't seem to hear.

"Melissa?" Selena said.

The girl did not turn around, but she quietly said, "Is that my name?"

"Do you want me to call you Missy?"

"Is that my name?"

"You tell me, okay?"

No answer.

"Are we playing?" Selena asked. "Is this like a name game?" No answer. "Is that what you'd like, to play a game?"

A shrug.

"You know, I'll bet Oscar the Grouch could tell me your name," Selena said. "Why don't you slip him on? It's okay if you don't want to talk, but maybe Oscar wants to say something for you."

Nothing. Then slowly, as though she barely had control of her movements, the little girl took Oscar the Grouch, slipped her hand in and pulled the long, furry puppet down her arm. She turned around. Oscar's mouth moved awkwardly. The child's mouth moved silently with it.

Together like that, Selena thought, the little girl and the puppet were scary as hell.

"Hello, Oscar," Selena said.

Oscar growled, and the sound, pinched and threatening, did not seem to emanate from the little girl's throat.

"Do you want to play a name game with me, Oscar?" Selena asked.

Again there was the tiny menacing growl, but this time, Selena saw something in the child's eyes.

Am I merely imagining it? Selena asked herself.

But it was there. She knew it.

It was a plea, a silent cry for help.

And she knew, too, it was neither normal eyesight, nor trained psychologist's vision that enabled her to see the sorrowful, yearning message in the child's eyes.

Deny it though she might, deny it though she had, it was her gift, her cursed birthright. *Dukkeripin*—the intuitive, paranormal, sixth sense of the *cohalyi*, the Gypsy wise woman.

She had a painful thought. Had Kris Heidmann sought help from that Gypsy *cohalyi*, would the teenager be alive right now? But the troubled girl had come to Ms. Selena Lazone, the liberated modern woman who after her name had those college-awarded letters to prove just how much she knew!

Kristin Heidmann died.

What of this child?

Could Selena Lazone help her? Selena Lazone, psychologist?

Or Selena Lazone, Gypsy *gule romni*, Selena Lazone, Romany witch!

"Name . . . game . . ." The little girl's lips moved, but the hoarse words appeared to come from the puppet's mouth in eerie ventriloquism. "You . . . know . . . her?   Know . . . her . . . name?"

Selena leaned forward. She pointed at the child. "Your name is Melissa Barringer. You are Missy."

Melissa Barringer's sigh was deep and grateful. As though reciting a magical incantation or a prayer, she said, "My name *is* Melissa Barringer. I live at 1302 Main Street, Grove Corner, Illinois. My zip code is 60412 . . ."

"No," interrupted the harsh voice of Oscar.

"I . . . I . . ." Melissa Barringer's head snapped left, then right, as though she'd been slapped. "I *am* Melissa . . ."

"No!"

"I am Lisette. I don't want to be, but Lisette . . ."

"No!" the puppet seemed to say, but not in the tone that a moment previous had belonged to Oscar the Grouch. This was a child's voice. It was furious and frightened and incredibly lonely.

And it was not Melissa Barringer's voice.

You cannot tell! It is a secret! A secret!

"I have to!" Melissa Barringer cried, choking on a sob. "I *want* to!"

No!

And as Selena struggled to hold her expressionless mask in place, the little girl and the puppet argued.

A furious voice.

A pleading voice.

Shouting.

Whimpering.

Multiple personality, Selena thought. Despite the notoriety of several cases, multiple personality was an extremely rare neurotic condition. Most psychotherapists never encountered even a single case.

Tshatsimo! The truth. She desperately wanted to believe that the child's affliction was multiple personality. That was a psychological aberration. That was crazy, but a psychologist could treat such a patient and such a condition.

But *Baht* had not brought Melissa to the office of Selena Lazone, psychologist.

Baht had nudged and pushed and led Melissa Barringer so that she might meet Selena Lazone, *ababina*, Gypsy sorceress.

But I am not an *ababina*, Selena silently declared to herself. No more of that!

Yet cautiously, Selena rose. The little girl was silent. Oscar was silent. But child eyes and puppet eyes focused on Selena Lazone as she approached. Selena moved like a slow motion mime or a trained soldier, on guard and alert.

"I must know," she said quietly, and she felt the entreaty of the child's eyes and the furious threat radiating from the eyes of the puppet.

Go away! You cannot! You will not!

Selena hesitated. She heard the warning without hearing words, the menacing promise flashing red and black in her mind. She wished a dozen futile wishes, and then she did what she had to do, what *Baht* commanded her.

She leaned down. Her lips lightly touched the center of the child's forehead in a kiss, a *cohalyi's* kiss. There was the heat, a blazing fever not of the body but of the spirit. And the taste of salt and sulphur was inevitable and awful.

Selena straightened. She was beginning to understand, and that knowledge filled her with tingling terror. The adrenalin rush triggered a nauseating roiling in her stomach; she took a deep breath, pushing away a feeling of faintness.

The *trushul*, Selena thought, the blessed cross, as she made the holy sign above the little girl's head. Once, twice, three times.

Eyes half closed, Selena whispered in Romany the ancient incantation:

> *Evil Eyes that have gazed on thee,*
> *May those Eyes extinguished be*
> *Evil Eyes that have gazed on thee,*
> *May those Eyes now cease to be.*

Is that a song? I know songs, too. Listen. Come along with me, Lucille, in my merry Olds-Mow-Beeyel . . .

The voice peeped, teasing and small, in Selena's mind, and in her mind, Selena responded. Who are you?

I am . . . Oscar the Grouch!

The puppet's mouth flapped stupidly, a moving caricature of a laugh.

Who are you? Selena demanded.

My name is Melissa Barringer. I live at 1302 Main Street, Grove Corner . . .

I want the truth, Selena insisted.

Do you?

Yes, Selena responded.

You know the truth.

Yes, Selena admitted. You are *diakka*.

A silence that seemed to echo with taunting laughter followed Selena out of the playroom.

She was sorry, but there was nothing she could do. There was nothing any psychotherapist could do. Yes, the doctors at Lawn Crest Hospital had been correct. There wasn't a physical problem.

Nor was there a mental/emotional problem.

Melissa Barringer's problem was spiritual.

That was when Warren Barringer arched an eyebrow. The Barringers and the psychologist stood cramped in the small observation room adjoining the playroom. "Spiritual?" he said. "You mean Missy ought to be enrolled in Sunday School?"

Selena ignored him. How could she expect him to believe that his daughter has been . . . obsessed by a *diakka*? Groping for words, she tried to explain.

"You know, Ms. Lazone, this is not amusing," Warren Barringer interrupted. "You'll notice I am not laughing. My wife is not laughing. We came here because we thought you might help our daughter, and you're handing us this nonsense about her being possessed . . ."

"Obsessed," Selena said. "An obsession is a spirit's attack on a living person. It can lead to total possession of that person. It's not to that point with your daughter. Not yet."

"Whoa!" Warren Barringer held up his hand, palm out. "I write fiction, but I don't live it, okay? Ms. Lazone, are you listening to yourself? Do you have any idea how crazy you sound?"

"Yes," Selena said.

Then Selena's eyes met Vicki's, and Selena knew she understood—and believed.

So Selena's next words were directed to the woman. "There's nothing I can do, Mrs. Barringer. Your daughter needs a minister, a priest, or a rabbi . . ."

"How about Shirley Maclaine?" Warren cut in. "Or maybe we can get Mary Baker Eddy's ghost! We'll certainly want to get Missy fixed up before she starts spitting green pea soup at us or spinning her head around 360 degrees!"

"I can do nothing more for you," Selena said.

Warren said, "Just for the sake of adding a moronic question to a ridiculous conversation, how do you know all this voodoo, black magic, poltergeist stuff anyway? Are you a witch, Ms. Lazone?"

"No."

That was all she said to Warren Barringer.

But to herself she admitted that once she was a *cohalyi*, but no longer.

Not ever again.

Bater.

May it be so!

THIRTY-FOUR

As soon as they got the car at the underground Grant Park parking garage, Warren started in. "I've never heard garbage like that in my life! Metaphysical babble! That Lazone woman has to be goofier than any of her . . ."

At the exit, he rolled down his window. "The ticket!" he snapped. "You have the ticket, right?"

She did. She handed him a ten dollar bill to pay the $7.25 parking fee. Warren snorted his annoyance at "Chicago, City of the Big Rip-offs."

Vicki thought he was upset in a way she did not understand. She was worried. She was worried about him, about Missy, about everything. She was worried and frightened and in her belly, behind the rib that still hurt, she felt an irregularly shaped, impossibly heavy weight.

Just as they were about to merge onto the Dan Ryan Expressway, they were cut off by an old Cadillac that lacked a rear license plate, a trunk lid and a back bumper. Warren swore.

In the back seat, Missy laughed.

Then Warren said, "The goddamned world is full of goddamned crazy people."

And you sound like one of them, Vicki thought.

Missy laughed. "Daddy is talking dirty!"

"Goddamn right Daddy is talking goddamn

dirty, goddamnit," Warren said. His hands were tight on the steering wheel. "Psychologist? She's the one who needs a psychologist. Maybe plug her toe into the wall socket and give her some shock treatments, goddamn crazy woman."

Missy giggled happily.

"Warren," Vicki said, "please."

"Sure," he said, "no problem."

Suddenly, he swung his head around, peering over his shoulder, his eyebrows question marks. His voice filled the car. "Missy, how about it? Are you crazy or what?"

"Warren, watch where . . ." Vicki sucked in a breath and tasted fear and dryness.

"No, Daddy!" A laughing response from the rear.

He whipped his head back to peer through the windshield.

That burning intensity on his face, Vicki thought, went beyond his drunken, vicious, the-hell-with-you and don't-get-in-my-way expression; it was madness.

"Warren, stop it," Vicki said tightly. "Just stop it *now*."

He did not. "Missy," Warren said, "do you have a nasty demon or anything like that in you?" His mocking and cruel tone was, Vicki knew, for her benefit.

"No, Daddy," Missy said.

"Goddamned right!"

"You're so silly, Daddy."

"I am silly," he agreed, "and that Lazone lady is a certifiable nut. And that is that."

"No, Warren," Vicki said. "I know what Ms. Lazone was saying, and I know why she was saying it."

Vicki did. One might pretend that all things were rational and logical, that simple-minded common sense was the key to all the workings of the universe, but it just wasn't so.

Melissa Barringer, their daughter, was being assaulted by a wicked spirit. *Diakka*. That was a word Vicki had never heard before.

But she understood. She believed in wicked spirits, and she had good reason. A wicked spirit had attacked her, tried to kill her. It was not— she would stake her life on it—her child!

Superstition? Foolish mythology? How could you watch television news or read the daily papers, how could you be alive in the twentieth century and question that evil as a force above and beyond human nature really, truly existed?

Vicki Barringer did not know how to combat the evil, the *diakka*, but she knew that God was more powerful than evil, that God could defeat evil, destroy evil.

She needed someone who knew and understood God. Someone who walked with the Lord and in His ways.

She knew of such a man.

And it all somehow made perfect sense.

Now was the time for a healing, and not only a healing for Missy.

. As soon as they got home, she would call Carol Grace and ask for the help of Evan Kyle Dean.

They were pulling into the driveway when she told Warren.

"What?" He slammed into "Park." "Bullshit! That goddamn charlatan, that snake oil salesman . . ."

Warren was positively screaming as they got out of the car. "Hi, you-all, I'm your Reverend

Jimmy Bob Jumpsuit, preaching my fat, phony ass off! Put your hand on the nineteen inch Zenith and I'll cure your cancer or your constipation!" Warren waved his hands overhead, doing a spastically ludicrous impression of a television faith healer. "Jay-zuss! Jay-zuss!"

Then Missy scampered out of the car and took Warren's hand.

As though a switch had been thrown, Warren instantly became calm. He shrugged and grinned apologetically. "Sorry, I guess that woman really got to me. I know I'm acting foolishly."

All Vicki could do was stare at him.

"Sorry," Warren said again.

Really, he assured her, anything Vicki thought they should do, why, that was what they would do. He had no problem with that. After all, they both wanted the best for Missy. Of course. No, no way he really thought there was anything to what Ms. Lazone had told them, but, okay, for Missy's sake, he would be open-minded.

He was speaking too rapidly, too soothingly. It was not genuine.

He was trying to put something over on her, Vicki thought.

You . . . fake! Anger flared within her. What did he think he was doing with his placating, condescending attitude?

Whatever he was up to, whatever his game and his reasons for it, Warren was not opposing her. For the moment, that was all that mattered.

In the house, Warren and Missy making themselves scarce, she called her sister and cried when she heard her voice.

Carol Grace cried, too.

With all there was to say, there really was very little to say—not on the telephone, anyway. "I am sorry." Both sisters said that. This was something that should have happened long ago. They both knew that.

Vicki needed her sister's help, the help of the man her sister had married.

Vicki spoke with Evan Kyle Dean. It was so hard to explain. It sounded, well, quite frankly, like she was utterly insane.

But she wasn't. I need God's help! I need this man of God, Evan Kyle Dean, Vicki told herself.

Despite her stumbling words, Evan Kyle Dean assured her he did understand. He promised he would help. He had encountered similar situations.

She was not to bring the child to him.

The evil must be confronted where it had beset the little girl. There, the wickedness must be banished from this, the rightful realm of God and His children.

Tomorrow, he would be there. For now, trust in God.

In Vicki Barringer's thanks, he heard a wet, heartfelt sob.

"God loves you," he assured her.

"Yes," she said.

He hung up the phone. "God loves us all!" Evan Kyle Dean sank to his knees. He folded his hands. He did not pray, did not speak to the Lord God, but instead listened with his most secret heart and his most secret mind.

God spoke to him: *Evan Kyle Dean, servant and prophet of the living God, in My name will you cast out evil? In My name, will you work miracles and wonders?*

In his most secret heart and his most secret mind, Evan Kyle Dean replied, "In Your name, Lord, will I cast out evil. In Your name, will I work miracles and wonders."

God spoke: *My name be your shield. My name be your sword.*

Evan Kyle Dean answered, "Blessed be the name of the Lord."

It was past one o'clock in the morning and he could not sleep. Just as he'd start to drift off, he would get this urge to laugh and had to stifle it. What struck him as funny?

Everything struck him as funny!

But no, he was not laughing, not out loud.

That doesn't mean he wasn't laughing inside.

Quietly, he slipped out of bed, although he was positive he could have unloaded a truckload of church bells without waking Vicki.

So what to do with these wide-awake moments? Say, he was a writer, right, so down to the writing room.

His room. His typewriter. His desk. In the drawers of his desk, some secrets.

The little doll!

Our secret.

He saw it was nearly three o'clock in the goddamn morning!

Time sure flies when . . . when . . .

When what?

A gear clicked, and within a part of his mind that had been blocked off, there was a shifting and a linking as he answered himself:

When you are fucking out of your mind! When you are hop, skip, and a jump crazy! When up looks like down and down looks like up and every way is sideways! When you've lost it, really lost it all, and your whole life is no deposit and no return. When she makes you do what she wants you to do.

The moment of clarity and its overwhelming feeling of loss vanished.

He stood up and left his room, remembering to shut off the light. He went up the stairs slowly, so slowly.

He walked into Melissa's bedroom and gazed down at the underwear clad child. She slept on her stomach. The blankets had been kicked away.

He did nothing but stand there in his daughter's room.

The child rolled over and sat up.

She was so beautiful.

"I love you," she said.

"I love you," he said.

Four: *O Drom Le Baht*
THE WAY OF FATE

The Romany are unfailingly light-hearted and optimistic, a joyful people. Often compared to carefree grasshoppers in a world of hard-working ants, Gypsies live by the creed: "Now is our moment and tomorrow will take care of itself."

The quotation comes from Travel on the Wind, *the book written by noted anthropologist and researcher Dr. Milos Bartok, who spent more than half of his life with the* Rom. *When the* Rawnie, *the great lady, Pola Janichka, was told of the doctor's assessment, she agreed. How could she not? After all, Dr. Bartok was only repeating what she had taught him.*

To the Gypsy, the world is dark and grim. Man is small and weak, helpless against natural and supernatural forces he can sometimes vaguely perceive but cannot understand. Animistic magic and shamanistic religion offer the Gypsy small solace and minimal protection in such a hostile universe. Philosophically, the Gypsy stands with head bowed in fatalistic acceptance of the whims and workings of a cruel cosmos.

The quotation is taken from Modern Man and Primitive Religions, *the textbook written by Dr. J. L. Popovich, the noted philosopher and sociologist who studied the* Rom *for over 20 years. When the* Rawnie, *the great lady, Pola Janichka, was told of this doctor's assessment, she agreed. How could she not? After all, Dr. Popovich was only repeating what she had taught him.*

Both doctors knew something of the Rom.

But neither doctor was Rom.

Thus neither doctor would have understood this swato *of Pola Janichka:*

"Puri *Tibbo? What is there that has not been said about old Tibbo,* Rom Baro *among* Rom Baros, *a* Rai, *a chief, a king! Strong? Why, once Tibbo lifted up a* grai *on his shoulders and, as the horse neighed its surprise at this turnabout of events, carried it all through the camp. 'After all,' Tibbo laughed, 'this horse has often carried me on his back! Why should I not return the favor?'*

"*Stories are told of* Puri *Tibbo's miraculous skill in foraging, his splendid luck,* bahtalo, *in always finding chickens and pigs and sheep and cows when others were fortunate to find even berries. Hah, the* kumpania *of* Puri *Tibbo never went hungry, you may be sure, and never once* did the Gaje policemen lell old Tibbo to jail for his foraging skills.

"Yes, Puri Tibbo was clever, so clever that he once sold a three-legged mare to a blacksmith! There was a cleverness in his hands as well. Puri Tibbo could juggle a dozen sharp tshcuris, no knife ever giving him even the slightest cut.

"And with such hands, you might think Tibbo was a grand musician, and so he was, but remember, one needs both hands and heart to make true music. When Puri Tibbo played the guitar, all people, Gaje and Rom, wept; when he played the mandolin, people and animals, crawling and flying, large and small, wept; and when he played violin, people and animals and vila, all manner of spirits, good and evil, wept.

"Puri Tibbo was a good man and a clever man, and you might think being good and being clever sufficient gifts for any man, but Puri Tibbo had wisdom as well—uncommon wisdom.

"What is wisdom, you might ask—and there are more foolish questions by far. The wise man sees what is as it is.

"And that is how Puri Tibbo saw everything. It is told how, when Puri Tibbo's oldest and best beloved son died of tate shilalyi, the chills and fever, old Tibbo wept and danced for three days. 'I weep in sorrow,' Tibbo told the kumpania, 'because my son is dead,' and all the Rom could understand this. But why did Puri Tibbo dance? 'I dance in joy,' Tibbo told the kumpania, 'because I had a wonderful son,' and, I am sorry to say, that not all of the kumpania had the wisdom to understand this.

"Ah, the wisdom of Puri Tibbo . . . It was said of Puri Tibbo that doctors sought his advice on how to dispense medicine, that judges sought his advice on how to dispense justice, that priests sought his advice on how to dispense salvation.

"Now, as must all people, Puri Tibbo died; only O Del, the good God, is eternal. Can it be too great a surprise that the death of a Rai, a noble and wise man, should be a noble and wise death?

"It happened that the kumpania of Puri Tibbo was obliged to pass through a land in which the Rom were despised and cruelly treated by the Gaje, a country in which Gaje law said Gypsies might be imprisoned or beaten or killed for the crime of being Gypsies. Thanks be to O Del, the caravan safely journeyed nearly the length of this wicked land, coming at last to a wide, rain-swollen, rushing river. Furious white explosions of foam burst against huge, jagged boulders in the path of the waters. The river roared like a thousand hells. It was a fearsome place and an awesome place, and on its bank, waving his hands in the air, was a Gajo dressed in the clothing of a farmer. He was screaming, 'My child! My baby! Someone save my little baby!'

"And there, far out in the water,

being swept downstream, was something small and pink.

"Puri *Tibbo* swept off his hat and stepped out of his shoes and started for the river.

"At that very second, Baht, fate itself, appeared to Puri *Tibbo*, and in such a way that Baht could only be seen by Puri *Tibbo*. Such a thing is strange and miraculous, of course, but as we know, much that happens in the life of each and every one of us is strange and miraculous. 'Tibbo,' Baht said, 'do not go into the river. You are strong, but the river is stronger. You see, this is my river, O Paya le Baht, *the Waters of Fate.* You are safe on the land. The water will surely kill you.'

"Roughly, Puri *Tibbo* pushed Baht aside and leaped into that awful river.

"A short but most violent time passed, and then, bones broken, lungs full of water, Puri *Tibbo* was hurled on shore far down river. Death, black and cold, was crawling within him.

"In Puri *Tibbo's* strong arms was a piglet, an eyeless freak with a split snout. The ugly piglet was the kind of sport the Gaje *thought* it bad luck to eat, and so it became sport, a killing joke on a Gypsy.

"Again, Baht appeared before the eyes, now growing dim, of Puri *Tibbo*. *'Tibbo, you knew you would perish if you went into the river. This time, Fate itself gave you a choice!'*

"'No,' Tibbo said, not at all regretfully, 'You are mistaken. You, Baht, made me

what I am. Mandi Rom. *I am a Gypsy man.
So I had no choice. I had to try to save a
drowning child.'*

"Then Puri Tibbo again said,
'Mandi Rom; *I am a Gypsy man. I have
lived a good life.'* For a moment, Tibbo's
vision cleared and above him he saw the
infinite blue sky; he would die outside,
befitting a man of the Rom.

"So he could say, 'Now I have a
good death,' which is what he did say
before he closed his eyes forever.

"May we all be able to speak so
when it is our time to go into the nation of
the dead."

THIRTY-FIVE

Walking along Michigan Avenue at 8:30, Tuesday morning, Selena Lazone felt a touch too warm in her London Fog coat. She doubted anything she could have worn would have been exactly right for today. It was chilly but not actually cold; today struck her as neither the end of autumn nor the beginning of winter. It seemed a day between seasons, a time between times, a temporary suspension of chronology and progression.

It was an ominous day.

She went into the Hamlin Building. Her first appointment wasn't until ten, but there were notes she wanted to check over. She anticipated her ten o'clock client. A nice, normal 26 year old woman, she thought. That is, a nice, normal, 26 year old neurotic who couldn't sustain a relationship because she was still working out all the old Oedipal schtick for her father.

She crossed the gleaming tiled lobby. She smiled at Hank, the soon-to-retire security man. Then she stepped into the empty elevator, pushed eight, and as the doors came together with their metallic whisper, she realized she was not alone.

The hairs at the nape of her neck rose as she turned to see Kristin Heidmann. For an instant,

Selena believed herself truly face to face with the girl, the living child.

No, Kristin Heidmann said.

Reality, Selena Lazone told herself, was the vibrating floor under her feet as the elevator rose smoothly and the hum of the overhead ventilator.

Reality was a *mulo*, this ghost child, who had come to confront her, to accuse her, to condemn her for her failure—as she had been condemning herself.

"Kris," Selena whispered, "I am sorry."

Sorry, yes, but not frightened anymore. *Mule* and *vila*, ghosts and spirits, had their roles to play in this world as they did in other worlds.

"It is all right," Kristin said.

Kristin touched Selena's cheek. The spectral fingertips felt like the tickly brush of seedling dandelions.

"I didn't give you the chance," Kris said, "but it's all right. It really is. Maybe it wasn't right to kill myself, but I've found peace now, Selena, peace and forgiveness, so it's okay. I can handle it, you know? I mean, Selena, I can handle being dead."

"Kris," Selena said, "if you accept your fate" —*Baht!*—"then why have you returned? Why have you not passed on?"

"I never said thank you, Selena," Kris said. "You helped me."

"I did try."

"You helped me, Selena. Things wouldn't be all right now if you hadn't. I want you to forgive yourself, Selena. You're not to blame for my suicide. And now, Selena . . ."

She knew what Kristin Heidmann would say

then. Selena could not even be sure she wasn't saying it to herself.

"There is a child who needs you. She needs special help."

Yes, there was.

"Help her, Selena."

Selena nodded.

"Then there's just one more thing I have to ask you to do for me."

Again, the comforting ethereal hand touched Selena's face, and Kristin Heidmann, *mulo*, asked Selena Lazone for a prayer.

Selena had a prayer. In Romany, the language of the truth of the heart, she whispered: "*Putrav lesko drom angle leste tu na inkrav les ma but palpale mua brigasa.* May the way be open before you in your world beyond as I release you from all chains of this Earth and my sorrow." To herself, Selena added, and as your forgiveness has released me from my chains of guilt.

The *mulo's* image seemed to flicker, then blur as though Selena were gazing at her through a rainy window.

"Kris, Kristin Heidmann . . . *Akana mukav tut le Devlesa.*"

The *mulo's* eyes flashed grateful understanding and farewell at Selena's words, "I now leave you to God."

The elevator's doors opened to the eighth floor.

Her ten o'clock appointment whined the usual whines. "My father just never seemed to have time for me, you know? Oh, he worked hard all his life, had to, really, to take care of my mother with her multiple sclerosis and all . . ."

She had only one other appointment for late

this afternoon, and she cancelled it. Then she called the apartment. David was in. Could he meet her for lunch at Bennigan's, just across the way?

She needed to ask him some questions. She had to talk about what she could not speak of last night.

An hour later, sitting at a window table in the bustling restaurant, she appreciated the noise all around her. Conversations and glassware clatter and the TV sets from the center bar blended together as a comforting curtain of sound that freed her to say anything. Of course, the vodka martinis also helped.

But most of all, looking into David Greenfield's fiercely black eyes, she thought, Yes, he is *tacho* rat. His soul is a Gypsy soul, and I can tell him anything.

"The Barringers, David. Vicki, Warren, and their daughter, Melissa. They came to the office. You know them."

"Yes." If he was shocked or surprised, he did not show it.

"I sensed that."

"*Dukkeripin*," he said quietly.

"Yes. I've tried to deny that sixth sense, or at least ignore it, but it's there and it's real. The Barringers, David, their little girl is obsessed by a *diakka*."

Selena went on. "I sensed a lot of other things, too, David. *Baht* itself brought the Barringers to me. Fate has a plan for all of us, for the Barringers and you and me, David. I sense the possibility of death for all of us—or some of us. And . . ." Her voice became less than a whisper, a voice that would have been incapable of speaking anything other than *tshatsimo*, the truth. "I am afraid. I could die, David. I am even more afraid that you could die."

He smiled mockingly. She understood he was not mocking her. Instead, he was taunting *Baht*. "And if you refuse to be part of fate's strategies?"

"Then the little girl, Melissa, will be . . ." Selena hesitated, searching for the word. It was not death; it was destruction of self—and worse. "The child will be lost." Then the Romany words came to her, far more precise and terrible. "*Detlene mulano*," she said "a lost child spirit, wandering lonely and afraid forever in the void, the gray realm between the world of the living and of the dead."

"I see," David Greenfield said.

"Tell me about the Barringers, David."

He did, briefly and brusquely, the way he treated all of his past. The past was the past, complete of itself, hardly worth consideration.

David denied being a Gypsy, Selena thought, denied being anyone except a man who looks at things and takes pictures of what he sees, yet in his attitude about living in the perpetual present, he was pure Rom. To the Gypsy, neither before nor after was of consequence, only now. "A candle is not made of wax but is all flame" was a Romany saying.

Even though she hated asking the question, she felt compelled. "David, did you love Vicki Barringer?"

"No," he said.

"Forget I asked that," she said.

Then, though she had already made up her mind, she spoke aloud. Saying it would validate it. "You know what I am going to do," Selena said. "It's what I must do."

"Of course."

"I have to ask you to help me."

"I will," he said. At that, she loved him so much it hurt.

David picked up the menu and opened it. As though they had been discussing import cars or the weather, he casually said, "Let's order, okay? I'm really hungry."

"Okay," she said. Trying to choose between seafood pasta or a California salad, she dared to think that this time David Greenfield would say, "Yes," if she asked, "Do you love me?"

THIRTY-SIX

He wanted to depart earlier, but the first Birmingham to Chicago flight he could book wasn't until late afternoon. He had a seat in the coach section. Casually dressed, without a tie, he was unrecognized, which he wanted to be, and alone, which he did not want to be. Certainly, there had been people at the airport who had thought they'd recognized him. There had even been several who had attended services at his True Witness Church, but when he greeted them with a quiet word or two, they had implicitly received his message and knew he didn't want to be disturbed.

It was time to fasten his seat belt. Already he missed Carol Grace terribly.

Later there would be a time for families to join together in forgiveness and love, but for the present there was danger—the gravest danger of body and soul. He could not allow Carol Grace to be in such peril.

Evan Kyle Dean was not yet sure how he would confront the evil because he did not yet know the true nature of the malign spirit that was attacking his niece.

His own niece! Could there be any doubt that the child was the lure, challenge and insult that Satan had put before him?

But he would conquer the evil. He would liberate the child from the bondage of wickedness. With the help of the Lord he would save her.

When the plane landed, with only his carry-on bag, he didn't have any luggage delay. The terminal was overheated, so he draped his coat over his arm.

From a telephone booth, he called his sister-in-law. He heard relief and hope in Vicki Barringer's voice as she gave him directions from O'Hare. It would be about two hours, she estimated, perhaps longer with the construction on the tollway. "Two hours . . ." she repeated, and he heard the catch in her throat.

"Just hold on," he said. "Keep your faith. I'll be with you soon."

At the Avis stand, he rented a car, and, 15 minutes later, behind the wheel of a Ford Escort, he drove south. He was one man in a compact car, but he knew he was not alone.

God was with him.

He would do God's work.

He's going to help me! He's on his way, right here, right now. He's going to make you leave! He'll get rid of you, Lisette, so there!

Say, would you like me to teach you a song, Melissa? It's been a while since I taught you a new one.

You listen to me, Lisette! He is so on the way, and he's super-special 'cause he's a minister.

Here is a good song. I always used to sing it. By the light of the silvery moon. . . .

He knows all about God, Lisette! It's like God is his very best friend! What do you think of that?

Poo!

Lisette, you know what?

Tell me.

He'll tell his friend God to kill you. That's it! God will kill you.

No!

You are going to die, Lisette. You will be dead, dead, dead, and then I'll be happy!

I won't die! I won't.

You'll see! My uncle, my very own uncle, is going to kill you. He is bringing God here, and they'll kill you together!

You think so? I don't know about God . . .

God is great, God is good, and He's so strong.

. . . but I know all about uncles!

The shades were drawn in the living room of the East Rogers Park bungalow, the only light the colored waverings from the three television sets that stood side by side. The tiny old woman sat on a sagging sofa, eyes half-open, watching, fingers resting on the three remote control units in her lap. If she saw something interesting, then she would turn up the volume and hear it as well.

The old woman wore a flowered dress that had fit better 40 pounds ago, before the cancer in her belly started swallowing her and eating her from within. There was a kerchief around her head, wispy white hair at its edges. Screwed into the corner of her mouth was a curved clay pipe. She looked a great deal like a living caricature of Mammy Yokum.

There! Channel nine had a commercial for Saturday afternoon's Creature Features, *The Wolfman*. That was a good one, all right—Lon

Chaney, Bela Lugosi, and Maria Ouspenskaya.
That Bela, yes, he was a *Gajo*, but he knew the
Rom, loved their music and treated them with
respect. Back in the old days, when horse drawn
vurdons roamed here and there, and Gypsies
traveled north and south, east and west, she had
gone out to Hollywood to work with Maria
Ouspenskaya. They were bit players in a foolish
musical adventure called *The Gypsy's Necklace*.
She and Maria Ouspenskaya had also been consultants for the film, explaining Gypsy customs
or, better still, fooling the ignorant *Gajo* director
by creating Gypsy traditions on the spot.

"No, no, no! The hero is an honorable Gypsy,
thus he would never begin to eat without first
washing his hands."

"Nor would he eat eggs. All Gypsies know that
eggs are slippery and weak substances that rob a
man of his strength."

"He must not enter the farmer's cottage without first stamping his left foot three times to
shake off any tiny devils that might be clinging to
him."

"That is not so! He would stamp but once as
he said a prayer to St. Sarah the Black."

"Stamp only once? Perhaps that is the custom
amongst the *Sinti Romany*, but among the better
bred *Kalderash*, even a child knows to stamp at
least twice!"

By the time the "hero enters farmer's cottage"
scene was on film, the poor actor was dancing a
jig at the doorstep.

Maria Ouspenskaya was a good Gypsy. That all
Gypsies might have the soul of Maria Ouspenskaya!

The old woman leaned back, settling into the familiar contours of the couch. She was sleepy all the time now, and one day she would sleep and not wake. Then it would be her time to journey *anda l thema*, to go beyond the waters into the nation of the dead. She had visited there before, both in dreams and in the spirit, and she did not fear it. It was neither a good nor a bad place, only a different one.

She took her pipe from her mouth and set it on the table to her left. She dozed, images from the televisions filtering into her mind and blending into dreams. Then she awoke at a knock at the front door.

"Joe! Joe, you get the door, okay?" On any given day, any number of nephews and nieces and cousins might be living in her bungalow. Names were important to the *Gaje*, not the *Rom*, and so she referred to all the men in her home as Joe. That way, she was always sure of somebody responding when she called out, "Joe."

A Joe answered the door. She heard men's voices and footsteps, then he entered the living room. She squinted. He wasn't too tall, but there was a good, well-balanced size to him; he seemed to belong in his own body—and so many people did not. He wore a hat; he had manners. She crooked a finger, beckoning him closer.

"Do I know you?" she said. "I think I ought to know you. I don't know. I'm old." When the old woman spoke English, she sounded like a polka band singer who'd been raised by B-movie gangsters of the 1940s. When she spoke German, she sounded, she had been told, like an angry pig peasant. She also spoke Spanish, French, Portuguese, idiomatic Russian, and some Hindi—all badly.

But when she spoke Romany, the true language, she spoke pure poetry.

"*Puri Dai*"—he respectfully called her "Old Mother"—"you might remember me. I'm a photographer. Some years ago, I took your picture for a book I called *Rom*."

"Yeah, yeah, I remember that."

He told her his name.

She nodded. "You didn't come to take my picture this time, did you?"

"No, *Puri Dai*," he said. "I've come because there is someone who needs your help. She needs your wisdom and your gifts."

"Hey, what you saying? You sound like 'This is a job for Superman' or something!"

The man's smile was serious. "No, but it is a job for the *Rawnie*, the great lady, Pola Janichka."

"I don't know, I don't know." The old woman shook her head. "I been sick lately." Her words trailed off and then, seeming to lose track of what they had been saying, she cocked her head and gave him a sharp stare.

"*Rom San?*" she asked. Are you a Gypsy?

"No," he replied.

She shifted to turn on the lamp, then remote controlled the televisions off. In the yellow splash of light, she leaned forward, demanding, "Your hand. I got to know who you really are, you know what I mean?"

He gave her his right hand.

She gazed hard, tracing lines with a shaking

finger, her breath on his hand. *"Rom!"* She said decisively.

. Yes, you are a Gypsy, Pola Janichka told David Greenfield. Maybe you don't know it or maybe you don't want to know it, but you are *Rom*.

So that she would know him, his heart and his soul, and thus know what to do, she read his palm. And then, because it is something we all must know if we are to be truly alive, Pola Janichka, psychic and sorceress, healer and witch, woman of knowledge, told David Greenfield who he was.

THIRTY-SEVEN

Stefan Grinzspan was a young Polish Jew. When the Nazis set about purifying the world for the master race, Stefan Grinzspan went to Auschwitz. National Socialism had a great deal of purifying to do, an awesome task that only *ubermensch* would dare undertake, and so, not only Jews went to Auschwitz and other such camps. You might find Slavs and Czechs and Russians, homosexuals and petty criminals of (1)any nationality, all the asocials and *untermenschen*.

Gypsies wandered the Earth, refused to seek gainful employment and had dark skins, so they were sent to the death camps.

The Gypsies at Auschwitz were ". . . the best loved prisoners. They loved to play, even at work, which they never took quite seriously. I never saw a scowling, hateful expression on a Gypsy's face. They would often play their musical instruments or let their children dance . . ."

This was written by Rudolf Hoess, commandant of Auschwitz, as he awaited his own sentence of death for war crimes. He stated he genuinely liked his Gypsies, and he found it quite painful and difficult to have 16,000 of them killed. He was, he explained, a sensitive man, and what was particularly hard on him was that he "knew almost every one of them individually. They were by nature as trusting as children."

Stefan Grinzspan did not see any dancing Gypsy children, but he did get to know one little Gypsy, a boy of perhaps six or seven, who was all over the camp, foraging for food. The child had brilliantly black eyes, and just once, Stefan would have liked to see him smile. Because Stefan worked in the kitchens, sometimes he could smuggle a rotting black potato or a turnip to the boy.

One day, luck ran out, as it had or would for most of the prisoners of Auschwitz. Stefan Grinzspan slipped the Gypsy boy half a piece of white bread, and then froze at "Nein!"

SS Lieutenant Hans Kraus, blond and youthful, was new to Auschwitz. A blanched face showed he was not accustomed to the pervasive stink of filth and burning corpses. His contemplative blue eyes, and sad, full mouth made him look as though the world had treated him unjustly.

"*Bitte,*" Lieutenant Hans Kraus said, "please, Jew, don't tell me that I saw you give the boy a piece of bread. I do not want to think ill of you."

Stefan Grinzspan thought, I am going to be killed. "Nein," he said. But Hans Kraus did not look like a man who could or would kill anyone. There were Germans who surreptitiously found ways to lighten the misery for the prisoners, even to save temporarily a few from the gas chambers. Even in the wickedest place on Earth, not everyone was wicked.

"Good," Lieutenant Kraus said. He crooked his finger, ordering the Gypsy boy to him. For a moment, it seemed as though the child would take flight, but then he approached the officer. "If the Jew did not give you the bread, little boy, then you must have stolen it." Lieutenant Kraus smiled conspiratorially, and the boy shrugged with comic assent.

The officer sighed. "This is not an easy time for children or Jews or any of us." Then he said, "*Ess der brote, klein kind.*" Eat the bread, little child.

In two ravenous gulps, the boy devoured it.

"Was it good?" Lieutenant Kraus asked.

The boy nodded that it was.

"I am glad," Lieutenant Kraus said. Then he grabbed the child and held him pinned tightly against himself, as he unsnapped the flap of his holster, took out the Luger and chambered a round.

As Stefan Grinzspan watched, the SS officer whirled the child away from him, seized him by the hair, put the pistol to the center of his forehead and fired. A bloody wad of brain hit Stefan Grinzspan on the chin and a hard piece of bone struck him in the ribs.

Stefan Grinzspan survived Auschwitz. Rather, something of Stefan Grinzspan was eventually liberated to come to New York. He had some money, reparations from a Germany forced to pay a pittance to those it had not been able to kill, and so he opened a small haberdashery.

He seldom laughed, and he never cried. He walked as though he were always tired and his feet hurt. Not infrequently, he dreamed of the Gypsy boy, saw him with a crumb of bread on his lip, his head shattered, and heard him accuse, "You murdered me."

The dream was true. He *had* killed the Gypsy

child. Stefan Grinzspan, the Polish Jew, became a devout Jew, an observant Jew, one who prayed at the neighborhood storefront *shul* morning, afternoon and evening. Daily, he sought forgiveness, and, on Yom Kippur, Most Holy Day of Atonement, he begged God for absolution—but did not receive it.

To be forgiven, to atone, to be at one with your fellow man, with yourself, and therefore with God, you must redress your wrongs and attain pardon of the one against whom you have sinned.

The Gypsy child was dead. Stefan Grinzspan was lost. Always he would know the joyless life of an automaton, a human impostor, always carrying the ponderous immensity of his sin. That is what he believed.

But that was not how it worked. He met a woman. Her name was Sarah the way the immigration authorities spelled it, but Sora in Yiddish, in the *mama-loschen*, the mother tongue. Sora understood this man who lived what was, at best, a half-life, because she, too, had a blue number tattooed on her forearm. Neither of them might ever know happiness, but, at least, when the nights were black and endless, he would not be alone and she would not be alone. It was reason enough to marry.

Happy was a word neither might have used, but they did feel as though they belonged together. And there were moments that seemed to sneak up on them, take them utterly by surprise, moments neither of them trusted because they were so nice. Once was kindling Sabbath candles, as the ancient, sweet, flickering light engulfed them both. Another time was when Sora spontaneously began singing a silly old Yiddish song, and he sang along, and then they each had a glass of wine, a little Mogen David, and that night they made very nice love.

They had a child, a boy. They named him David or *Duvid*. The eighth day after the birth, at his son's *bris*, Stefan Grinzspan got tipsy on *schnaps* and wept and danced.

He loved the boy. He was surprised by his own ferocious love, its penetrating intensity. He was totally astounded that he could love. But, oh, he loved this gurgling, drooling, baby boy, this David. He loved him. He loved his wife. He had given over unto despair—and now, he was raised up. Now he understood that surely goodness and mercy, as God had promised, were to be his.

Then, when David was four, Sora caught cold. She got tired with a tiredness that would not go away. From diagnosis to death, her acute leukemia required three and a half months.

The child could not be comforted. He cried ceaselessly; he could not understand why his mother was gone.

But Stefan Grinzspan understood. Happiness or any thought of it was cruelly taunting illusion. It was not meant for him nor for his son, while, upon his head and his soul was blood sin. He was damned and damnation descended even unto the seventh generation.

Then salvation presented itself, although he did not at first realize it.

A family of Gypsies, with the Hungarian name Hovarth, moved into the store across the street from Stefan Grinzspan's haberdashery. The storefront became *ofisa*, a fortune telling parlor with living quarters in the rear. Signs proclaimed that "Madame Tona Hovarth, Psychic Adviser to European Royalty and Hollywood Stars" was giving consultations. On the streets for blocks around, Hovarth children, aged six to 12, passed out handbills and panhandled.

Everyday, from his store, Stefan spied on the Gypsies. At first, he tried to tell himself he hated them because they made him hate himself even more than he had thought possible.

Then one day, Stefan saw the Gypsy man lounging with a cigarette at the *ofisa* entranceway. That seemed to be his sole occupation. Loafers and thieves, Stefan forced himself to think.

The Gypsy was barrel-chested and barrel-gutted, swarthy, perhaps 50; he had a gray and black walrus mustache and wore a hat, a comic, droopy brimmed Panama. He was an unremarkable enough Gypsy, not differing greatly from many you might find in numerous American cities, but on this fair warm day the sleeves of the man's none too clean white shirt were rolled up to the elbow, and Stefan noted the blue numbers on the man's heavy forearm.

Stefan Grinzspan closed his store and crossed the street. He stood in front of the Gypsy. The Gypsy smoked a Lucky Strike and said nothing.

Stefan rolled up his own sleeve.

The Gypsy nodded. "*Hitlari* bastards," he said. "In your name and in mine, for all the innocent who suffered, I call down an *armaya*." His tone was reverential as he pronounced the Romany curse. "May the brains of the *hitlari* burst, and their blood pour out of their ears and their eyes, and may even their shadows know pain and cast a stink in the nostrils of good people."

The Gypsy flicked the butt of his cigarette onto the sidewalk. "You a Jew?"

Stefan said, "Yes."

"Jews are okay," the Gypsy said. He pointed to Stefan's ever present *yarmulke*. "Jews got sense about important things. Like us Gypsies. You know you keep your head covered to show God you got respect for Him."

The Gypsy held out his hand. "I guess we want to be friends, okay?" Stefan Grinzspan told the Gypsy his name and learned that Big Hovarth was as good a name as any for the big man. Because, Big Hovarth said, it was what friends do, they went into the *ofisa*, the women hurrying to serve them brandy and then hurrying out of the way so as not to annoy the men. In the back, they sat and they talked.

Many days they talked like this. The more Stefan got to know Big Hovarth, the more sure he was that God in His mercy had granted him the opportunity of redemption. At last, he had a chance to atone, to set right the balance of his personal universe.

There was no question that Big Hovarth and the Hovarth clan were good people. There was no question that Big Hovarth loved his sons and his daughters. That was the *Romany* way. "We Gypsies love our kids and we honor our old people. Maybe that's why we don't always get along with the *Gaje*, heh?"

"I, too, love my son David very much," Stefan Grinzspan said. "And I worry about him. I have to do what is right for him, you see?"

Not fully understanding, Big Hovarth still

nodded solemnly. Doing what is right was how a *Rom* was obliged to live.

"I want my son to be cared for. I want him to be with people who love children, people who will be kind to him and teach him to live properly."

"That is what all good men wish for their sons," Big Hovarth said.

"But I must do more than wish," Stefan said. "I must insure that this will be his fate, for you see, my friend, I will soon be dead."

Big Hovarth stroked his mustache for a time, then said, "You are going to die soon?"

"Yes."

"You sure?"

"Yes."

"I will regret it," Big Hovarth said. "I will light candles in memory of you."

"I must ask more than that of you, Big Hovarth," Stefan Grinzspan said. "I want you to take my David and raise him as your own."

Once more, the Gypsy took a long time to respond. "Is this what you truly want?"

Stefan Grinzspan thought, My son is dearer to me than my own life. I must give him up, for his sake and mine. Atonement. "Yes," he said. "I have money. I will give you money."

"You have asked a favor of me. I am your friend. Whatever a friend requests is a Rom's obligation and his honor." Big Hovarth nodded. "Three days, the Hovarth *kumpania* moves on. Detroit, maybe. Chicago. Your son will be with us."

That night, Stefan tried to explain to his David. He told the boy that, like Mama had had to go away forever, soon Papa must go as well.

Hysterical, arms around Stefan's neck, his tears soaking his neck and cheek, the boy screamed, "No, I love you! You cannot leave me!"

"I must," Stefan said. "You will be taken care of. My good friend, Big Hovarth, and his family will look after you. You will be a son of their family, a Gypsy boy."

As I have taken a child from the Gypsies, now I restore one!

"You will see, David, they will love you. You will love them."

David jerked away from his father. "I loved Mama and she left me! I love you and you are going to leave me! It hurts here and it hurts here." He drummed his fists against his chest and belly. "It hurts too much. Too much!" He beat himself harder. "No! I won't ever love anyone again. You hurt too much when they . . ."

Stefan grabbed the boy's wrists. "Stop it! Stop it now!"

And just like that, the child did stop. Though his face stayed flushed, his black eyes grew cold and tearless. "I do not love you, Papa. Not anymore. No one ever again. Nobody will ever leave me and hurt me like this again." The boy's cold smile twisted Stefan's guts.

On Friday, David silently accepted his father's kiss, then, with nothing on his face or in his eyes, calmly took Big Hovarth's hand and drove off in the *kumpania's* modern day caravan of two Lincolns and a Cadillac.

Stefan Grinzspan, his heart a dried pit in his chest, went back to his apartment. The Sabbath began at sundown, and this time, he did not welcome the day of peace with candles and prayer. He waited until after sunset, when the tentative dark was upon the city, and then he turned on the oven. He could not light it; you were not to strike a fire on the Sabbath.

In his *yarmulke*, his white and blue *tallis*, the prayer shawl of observant Jews, draped over his shoulders, he sat at the table. After a while, he felt somewhat dizzy, as though his soul were trying to loose itself of his body. He breathed deeply and felt himself become light, relieved of the pressing weight of sin. He arose, weightless and innocent and free. I have given my son to the Gypsies, and I am giving my soul to God.

The vows we make when we are youngest and most foolish are the very vows we most strive to keep as we grow older and more wise. The Hovarths taught David Grinzspan Romany ways and loved him like a true son. David Grinzspan learned Romany ways and did not love the Hovarths. He gave them respect. He treated each and every one of them with proper courtesy. He made it clear to them and to himself that he was with them but not one of them.

The Hovarths felt hurt.

David did not share that hurt.

David did not feel.

As a young man, David discovered photography. He found satisfaction in the way it let him clinically gaze at the world, providing clean, objective distance from what he saw.

He no longer called himself David Grinzspan. That was a Jewish name, and he was no Jew. His father had given him to the Gypsies. He did not call himself by the name Hovarth. That was a

Romany name, a name for a man of *tacho rat*; but a *Rom* is a man of deep feeling, one who lives by his passions—and David had no passions.

David Greenfield was a relatively euphonious name. It signified nothing.

Nothing. No one.

It was a fitting name for the man he saw himself as, the man he had chosen to be.

All this and more, his past and his future, Pola Janichka learned from David Greenfield's palm. "*San Rom*," she said again. "You are a Gypsy. Your soul is a Gypsy soul. Your heart is a Gypsy heart, and it beats with the great heart of your people."

David shrugged. "The curse," he said.

"I know, I know," Pola Janichka said. Of course, she had seen Selena in his palm, too.

"I speak for her as she is forbidden to speak to you. The curse, *marhime*, must be lifted. She begs this of you. She begs to learn from you once more, to be given your knowledge of *draba* magic and charms."

"*Mong, fuli tschai, mong!*" Pola Janichka said. "Beg, you foolish girl, beg! I loved her. I gave my love freely. I gave my gifts freely. Then Selena Lazone broke my heart."

Pola Janichka closed her eyes. Her mouth worked on the stem of her pipe. Finally, she said, "I will see her," she said. "Bring her to me. Now."

THIRTY-EIGHT

"**T**hank God!" Vicki hugged him and burst into tears.

Warren perfunctorily shook his hand and took his coat. He offered a bland, vaguely appropriate greeting; beneath an obviously forced smile lurked a look of mildly amused disdain.

Shoulders quaking, Vicki sobbed, "Oh, thank God, you're here!"

Here was the setting of the most momentous undertaking of his ministry, of his life. Here would he prove himself. Here would he encounter, combat and defeat the evil, proving himself the Lord's true champion.

Evan Kyle Dean could feel it, standing in the foyer, a few minutes past nine, with these two people that genealogy, chance and God Almighty had brought together.

Here was the testing place of Evan Kyle Dean. All his senses were receiving intimations of the past, present, future—and of eternity.

There were secrets here. There was secret sin, crimes contemplated and crimes committed, crimes against others, crimes against self, crimes against God. Teasing flashes played on the keen receptors of Evan Kyle Dean's awareness.

His heart raced. He was dry-mouthed and

light-headed, his blood and his power burning throughout his body.

"Vicki, Warren," he said, "let's talk."

The words came spilling out of Vicki as she sat at the table with Evan Kyle Dean. He did not interrupt. Nor did Warren, who had not sat down but was pacing about the kitchen, sometimes slipping within the periphery of Evan's vision, to favor him with a tight-lipped mocking smile, sometimes moving behind him, momentarily out of sight as he circled the table and the two of them. Warren might have thought himself a phantom observer from an alien planet, curious about their discussion, able to comprehend little of it, even as he ridiculed them for not recognizing his presence.

"That's it," Vicki said. "That's all of it."

"I see," Evan said. Suddenly, he cocked his head, caught Warren's eye and froze him in his tracks. "I've not heard from you, Warren. What do you think of all this?"

Warren glared and, for an instant, Evan Kyle Dean expected his brother-in-law to leap for his throat. Then the moment of tension passed with Warren's laughter. He leaned back against the counter, arms folded.

"I think it's nonsense," Warren said. "Bullshit."

"Warren!"

Warren straightened up, wagging a finger at her. "Nope, Vicki, I have been patient. I'll go along with it because it will keep you happy and it can't do the kid any harm."

He sighed, as though he were the most put-upon man who ever lived. "The kid needs some shrinking, so we go see the lady shrink. Turns out Ms. Freud is missing a few cards in her deck but has replaced them with moths and butter-flies, and she tells us our kid has a wicked spirit, a *diakka* or some damn thing in her soul. So of course, we just have to get in touch with a professional exorcist. Makes all the sense in the world! And hey, no need to check the classified advertising in the *National Enquirer*. After all, my very own yokel brother-in-law does demons, yessir!"

"Warren!" Vicki got to her feet.

Warren ignored her. Frowning menacingly, Warren strode towards Evan Kyle Dean. "Hey, brother-in-law, will we get a family discount rate? Double demons for your dollars? And can we pay by credit card?"

Vicki brought her fist down on the table. "Warren, Evan came to help us!"

"Right, right," Warren said. "And just because I'm such a fine guy, I'm going to tolerate his help tonight, and that is it. The End. Then the most holy reverend can take his Save Your Soul show back on the road and out of my face!"

Warren grinned theatrically at Evan Kyle Dean. "Get the message, Preach?"

"You don't have sole say in this, Warren! Missy is *our* child. This is *our* house."

Evan Kyle's Dean's solemn voice stilled hers. "You're afraid, Warren," he said. "What are you afraid of?"

Warren Barringer's face flashed white, and for an instant his eyes rolled back as though he were going to faint.

Then he rasped, "Goddamn you . . ."

Evan stood up. "Are you afraid of God, Warren? Are you afraid of yourself?"

Warren lurched at him.

Knuckles hard against her teeth, Vicki pressed down a cry. Then she sprang at Warren and grabbed his upper right arm, sinking her fingers into the muscle.

Ignoring her, Warren brandished his left fist in Evan's face. "Afraid? I'm afraid I might knock your pious ass into the middle of next week." Warren twisted and pulled back, freeing himself of Vicki's grasp.

"You have your faith healing party tonight," Warren said, "and then you take your holy nose out of our business or I'll . . ." He backed out of the kitchen, eyes shifting paranoiacally from one to the other.

The threat hung in the air, the more menacing for being uncompleted.

"I'm sorry," Vicki said, eyes down. "He's upset."

Yes, Evan Kyle Dean grimly decided, but his brother-in-law's fear and fury were somehow linked to the living wickedness in this house. Like heavy invisible fog, evil filled the rooms of the Barringers' home. He felt it clinging to him, could smell its sour corruption with each breath, hear it whispering lewd promises and hideous threats just beyond the range of normal hearing.

That evil had in some way touched Warren Barringer.

But not Vicki Barringer. He saw that. His sister-in-law's innocence might have been an aura, a pure light emanating from a soul that had no secrets.

He would discover the secrets. He would command all that lay hidden to become known!

He would cast the devils of this house back into the pit of darkness.

"Warren doesn't mean anything," Vicki was saying. "Sometimes he can . . .''

"Don't apologize, Vicki. I do understand. It's all right." Evan gently took her hand. "Now, I'd like to meet my niece, Melissa."

That is what he said.

What he meant was that he was ready to vanquish evil.

As he went down the hall, his heart pounded so much that he feared it would pop the buttons off his shirt. A savage, rough-edged pressure roared in his ears. He wanted to kill, to take his bullshit brother-in-law by the throat and squeeze and squeeze and squeeze until those fucking sincere eyes popped out of that cornpone face!

Brother-in-law Evan Kyle looked at him and somehow saw right through him. It was as if Warren Barringer could not conceal anything from the fucking minister!

The moment he closed the door of his study behind him, he felt better. Sanctuary! He switched on the light. He could breathe now. He felt okay—no anger, no fear. Another deep and calming breath. He had to admit he had come near to freaking, but it was his house, and he was in charge.

A place for everything. Everything in its place. All right. Work on the book a little? His secret and wonderful, audacious and true book!

He was tackling this one in an unusual way, just letting it flow without elaborate plot outlines or character sketches. Nothing but what popped into his head was transferred directly to the page. Later, he would compile it and put it all together so that it made sense for a reader.

Right now, the book had to make sense only for him.

He pulled back the desk chair and sat down. Again, he assured himself that he had nothing to hide, nothing to be ashamed of, nothing to fear. He was Warren Barringer, respectable college professor and respected writer. He was god-damned Mr. Clean. Didn't smoke, didn't drink, no vices to speak of . . .

Warren Barringer, family man, was a decent provider, a thoughtful and considerate husband, an attentive father.

He rolled a sheet of paper into the Underwood.

He loved his kid.

He loved kids.

His fingers went to the typewriter, but they didn't move, fingertips rooted on the keys. Nothing flowed from mind to paper. His mind was empty.

He slid open the right hand desk drawer. He took out the white china doll, the little girl with the bonnet and basket of eggs . . .

He knew what he had to do. He knew what he would do.

He remembered the promise he had made, and the loving promise she had made.

His brain was bursting with things he had to say. With a very few words, he said all of them:

> *He loved the little girl.*
> *He could not help himself.*
> *He was what he was.*

He studied the three sentences.

He read them aloud in a monotone.

It was said, and there came to him an instant of perfect understanding as he abandoned his last vestiges of hope in the lie called free will.

Warren Barringer was lost.

And he knew it.

THIRTY-NINE

She turned her head and looked up from the *Snow White* coloring book. A lovely child, he thought, just lovely.

Standing beside him, just inside Melissa's room, Vicki said, "Melissa, this is your Uncle Evan."

"Hi, Uncle Evan." The smile came immediately with no hint of shyness. Her eyes shone. "Everyone calls me Missy, except sometimes Mom when I'm bad."

"Hello, Missy," he said.

She put the red crayon down on her table and stood up. "I didn't have to go to school today, and we bought this new dress this morning 'cause you were coming." She smoothed her dress, dark green corduroy with lace collar and sleeve trim. "You know, I usually just like to wear my jeans, but this is a pretty neat dress. Even though it's brand new, there's something kinda old-fashioned about it, isn't there?"

"Yes," Evan Kyle Dean agreed. Something old-fashioned about the child herself, he thought. With her golden hair combed simply back and the wispy lace about her pale, swanlike neck, she reminded him of an antique cameo portrait, an idealized artistic image of the way children ought to be.

This was a mistake, he thought. He did not belong here. His niece had no need of his power to bring healing, to cleanse souls. As rude as Warren had been, his brother-in-law, it appeared, had accurately assessed the situation. And Vicki had been deceived by others or by herself in this age of high anxiety, tabloid terrors, fundamentalist fanatics and false prophets.

Why, look at the little girl! Melissa Barringer, guileless and bubbling, absolutely glowed with physical and spiritual well-being. Could he believe that she . . .

He tensed. Evan Kyle Dean cautioned himself to take a moment for the most profound consideration. First impressions, that was all! First impressions gathered only by his five senses, not his soul-sense, the intuitive, godly feeling within that unerringly discerned truth from falsehood.

The nice little girl standing before him was a lie! A blackness, thick and menacing, pressed down on him. He felt it. There was evil here. It shook his confidence, so easily had he almost allowed himself to be gulled by this deception! The home of the Barringers, his in-laws, was a temple of lies, all of them stemming from the father of lies who had dared him to test his soul's mettle against the powers of evil.

Melissa put a hand to her head and wound a strand of hair around her first two fingers. She gazed at him placidly, and this time, he truly gazed back and looked within her. What he saw was not innocent and young and untainted. What he saw was not beautiful.

In the child's eyes burned depravity, a relentless will that acknowledged neither the evolving ethics of Man or the eternal laws of God.

There was something else there—a cold and confident dare. *I will do as I want. Who are you to oppose me?*

He spoke the answer only to himself. *I am the blessed and chosen of the Lord God Almighty. I will prevail.*

He gently took Vicki's elbow and steered her from the room. "Missy and I need to get to know each other," he said. "Don't worry about us. We'll be fine."

The little girl untwirled the spirals of hair around her fingers.

With the door closed, he said, "Now we can talk, just you and I. Uncle Evan and Missy."

"Sure," she said, "but is it okay if I finish coloring my picture?"

"Is that what you want to do?"

"Uh-huh," she said. She seated herself again at her little table, concentrating, lips pursed, guiding the tip of the red crayon precisely within the outline of the apple the warty-nosed, black-cowled woman offered Snow White.

He stood behind her, looking over her shoulder. The apple grew ferociously red. Without turning her head, she said, "I'm glad you're here, Uncle Evan."

"Are you?"

"Yes," she said. "I get to stay up late an' everything. I'll get to finish this picture tonight. And Mom said I won't have to go to school tomorrow." She giggled. "I've missed a lot of school. I could care less. You miss a year, and all you have to do is three pages from your workbook and you're all made up!"

"You're doing a fine job of coloring," he said.

"Thanks," she said. "I do pretty good, I

guess. My friend Dorothy Morgan says she's the best colorer in the whole second grade, but I am. No brag. Just fact."

"Is that who you are?" Evan asked. "The best colorer in the second grade?"

She turned around to look at him and grinned. "Yup, that's me." Then she tapped the crayon tip on the nose of the hag. "And she is a little old lady, except she really isn't. Sometimes she's a wicked witch. And sometimes she's the evil queen. Isn't it funny how she can be two people at once like that, Uncle Evan?"

"Do you think it's funny?"

"Kinda. It's like she's got this big secret, and she's fooling everybody!" She put down the crayon. She began to play with her hair, winding it around her fingers.

"What about you?" he asked. "Do you have a big secret?"

She hesitated. "Maybe . . ." she said, her tone noncommittal.

But now on her face, he saw the plea, the desperation and hope that the dark furies within her eyes might be cast out. Had she been speaking to him, he could have heard her no more clearly: *I have secrets, terrible sinful secrets. Bring these dark secrets before the holy light of God that is yours, Uncle Evan, and they will disappear. Help me, Uncle. Save me.*

I will, he vowed.

Her fingers curled a strand of hair.

"Do you want to tell me your secret?"

She nodded, then her face twisted, lower lip curling down like a crescent of raw flesh, eyes brimming with tears.

He picked her up, and she clung to him. It felt

as though he were holding a living, sobbing, block of ice. Evil had attacked her, was inside her and attacking her at this very instant. He felt that.

"You cry, Melissa," he said. "Tears will help." He sat down on the foot of her bed, holding her on his lap. "And when you've cried as much as you need to, then we'll fix it all."

He shivered as she squeezed tighter against him. His arms encircled her—and he could not see the too-wise, most unchildlike grin she pressed into his shirt.

She cried. She wanted to laugh, but she wept. Uncle was patting her back, telling her it was okay for her to cry.

Of course. Uncle wanted her to cry. Uncles liked tears. If they didn't, would uncles know so many ways to make you cry?

But she was smart. She had learned the lessons she needed to know to survive. She knew all about mamas who went away and mamas who had no love for you, and she knew all about uncles who could hurt you even while they were saying how much they loved you.

Now she knew games and secrets and tricks to stay alive.

I will not die! Never!

She sniffled. She crawled her right hand up his chest. Almost invisible between the pads of her thumb and index finger was a single blond hair plucked from her head, charged with her life force and will and energy.

As he told her he would help her, that he would free her, that he would return her to goodness, she carefully slipped the hair inside his shirt collar.

"Uncle, do you love me?" she asked.

Certainly he . . .

Of course he loved her. There are ways to make the men love you, to make Uncle love you.

. . . loved her. She was his very own niece, and she was one of God's children.

"Come with me," she said to him.

And holding her hand, he did.

He heard his blood hissing in his veins. He had gone beyond the restraints of mundane self and mortal flesh. He felt exalted and radiant with a peculiar grace that was his and his alone, the grace of goodness that was the gift of the servant of the Lord, Evan Kyle Dean.

Holding the child's hand as she led him downstairs, he did not doubt that now would come his battle with evil—his battle and his victory.

He had no intimation of the form evil might take nor of how it would rise up to attempt to destroy him, but Evan Kyle Dean did not doubt. He had faith. He knew what manner of miracles he had worked and could work, he knew among his gifts was the powerful gift of casting out unclean spirits, he knew that he was above all a good man, a righteous and true man.

In the living room, Vicki Barringer started to rise from the sofa. He saw the worried questions on her face.

"It's all right," he told her.

The child took him down another flight of stairs to the basement.

Television, comfortable lounging furniture, a

wet bar and a stereo system were all supposed to make it the family room, but it was the basement, and he felt the chill and the cold, smelled the wet and the lingering black odor of coal, the stomach-turning stink of rotten food and urine and feces and sickness. Though the lights were on, there was no light, only in the pungent, cruel dark glow of her eyes.

And Evan Kyle Dean knew. Transcendant, he had freed himself from the prison of the present, and he had journeyed into the past, as real for him as this instant's present.

He understood now that this singular manifestation of evil came into this world in the past.

Right here, in a cold and damp basement, was a place of torment and perversion, wickedness and death, and what had happened here, like the memory of evil, could never entirely disappear from the universe.

I'm so alone, Uncle. I'm afraid and alone. Please be good to me . . .

Did Melissa say that? He thought she did. Something like confusion wriggled in the back of his mind. Melissa had changed. She looked the same—but not the same.

But she was alone and afraid, and he had to give her comfort and shield and protect her from the evil surrounding her . . . surrounding them.

"Please, won't you hold me, Uncle? Be nice to me."

Like a man coming out of anaesthesia, he was disoriented; past and present, reality and illusion were a soft fuzz. But in the floating uncertainty, he did know one thing. Hold her. Be nice to her.

He had to do what she'd asked.

So he sat on the sofa, rocking her on his lap, and she was whispering to him, her breath a warm wind in his ear, petting his face, whispering in his ear, wiggling on his lap, patting his back, whispering warm secrets in his ear, whispering . . .

He felt tired, as though he were on the verge of badly needed sleep. No, it was more like he had dropped directly into dream without first drifting into slumber.

And she whispered in his ear and whispered. Her voice was wetly sweet with promises. She promised to be nice to him. She promised to love him. She promised to be good to him. She promised to make him happy, to make him very, very happy.

A lovely child, a dear little girl. It was a wavy, feathery thought, exactly like a thought in a dream. He did want her to love him. He would be gentle and kind to her and she would always love him.

She slipped off his lap and stood between his knees. Then she knelt.

His mind lay buried beneath lazy dream weight, but in his belly and below was a stirring, a tingling of arousal.

She unzipped his trousers . . .

Yes!

. . . and her hand, small and warm, reached for him.

Something like lightning flared in his brain and he rocked forward, sinking his fingers into her shoulders, paralyzing her with his grip. "What are you doing?" he demanded.

"I love you, Uncle. Don't hurt me!"

Hurt her? He wanted to kill her! He wanted to use his fists, to feel her body break and tear as he hit her and hit her and hit her. He wanted to work her destruction with his own bare hands. She was a temptress, a monster! She was a . . .

"Whore! You whore!" He was a good man, and she was a whore who sought to ruin him, to destroy him, and he would punish her for that. He would kill her. He sank the fingers of his left hand deep into her shoulder, and she writhed in his grasp as he balled his right hand into a fist and drew it back.

She smiled.

He groaned. He released her. With a knee, he unintentionally pushed her back on the carpet as he got up. Fingers palsied, he yanked up his zipper, then he reeled up the stairs. He heard her call after him. "Uncle! You want me . . ."

Then he was in the kitchen.

With a deep breath, he understood. He had gone down to the basement to learn about the wicked spirit that threatened his niece, to meet the evil of the Barringer house.

He had indeed.

And somehow the evil had invaded him.

He could not deal with it now. He felt as though he had been beaten with clubs. He was exhausted. He needed to sleep.

Then she was there, standing at the head of the stairs to the family room. Her look was one of studied innocence even while it proclaimed that they shared a guilty secret.

She was there, too, a few minutes later, as he stood with Vicki and Warren in the foyer. There were things he had to think about, to consider, he said, and so for the time being, he didn't want to say anything.

Vicki said she understood, but her expression told him she didn't, not at all. "Have faith," he told her.

Then Warren, surprisingly, stepped forward with an apology. He was sorry. He was out of line.

He knew they all wanted to do the right thing for Melissa.

"So, please, forget all the earlier brouhaha and stay the night."

"No, thank you," Evan Kyle Dean said. He needed distance from this place, he thought, and from the child. He needed to rest and gather his strength.

Warren got Evan his coat. He thanked him, and Evan thought he sounded sincere.

"I'm glad you came, Uncle," the child said.

Evan Kyle Dean said, "I'll come back tomorrow."

The little girl smiled.

FORTY

It was ten-thirty when David brought Selena to the house of Pola Janichka. "The *Rawnie* awaits you," said the sullen Rom who admitted them. The man stood back so that Selena Lazone might not defile him by even an accidental touch of her clothing. Selena Lazone was *marhime*. With his right hand, thumb thrust between first and second fingers, the Rom gestured to ward off evil.

David spoke in Romany. He was shocked. He was hurt. He was insulted. Such rudeness from a Rom was a grievously painful thing; throughout the world, the Romany were justly praised as the most hospitable of people. David's words oozed irony.

Hanging a step behind him, Selena said nothing, her attitude and clothing, a utilitarian car coat over a simple, dark blue dress, was that of a supplicant and a penitent.

The Rom shrugged apologetically. He meant no offense to David. As for the *marhime* woman, she was unclean, outcast from those of *tacho rat*, and her feelings need be of no more concern to him than those of a plant or a bug.

David glared.

The Rom said to go down the hall, which, like the bungalow itself, was long, narrow and dark.

David led the way to a large, impossibly cluttered room.

Dozens of candles provided shadow-dancing illumination. Some were in golden candelabra or silver or brass candlesticks; others were waxed to ashtrays or peanut butter jar lids. There was a lumpy sofa and against a wall stood a row of steel-tube armed chairs like those you used to find in budget shoe stores. There were plastic TV trays and an old sailor's trunk, orange crates and slatted wooden folding chairs. On one wall hung an unframed painting depicting the signs of the zodiac; next to it was a poster for *Superman* showing Christopher Reeve in flight. Another wall had an elaborate religious tapestry depicting The Holy Virgin, Jesus, and St. Sarah the Black, the patron saint of the Gypsies, although not a saint recognized by the Catholic Church.

On an antique sideboard with elaborate hand-carved scrollwork stood a framed picture of Gypsy guitarist Django Reinhardt and his musical colleague, Stephane Grappelli. It was inscribed, "Pola Janichka, thank you for blessing our music." Grappelli's signature was a typically artistic scrawl; Reinhardt's was a typically Romany "X."

Pola Janichka sat slumped, head bowed, perhaps dozing, at a card table that wouldn't have brought six cents at a garage sale. The table was covered with a century-old, handmade lace tablecloth from the village of Brugge, Belgium. The crystal ball stood in the center of the table. In the past, Pola Janichka had said that the crystal ball originally belonged to Madame Blavatsky, Arthur Conan Doyle, or Jean Dixon; actually, she'd ordered it from the Johnson Smith catalog in 1947.

"*Puri Dai*," David said quietly. "I . . ."

The old woman did not raise her head. "I know you're here, sir. I know who you got with you. What does the *marhime* want?"

Selena whispered, "*Mandi . . . te potshinene penge lajav . . .*"

Pola Janichka raised her head, her angry eyes cutting off Selena. "No," she said, "don't you talk Romany. Romany's not your language, not now and maybe not ever. You went away to be Ms. *Gajo*. You learn the *Anglai* so good that maybe you think someday you get to turn the letters when Vanna gives up the job. For right now, you got something to say to me, you can talk *Gaje* talk."

"I am here," Selena Lazone said, translating from the Romany, although nothing like an exact translation was possible, "to pay for my shame. I beg you to lift the curse of *marhime*."

"A curse? A curse?" Pola Janichka sniffed. "That's silly superstition, my fine *Gajo* lady, the kind of thing those ignorant Gypsies believe in. But a smart *Gajo* woman like you, a woman who reads books and everything, no, you can't really believe in foolishness like a Romany curse."

Quietly and slowly, Selena said, "I believe there is good and I believe there is evil. That is not superstition; it is Truth for both *Romany* and *Gaje*, for all who live and all who will ever live. People are different and so they see good and evil in different ways, but all must choose one or the other in their own way."

Selena paused, then continued somberly, "My

way is the *Romany* way, *Rawnie*. I understand this now. So that I may do what is good, so that I may serve *O Del*, I must be the *Rom* I was born to be."

Pola Janichka said, "You are sincere in what you request? You truly wish to be Selena Lazone *juvel Romano, yilo tshatsrio, y tacho rat*?" A Gypsy woman, one of true heart and true blood.

Selena hesitated. "English will not let me say what I wish to say. May I speak Romany?"

"Whatever." Pola Janichka sounded bored.

In Romany, Selena pronounced an inviolate *armaya: "Te shordjol muro rat may sigo sar te may khav."* She said that if she were not sincere in her request and in her repentance, "May my blood spill and my life thus end even before I have another meal."

Candle flames danced; reflecting them, the crystal ball became a miniature of the heavens encircling the world, golden stars winking and flashing in no meaningful pattern. There was the warm, airy silence that one never finds in life but only in fantasy, and the silence stretched and stretched.

Until finally, in a voice that seemed not hers but that of a very old and very tired woman, Pola Janichka said, *"Bater."*

May it be so.

"Bater," Selena said.

"You go on, you get out of here." As though she only now remembered his presence, Pola Janichka animatedly spoke to David. "You like beer? I got beer. Blatz. In the refrigerator. You go drink a beer and watch the televisions. I got HBO. I got Sportsvision." The old woman made a shooing gesture.

As he started from the room, Pola Janichka told him to wait one second so that Selena could give him her coat.

And he'd better make himself comfortable, she told him. There was lots of beer. Channel seven had some good old movies.

She and Selena, they might be a while.

Then Selena Lazone and Pola Janichka were alone. "So sit down."

Selena pulled a chair to the table.

Pola Janichka said, "You know, *tschai*, I loved you and I still love you, and I meant to give it all to you, everything, to teach you everything I knew. Then you ran off. Selena, that killed me a little bit."

Selena did not reply.

"Selena, the *draba* powers, the magic that is yours . . . *O Del* gave you such a gift! And the teaching I gave you, another gift. And you said 'No!' And you throw my gifts in my face and you throw God's gifts in His face."

Pola Janichka half-rose. She leaned across the table and slapped Selena.

Except for an involuntary blink, Selena did not respond.

"Did that hurt?" Pola Janichka said.

"Yes."

"Good," Pola Janichka said. She slumped back upon her chair. "I wanted to hurt. You hurt me, now I hurt you." With a weary sigh, Pola Janichka changed to *tshatsimo Romano*, the language of truth. "You must greatly love one who hurts you and makes you cry. You made me cry nights and days and more than that, Selena Lazone."

"I am sorry. Pola Janichka, I did not mean to

cause you pain. I wanted only to learn . . ."

"To learn what?"

"To learn who I was. To discover my place in the world. And I feared that would be denied me if I lived my life as the sorceress, the *ababina*, the Romany said I had to be." Selena Lazone looked into the ancient and mystery-laden eyes of Pola Janichka. "I did not mean to cause you pain," she said. "For that, I am sorry."

Pola Janichka said, "I am pleased you are sorry. A day will come and yet once more will I weep for you, Selena Lazone, but for those tears, you will not owe me nor your people an apology. They will be sad tears and good tears."

"I do not know what you mean."

"Then you are not meant to know what I mean."

"As you say, *Rawnie*."

"As the good God, *O Del*, wills, Selena Lazone."

"*Bater*."

"Now we have much to do."

"Then let it be done."

"*Bater*," said Pola Janichka.

In a low and holy voice, Pola Janichka invoked the *Rom*, called on the collective power that beat in the living heart of the Gypsy people. She invoked the *mule Romano*, the spirits of the Gypsy dead, Gypsy spirits who would remain alive as long as they were remembered by the living. Pola Janichka invoked those who had come before, those who were and those who would come after. She invoked all *Rom* in the name of *O Del*, the living God, and in the name of a contrite Selena Lazone and in her own name, Pola Janichka.

In Romany, Pola Janichka said, "Wrong can be forgiven but it should never be hidden."

"Nor can it be hidden," Selena Lazone answered, as Pola Janichka had long ago taught her to answer.

"Then together let us find the truth for you," Pola Janichka said, not without a note of sorrow.

The holy *solakh* commenced, the sacred ritual of truth and confession.

Of forgiveness and redemption.

FORTY-ONE

As he drove west on the unfamiliar US Route 30, Lincoln Highway, Evan Kyle Dean shivered and not only with the chill of weariness. The night had become almost insufferably windy and cold, and the rented Ford Escort's heater produced gurgling and wheezing but virtually no heat. He wished he had put on his coat before getting behind the wheel.

He yawned and waited for the increased rush of oxygen to revive him, but it did not come. He heard the wind's cold muttering on the glass and steel surfaces of the automobile. He felt alone. It was a strange, almost unreal, torpor that, like freezing smoke, seemed to be swirling sluggishly in his arms and legs and chest and belly and brain. It was unnatural, like nothing he had ever before experienced.

He was afraid he would fall asleep. The wind was a demonic lullaby urging him to nod off, to just let the car go where it would. But he had to keep driving, had to put the miles between himself and the Barringer home. He could rest only when he was so far away he could no longer sense the evil, invisible tentacles reaching for him.

How many miles behind him were the

Barringers, his sister-in-law, his brother-in-law, his niece? Melissa, what was she? Innocent child or impious child? Victim? Victimizer?

Change lanes. Stay awake. The standard advice is, if you feel sleepy, you roll down the window and let the air blast you in the face, but he couldn't bear the thought. It was so cold tonight, so damnably cold. So play little driving games to give yourself something to do. Move over a lane. Shift back. Speed up. Slow down.

It was almost midnight, and he was exhausted.

Then he saw it, the promise of rest—a neon-bright Holiday Inn sign no more than a mile or so ahead.

The desk clerk politely took his Mastercharge card and gave him a room. It smelled of room freshener that couldn't completely mask old cigarette smoke. He dropped his travel bag on the rickety luggage stand and hung his coat on the clothes rod. No surprises at a Holiday Inn— and no closets, either. He did not mind. All he needed was a bed.

He yanked down the bed coverings. Fully dressed, except for shoes and socks, he slipped between the sheets. In under 30 seconds, he was asleep.

And dreaming.

The relief is so overwhelming he thinks he might cry. He has escaped from an oily blackness into a world of familiar light. He is home. He is in his own living room with his own wife, Carol Grace.

He kisses her passionately. He needs her. He loves her. He loves her. But . . .

Carol Grace is not Carol Grace. She is Vicki

Barringer, who says, "I need you."

The complacency with which he accepts the impossible metamorphosis assures him this is a dream. He need fear nothing that happens, because it is not truly happening; a dream comments on reality but is not reality. So let the dream proceed in its own dreamy way, and should anything prove too disturbing, he will end the dream.

There is neither surprise nor transition before he is transported to bed with Vicki, kissing her breasts, kissing a meandering path down her belly, tasting salt on a rising and falling satin surface. He has no guilt. This is but a dream, and he is a dream adulterer. Conscious thought might be sinful, an affront to your fellow man and yourself and God, but dreams sprang from the unconscious and were beyond your rational control, often beyond your understanding.

"I'm your girl. I'm your own little girl," she tells him.

That is right. She is his own little girl. He has always wanted a little girl, his own little girl.

He wants to possess her. He will. His will be done. Now.

He is inside her, inside her heated core, the clutching ooze and heat and clinging flesh. He feels a moment of foolishness as he is looking down at himself and Vicki, his little girl, watching the clumsy gyrations of his own naked buttocks.

Participating in the dream as well as observing it, Evan Kyle Dean is experiencing the wildest, most frantic lovemaking he has ever known.

She squeals and begs for more. Harder. "Give it to me! Oh, Daddy! Oh, Uncle! Give it to me!

Give it to me! Oh, fuck me! Fuck meeee . . ."

Then she turns her head to look back over her shoulder in salacious victory.

With sinking dread but no surprise, he sees Melissa peering at him as he skewers her, as he fucks her, and she is laughing, and so, just as a test, he tries to stop fucking her or to make her change to Carol Grace, but he cannot do that. He cannot quit fucking the little girl.

Evan Kyle Dean awoke.

He sat up in bed.

Dreams, he told himself, neither holy revelation or self-condemnation. A pornographic fantasy staged on his mental movie screen, and given recent events, one with none too ambiguous symbolism! There was, however, he mused, nothing symbolic about the erection he still sported. There was no reason for concern, though; indeed, it made him feel he was not so many decades removed from that youngster who'd awakened each and every morning with his manhood at attention!

Evan Kyle Dean lay back. He fluffed his pillows and, beneath the warm comfort of the blankets, folded his hands on his chest. Eyes closed, he concentrated on nothing and felt his breathing deepen so that each exhalation came all the way up from his toes.

He was not sure when exactly he went from waking to sleep, but he knew he was dreaming because what he saw could not be real.

She is an angel, an ectoplasmic imitation of flesh. She burns with divine light. She is naked, of course, but there is nothing in the least sexual about her nakedness. She is the perfect image of a perfect child, the Angel of Innocence, and he knows she has chosen this form to suit him.

"Evan Kyle Dean," the angel says, "will you be the beloved and chosen of the Lord?"

"I will."

"You are a good man?"

"I am."

"You are a righteous man?"

"I am."

"Then save me, righteous and good man who would be the Lord's beloved, the Lord's chosen. Save me, and I will reveal to you my name."

He thinks of the Old Testament's Jacob who wrestled all night with the angel, who strove to learn the celestial being's name and did not. Jacob became Israel, the Father of Nations, of the Chosen People.

Now he would be told the mystical name of his angel. He will learn her name and will come to learn the secrets of the seraphim.

"Save me, Evan Kyle Dean, save me and be honored among the most godly."

He sees it then, surrounded by blackness. It has a naked man's flabby body, made all the more sickening by its pink-whiteness, and its erect penis is a purple-capped weapon. Its head is not the head of a man, but of a rat. The rat's fangs gleam yellow and wet. The sharp nose twitches, whiskers testing the air.

This is the enemy; this is the hideous shape evil has chosen to assume. The Rat.

"Take me from here, Evan Kyle Dean," says the angel.

He will. He will take her wherever she wishes to go.

She wants to go out.

But it is cold out, so cold.

The Rat is coming for her. Help her. Save her. Learn the angel's name.

Evan Kyle Dean got out of bed. He did not want to be cold. He could not stand any more cold tonight, so he took his coat and slipped it on. He did not, however, put on his socks and shoes. He looked at the green LED clock numbers on the television's top panel. It was 5:48 in the morning. His conscious mind registered that. He opened the door of the motel room.

Where is she? Where has his angel gone?

Here, Evan Kyle Dean, I am here.

He put his hand in his right hand coat pocket. His fingers touched something smooth and cool. He took it out.

His angel has changed. She is small and perfect. He can hold her in the palm of his hand.

Coat flapping, Evan Kyle Dean walked barefoot through the parking lot of the Holiday Inn. The icy wind whirled viciously around him.

Angel's eyes shine so very bright. Her eyes become bigger. Their radiance fills him. There is nothing but the light of angel eyes.

He hears her laughter.

And he knows, held captive by her growing, gleaming eyes, that she is not an angel, but a spirit who means his destruction. He knows he is betrayed.

The wind was encircling him, holding him, paralyzing him.

He understands he has betrayed himself. The admonishment from Proverbs 3:5 comes to him. "Trust in the Lord with all thine heart; and lean not unto thine own understanding." A good, righteous man. That's what he arrogantly thought himself. He thought himself "God's anointed," but the anointing was by Evan Kyle Dean and not by the hand of the Lord. He asks the question of himself that King David the Psalmist asked of all men: "How long will you love vanity?"

Huge, glowing, hellish eyes accuse and condemn him like a mirror.

A whisper—*"My name is Lisette . . ."*

The dream ends . . .

. . . but he could still see the enormous eyes. He stood in the center of the eastbound passing lane on Route 30, a prisoner of the wind and the night and the evil. In his right hand, he held a china doll, the figure of a little girl in an old-fashioned bonnet, a basket of eggs on her lap. He felt drained, without strength. He could not move as the truck bore down on him, headlights looming larger and larger. A horn blared, a loud and lonely and futile sound.

Humbly, Evan Kyle Dean prayed to God: If it is Your will, save my soul.

He thought he heard God's voice: *I will.*

Then the truck hit him.

FORTY-TWO

*S*olakh.

Pola Janichka walked out of the room, saying, "Wait until I call you, then come to me."

Time passed. Time that did not feel like time passed and made her feel dreamy, awake and dreaming.

Selena heard Pola Janichka's call.

Selena stepped into the hall. The hall was black. Here light dared not invade. She began to walk in the direction from which she thought she had heard Pola Janichka's summons, but then the lingering echo of Pola Janichka's voice was all about her. She stopped walking. She did not know which way to go, and she was lost and afraid.

You need never be lost. Life is not geography. It is far more simple and thus far more difficult. You can go ahead. You can go back. You can stand still. Those are your choices. You have no other.

Choices, Selena Lazone? There is only one choice. If you are alive, you must go forward. That is what life is. Moving ahead. Moving onward. Life is movement and continuance, a progression.

So then come to me, Pola Janichka said—or

Selena Lazone thought she heard her say.

Now the darkness receded from the path she walked, and her fear receded with it. Pola Janichka appeared, not so far off, not so faraway at all. She beckoned.

But Selena could not come to her, because at her feet lay a chasm, wide and deep and terrible, an impossible distance separating her from Pola Janichka.

What separates is evil, what unites is good.

Tshatsimo, thought Selena. That is the truth. And what is the truth that may unite us?

Selena cried out, "I cannot come to you. Between us there is a barrier."

"There is nothingness," Pola Janichka said, "but can nothing be a barrier between those who desire to be together?"

"It can be," Selena Lazone said. "It should not be."

"Why does an uncrossable abyss lie between us?"

"Because I see it there and because I have said it is there," Selena Lazone said.

"And because I see it there and because I have said it is there," said Pola Janichka. "But if neither of us sees it and if neither says it is there, then it is not there."

"There is nothing, and nothing cannot keep me from you or from my people," Selena Lazone said.

"Then come to me," Pola Janichka said. "Come to us."

Selena stepped forward and did not fall.

There is a solid foundation under my feet. I walk the pathways that others of my people have walked. New road or old road, as I journey, I follow their *vurma*, their signs and roadmarks they have left to guide me.

Solakh.

Together, they went on. "Where are we going?" Selena asked.

"Where you must go," Pola Janichka answered as they walked into the past, into the sometimes misty, sometimes too vivid realm of expectations, disappointments and remembrance.

In the past, Selena watched herself . . .

. . . being born, the caul clinging to her face, heard her own first wail, a cry against what she was meant to be, a scream against *Baht*, fate itself? . . .

. . . her mother, bloody and weary, saying with pain-bitten lips, "The seventh daughter of a seventh daughter. Great her *draba*, her *dukkeripin* gifts. No less great, her burden."

. . . her father, surly but handsome, with the edged hardness that is found only in weak, frightened men. Grigor, drinking whiskey and smoking and laughing with the men. Ah, sometimes he had been known as Dark Fortune Grigor and sometimes Cloudy Days Grigor. Three times had the police, the *Gaje shanglos*, *lelled* him off to prison, but, from this day on, you could, call him *Bahtalo Grigor*, Lucky Grigor!

Seventh daughter of a seventh daughter—and one born with the caul! *Cohalyi*, sorceress, magic her birthright. And when his daughter was of an age to be married, what a bridal price she would fetch! He would sell her to one of the rich tribes, like the Adams . . . no, the Volkos! Ah, so much money, *lowe*, those Volkos had!

My father was a cruel and hateful man. I was only a piece of property to him.

"Your mother was a seventh daughter, Selena," Pola Janichka told her, "and your father was an unfortunate ignoramus. Never blame on wickedness what is more properly the work of stupidity."

Solakh.

Selena watched her life, her childhood as time sped by.

To see where you are going, you must sometimes see where you have been.

A series of automobile rides blurred together, roads north and south and east and west, no destination ever as important as the going. Los Angeles. New York. Atlanta. Chicago. Miami. A summer in France in the Camargue. Once a very short stay in Limerick City, Ireland. Grigor couldn't stand it there. Too many of the Gypsies of Ireland were abandoning their nomadic existence and living in houses, even paying taxes on them.

With her sisters, Selena begged on the streets of cities and towns. Her mother *dukkered*, told fortunes for the *Gaje*, and Grigor took what money she earned and vanished for days at a time, and the money vanished permanently.

And now her mother wept, her tears streaming down her cheeks, and her sisters pulled at Grigor's clothes, begging him, but Grigor had done it; he had made the arrangements. Selena would be the bride of Tene Volko's grandnephew. Selena was 11, going on 12. $10,000, that was the price for her.

Pola Janichka said no. Of course, she had

known of the seventh daughter of a seventh daughter. Was there a Gypsy on this side of the infinite *Paya*, the Atlantic Ocean, unaware of such a momentous event? And now Grigor, fool that he was, meant to sell the child for $10,000 so that perhaps she could run *boojoo* swindles on foolish *Gaje* to support a lazy dolt of a Volko.

It would not be permitted. Pola Janichka forbade it. The *Rawnie*, as venerable, loved, and feared as any Romany chieftain, was adamant. A far more important destiny awaited Selena Lazone.

Grigor fumed. He was the child's father.

So? Pola Janichka replied. A tomcat can be father.

Ah, the great lady did not understand. Grigor had the girl's best interests at heart. The Volkos were well-to-do. Selena would prosper as a Volko. He wanted a good life for his daughter.

Pola Janichka said, "I offer you the ten thousand dollars and ten thousand more. Sell the child to me."

Grigor did.

"I think I know now, but I need to have you tell me, Pola Janichka. Why did you want me?"

"So that I might teach you, Selena Lazone, and so that you might grow in wisdom. So that you might help those who needed help. So that you might become *gule romni*, a wise woman, one who knows and understands others because she knows and understands herself.

"There was yet another reason, Selena Lazone. Within me, was an abundance of love. So great a love, yes, but worthless as long as I gave it to no one. Love, like money, should not be hoarded. It should be given away freely. I wished to give that love, all of it, to you.

"So I taught you the *Darane swature*, and the *paramishta* and the *djili*, and more, taught you the *draba* charms and *armaya* . . ."

You did, Pola Janichka.

". . . taught you to *dukker* with tea leaves and palms and cards, taught you to look into the heart and mind and soul with your heart and mind and soul, to heal, to bring comfort and wholeness . . ."

All this you taught me, Pola Janichka. *Kako*. Thank you, Pola Janichka.

". . . and it was not enough for you . . ."

Out in the *Gaje* world that surrounded us, a world from which we were excluded and from which we excluded ourselves I thought I saw so much more!

Pola Janichka, because you gave me love, I learned to love. I learned to love people. And I learned to love learning. That love of learning became a fierce thing within me, Pola Janichka. I wanted to learn all that I could and to use my knowledge to help people.

At 15, Selena looked older, mature, as much because of the confident way she conducted herself as her appearance, but still, she was too young to be wise. *Cohalyi*, yes, but she certainly could not yet be called a *Rawnie*.

She came to Pola Janichka, her teacher. "I want to learn to read," Selena Lazone said. "I want to learn to write. I want to go to school. I want to learn everything."

Pola Janichka said, "I hear your words, and I also hear what you truly say. You wish to be a *Gajo*."

She did not mean that, not at all, Selena

protested. Why should it be forbidden for her to become literate, to gain the knowledge that the world had to offer, while yet remaining a true daughter of the *Romany*?

Pola Janichka said, "If a dog sets out to learn to meow, I have to think it wishes to be a cat."

"But . . ."

"*Yekka buliasan nashti beshes pe done grastende,*" Pola Janichka said. "With one backside, you cannot sit on two horses."

That ended the discussion with Pola Janichka. The discussion with herself, with what she knew and what she wanted to know, with who she was and who she dreamed of being, continued for a week. Though it brought her pain, though she realized it would bring pain to Pola Janichka, she had to be true to herself and to the promise of the person within her she felt she could be.

She tried to explain that to Pola Janichka.

With the edge of her hand, Pola Janichka chopped the air and cut her off. "If you choose to be one of them, the *Gaje*, you likewise choose not to be one of us. You become outcast. Banished. You call down upon your own head the curse of *marhime*. Know this, Selena Lazone."

"No," Selena said. "If I am to be *marhime*, then it must be Pola Janichka who condemns me."

The moment that followed Selena's statement and plea lasted forever.

Then Pola Janichka said, "*Bater.*" She spat at Selena's feet. In a thickly wet voice, Pola Janichka solemnly pronounced the curse— "*Marhime!*"—and turned her back on Selena Lazone.

Selena Lazone turned her back on Pola Janichka and on the Romany and fled. In the *Gaje* world, she could not accomplish what she wished to if she were seen as a child, and so, sometimes implicitly and sometimes overtly, she declared herself a woman—and as a woman, she found work and earned enough money to live and to learn.

And now . . .

Solakh.

"I have returned."

The search for knowledge had brought her here. The search for self had led her to the *Rom.* The past had brought her to the present.

"*Te aves yertime,*" Pola Janichka said. "I forgive you, and may forgiveness flow like God's grace from *o juvindo Romano, o muli Romano,* our living Romany brothers and sisters and from the spirits of our honored dead."

Selena Lazone was no longer *marhime.*

She was Rom. She was *ababina. Cohalyi. Gule romni.* Sorceress, witch, magic woman.

She was Selena Lazone—healer.

Sitting at the table, the crystal ball between them, Selena asked, "What must I do, *Puri Dai?* How can I save the child, Melissa Barringer? How may I bring peace to the *diakka, Puri Dai?*"

"It will require great strength and power, Selena," Pola Janichka said. "I mean no insult, but I simply do not know if you have such strength and power." She sighed. "And as I am now, no matter the respect others afford me in my age, I could not confront this *diakka.* I do not have the strength. I do not have the power."

Selena brought her hand to her mouth, knuckles tightly pressed to her teeth. At last, she dared to say what she had sensed since first coming tonight to the home of Pola Janichka. "*Puri Dai*, you are dying."

Pola Janichka nodded.

"Is there nothing that can be done . . ."

Pola Janichka smiled. "I get the Christian stations on cable, but the *Gaje* preachers have done nothing to cure me." Then she grew serious. "There is one sure death guaranteed everyone. It happens because it must. *Baht*. It is that sure death that dwells within me."

Tears burned Selena's eyes.

"Do not weep, *tschai*, my own little girl," Pola Janichka said. "There are beginnings and there are endings. There is completion. You are complete because you have found your people and yourself. And I am complete because you have returned to me."

Pola Janichka smiled. "What God wills, Selena, what God wills. We will trust *O Del* and rejoice."

"*Bater*," Selena Lazone said.

"You will need help," Pola Janichka said. She took Selena's hands and held them, her grip warm and strong. "Your man, go get him now. He will stand by you in this. He is *Rom*. He is *tacho rat*. His heart is good. There is much we have to talk about, much that I must teach you about *draba* and *vila* and *O Del* and *O Beng*."

It was morning when Selena Lazone and David Greenfield departed. At her front door, Pola Janichka watched them walk into an ugly gray-black dawn. The wind blew fiercely from the north, a night wind that would not be banished by the day, cold and angry and strong.

"*Akana mukav tut le Devlesa*," Pola Janichka said.

"I now leave you to God."

FORTY-THREE

It was a quarter to nine. He said "I'm leaving a little early today. A few things to take care of at school. I'll be home around the usual time, okay?" He smiled and saluted with a casual hand to his forehead. In his blank expression there was no sign there was anything at all worrisome, bothersome, or even annoying in his complacent, perhaps humdrum life.

For a moment he simply stood there as Vicki tried not to stare at him. In a gray-blue housecoat that felt particularly drab, she sat at the kitchen table. Distractedly, she thought, Who is he? This is my husband, and I do not know who the man is. She wanted to be more upset by that thought, but she was not. It was not the first time in the past few hours she had had it.

Warren had slept beautifully, while she had been awake the entire night. She had fitfully turned from side to side, trying to force herself to relax. She discovered itches and minor aches that ordinarily she never would have noticed.

After a while, she tried thinking of absolutely nothing. No luck. Her imagination conjured up abstract, shape-changing horrors and inky, lurking fears. She attempted to picture soporific scenes of golden sandy beaches and green woodlands. Her mind's eye could see only desolate snow or flickering, black-tinged flames. She tried to pray. The words, the pleas to God, had been in her mind, but despite her sincerity had been hollow and floating and utterly futile.

More than anything else, though, it was the wind, as all night long it encircled the house, awful and threatening.

Awake, so horribly awake, she lay beside her husband. Warren, damn him, slept like there was absolutely nothing at all wrong with the Barringer family, nothing whatsoever troubling Missy.

Some time between three and four in the morning, she thought surely she would start to cry. She reached out and touched Warren's elbow, then his hip. His breathing did not change.

"Warren."

No answer.

"Warren?" She wanted him to awaken and hold her.

Warren did not awaken. He would not. He rolled heavily onto his side, his back to her.

She felt like shaking him, striking him, slugging him with her fist right between the shoulder blades, but then the moment passed. She had no right to expect anything of him because he was a stranger.

At the door now, seemingly puzzled by something, Warren asked, "You okay, Vicki?"

"Sure, okay," Vicki told the stranger—and he left the house. Her pinched laughter surprised and frightened her.

Losing my mind, she thought, but there was no panic at the thought. Panic required energy, and she was drained. But she was going out of her mind. She felt distanced from everything, set apart from all those things and all those people that had once been a familiar microcosm of her world.

A few minutes later, with another cup of coffee, she listlessly peered out the window at the gray day. She heard the television set playing in the rec room beneath her feet, violent and demented cartoon-frenetic sounds she could feel rather than hear. Missy was down there, with coloring book and the morning kiddy shows. For the moment, she did not even want to look at Melissa . . .

Missy was another stranger in the house. I admit it. Right now, she scares hell out of me. Right now, I wish she were gone!

Vicki felt as though she had been viciously and irrevocably cut free from everyone and anyone to whom she had ever been emotionally tied.

In a world too full of people, she was alone. No!

She did have a friend, a good friend, Laura Morgan . . .

Or she had had a friend.

After that awful Sunday, there had been a rift in their friendship.

As she had told Laura, Vicki had not gone in to work at Blossom Time on Monday. But then, five minutes after she had told Laura that, everything went berserk.

So Vicki had not gone to work on Tuesday nor Wednesday nor the whole week.

But Laura had not called her. Laura didn't seem to care.

No! Laura Morgan was a friend—a true friend.

Vicki called Blossom Time and, when Laura answered, Vicki said "Hello," and that was the only word she could say without a stammer. Laura sounded cold and businesslike. No, she was actually more wooden and brusque than that; Laura would have had a professionally courteous tone had she been responding to an inquiry about the price of tea roses or even to a wrong number.

Vicki tried to explain what had happened.

Then she stopped talking. I . . . I sound insane, Vicki said to herself. I know I do.

Laura Morgan said, "I'm sorry, Vicki. I don't know what your problem is. I'm not so sure I want to." Laura's voice was as thin as the edge of a sheet of paper. "I've given this a lot of thought. I don't like what I'm saying, Vicki, but it's the truth. You see, you didn't get in touch with me. I didn't get in touch with you. I think that's the way I wanted it to be."

With a sinking heart, Vicki listened to a long silence, and then Laura said, "and I am afraid that's the way I still want it to be. For now, anyway."

"I see," Vicki said, as she thought, I want to cry.

"Vicki, I've got to think of my child," Laura said, her tone softening. "You understand."

Again Laura paused and then said, "Vicki, there is something seriously wrong with Melissa. I think we both know that."

She knew Laura was speaking but she did not hear an intelligible word. This is it, Vicki thought, the moment in which I snap and go stark raving mad.

She did not cry but forced herself to tune in Laura Morgan. "Maybe I'll feel differently after a while. Maybe we can get together then, sort of play it by ear . . ."

"Yes, I do understand," Vicki interrupted. And with Laura's voice still coming from the receiver, she hung up.

Then she looked at the telephone and studied its shape and color, then touched its smooth plastic. Reality! She had to concentrate on the real world and nothing but if she were to maintain her sanity. She had to use her five senses and only those senses. No imagination.

And no memories. Not now. Cross out memories and imagination. Look there. A single blip of water hung from the kitchen sink faucet. She gave all her attention to it. When it swelled to drop size and tore free, she tracked it all the way down. It fell at a normal realistic speed, not too fast, not too slow. No special effects here.

Reality. The world as it is. No problem. No craziness.

God, Vicki prayed, please help me. Help us!

The telephone rang. She clenched her teeth and answered it.

"Yes?" She thought she sounded rational and calm.

It was her sister, Carol Grace.

"Yes, Carol Grace and how are you?"

Carol Grace had just been contacted. They had notified her as soon as possible. It was all so confusing, she didn't know . . .

Yes. What had happened? What was it?

It was Evan, Carol Grace explained, telling her

all that she knew, which was not really all that much. She'd be up on the next flight and . . .

As though someone else with a humanlike intelligence had taken over her body, Vicki found pencil and paper and scribbled down the information Carol Grace shakily presented.

Oh, God! Vicki hung up the phone. She remembered the awful night wind, that wind of insanity and nightmare. She felt that wind now as, powerful and deathly cold, it blew through her.

From the rec room below came the muffled sound of the television. Faintly, the sound of chilly metallic synthesizer music came to her—the standard all-rhythm, no-melody, kids' show soundtrack.

Missy. All right. Missy. God help her. God help me! Damn!

Those were Vicki Barringer's more coherent thoughts as she went downstairs.

Missy sat cross-legged on the floor less than three feet from the television. The program, a syndicated rerun of *Hulk Hogan's Rock 'N' Wrestling*, was jumping reds and blues and blockily drawn characters without shadows. Their figures moved in grossly stiff animation against the background of a sterile two-dimensional world. The television picture kept intruding on Vicki's peripheral vision as her daughter ignored her.

"Missy," Vicki said.

The little girl did not reply as the thin shifting colors of the TV screen played on her face.

"Your Uncle Evan . . ." Vicki said.

". . . We were hungry," said a cartoon Nicolai Volkoff, "So-vi-et. Get it? So. Vee. Ett! Ha, ha!"

Missy laughed.

"Something happened to him, something very bad . . ."

Missy kept on laughing.

Vicki moved in front of the television.

"You're in my way," Missy said, and she sounded annoyed, even threatening.

The little girl smiled.

Vicki looked at the child's face and turned to ice, afraid of what Missy might do to her.

And no less afraid of what she might do to this inhuman clone of her child.

Above her and seemingly very faraway, there was the too cheerful sound of the doorbell.

I have been programed to respond to doorbells, Vicki thought, as she went upstairs. She opened the front door.

She saw them, the woman and the man, and flickering, angled sheets of light cut into her mind. The world tilted on its axis. She thought, I definitely have gone crazy.

"Hello, Vicki," David Greenfield said.

FORTY-FOUR

David Greenfield tensely waited in the hall by the closed bedroom door. *Baht*, he thought. This was where fate had brought him, had brought all of them. It would have been a lie to say he understood much more than that, but that much was enough for him.

And what did Vicki Barringer understand? he asked himself. Pleasant, shy, soft-spoken, too serious Vicki, one of the women from his womanizing days. He couldn't, in all honesty, remember much more about her, about the Vicki Barringer of his past, except that she wasn't one who had caused him any problems. There had been no attempts to define herself through her association with him.

Vicki had been okay. He decided it was a compliment to be able to say that about any of his affairs during that period of his life.

Poor Vicki Barringer. She had obviously been shocked when David and Selena had appeared at her door. It was apparent that this was only the most recent shock in a series of shocks. Fluttery tics along her jawline, eyes too big for her face, Vicki looked like she had just that moment been released from several months' solitary confinement.

They spent nearly an hour talking. That is,

Selena had done most of the talking, trying to explain and often having considerable difficulty in telling Vicki what she knew and how she knew it.

In the end, though, Vicki made it plain she understood all she needed to. In a tired voice, she said, "I couldn't explain how I know it, but I believe, I really believe God has sent you to help my child."

"Yes," Selena said.

No, Vicki could not take part. She must not. She might be hurt, or she might bring about harm to others—David, Selena, or even her own daughter.

She had to stay out of the way. She could see that they were not disturbed. She should pray. She should trust in God and in God's Truth. Good was more powerful than evil. That was what the Romany believed, that was what the *Gaje* believed, that was what all good men believed, even those who were unwilling to profess belief at all.

Truth to tell, David mused, he had scarcely a more active role than Vicki Barringer. He was to guard the door.

And in his hands he held the *mulengi dori*, the Romany string.

The Romany know of many magical *draba* charms and amulets, their power appropriate to the situations in which they are employed. Garlic, the Romany believe, affords protection against evil changelings even as it strengthens the blood. A silver knife, a *tschuri*, can be a weapon against minor wicked spirits. Sea shells ward off lesser, ordinary misfortunes, but a NAV sea shell, one which miraculously bears the name of God in its chambers and swirls, provides good luck for all of one's life.

Far more potent than any other *draba* charm, though, is the *mulengi dori*, the Romany string. *Mulengi dori* could be more precisely translated as "dead man's string," but certainly no Rom who values his well-being would call it that. The *mulengi dori* is an inch and a half wide strip of white cotton (white is the Romano color of death) which measures the coffin of a Rom. The cloth strip is then cut into lengths of about 18 inches, each with a knot tied in the center. These *mulengi dori* are given to those who have reason to honor the *mulo*, the dear dead one, and to call on him for protection in the most threatening times.

The *mulengi dori* David Greenfield held had measured the casket of the father of Pola Janichka.

The *mulengi dori*, Selena had told him, would mean the destruction of the *diakka*—and Selena's own salvation.

It was David's responsibility to use the *mulengi dori* when it was needed; Selena could not call on its great magic herself.

She would not be here.

She would be in a world between worlds, a world that was neither the land of the living nor of the dead. She would be in the void with the *diakka*.

"What do you want? This is my room. You get out! I don't want you here!" The little girl was sitting at her small table when Selena entered.

Selena said nothing but approached cautiously. The child eyes beamed hate and distrust.

From her pocket, Selena took a half-ounce plastic squeeze bottle.

"What are you doing? Hey!" the little girl protested, hands coming up too late as Selena dribbled the water taken from a clear running stream onto her head.

In Romany, the language not only of truth but of magic, and therefore the natural tongue of an *ababina* sorceress, Selena prayed:

> *As the water is pure*
> *May the child be pure*
> *May her soul be pure*
> *As the water is pure*

She passed her hand over the child's head.

> *Spirit, I implore you, take your leave and*
> *cause no more to grieve this child and*
> *those who love this child, this tschai*
> *may she be free of you*

The child's eyes glazed over. Her mouth opened slackly. She was no longer the same; something had left her.

No!

The voice snapped suddenly, not in Selena's mind but in a domain of special consciousness that was hers by birth and learning.

I want to live! I must live!

Without uttering a sound, with her heart and her spirit, Selena answered the *diakka*. In a way that was not speaking but was ever so much more direct than speech, she said, "You cannot live. Now is not your time to live."

I live and I will live!

". . . but I can help you." Selena spoke simply to the spirit child, her voice that was not a voice colored with the compassion she gave her clients in her work as a psychologist. "I can help you to get rid of all the hurt inside you. I can help you to find peace."

Peace? I don't know what you mean! I want to be alive! I want to be happy!

"Being alive doesn't always mean being happy. You know that . . ."

Maybe I do. So what?

"I came to help Melissa. And I came to help you, Lisette. You told me your name. Do you remember?"

Yes . . .

"Lisette, there was more you wanted to tell me, more you needed to tell me. I know that. I am sorry. I could not listen to you then. I was afraid. Now I am not afraid. I know you have to get your hurt out of you, share it with someone else, if you want your hurt to go away."

I don't know. I just don't know.

"Let Melissa alone, Lisette. Give her back her life. Let me help you to leave behind your pain and your anger and go where you will find peace."

"Lisette?"

There was a pause, an endlessly expanding moment in time, then hesitant and hopeful the voice came.

Help me . . .

Selena stroked the head of the dazed little girl seated limply at the play table. Her touch told her the child was Melissa Barringer and no one else.

"Sleep, Melissa Barringer," Selena said. As though hypnotized, Melissa folded her arms on the table and rested her head on them. She slept instantly and deeply.

Please. Help me . . .

Selena sighed, squeezed her eyes shut, then opened them. "I will come to you." Selena sat down on the foot of the bed. She wove her fingers together in her lap. She squared her shoulders.

And she willed her spirit to loose itself from the confines of her body and this earth and this time . . .

. . . as the soul of Selena Lazone traveled to a place that belonged neither to the living or the dead but to the lost and lonely . . .

The Void . . .

. . . where the *diakka* awaited.

FORTY-FIVE

Where the spirit of Selena Lazone journeyed, the Void, Nothing was the rule and the reality. Selena Lazone, her essence unfettered by flesh, felt herself engulfed in Nothing, enveloped by it. She experienced in somber waves the dread and desolation, the cold discontent of those souls condemned and exiled here, the enduring and infinite unhappiness.

A sound came from everywhere/nowhere. It was an atonal chorus of those souls who lingered here, neither alive nor dead. Most sorrowful were the voices of the *detlene*, the souls of lost children, crying out in eternal loneliness for mothers and fathers and brothers and sisters and friends.

And she heard one voice, singular and distinct from all the others.

Help me . . .

I am coming.

While here existed neither geography nor three-dimensionality nor time, the human mind cannot abide a vacuum, cannot cope with or make sense of sheer nothingness, and so Selena's perception of everything was determined and prescribed by the familiar shapes and forms of the physical plane.

She saw herself, the spirit of Selena Lazone, as simply . . . herself, Selena Lazone. There was nothing at all *mulano*, ghostly, about her. She walked along a narrow path of twists and turns as sudden and sharply angled as comic strip lightning bolts, a path that led through black nothing and gray nothing and smoky nothing, non-colors that camouflaged flitting forms, lost souls of beseeching eyes, uneasy spirits that performed skittering staccato dances of despair, that imploringly reached out to her—and could not touch her.

Then Selena saw the *diakka*, as it appeared like a developing print coming into focus on photographic paper.

She was delicate and blonde, finely featured, clad in the too elaborate, ruffled dress and ankle shoes of a long-ago America. As Selena approached, she felt waves of emotion emanating from the *diakka*—the loneliness, of course, always the loneliness, and the rage, the outrage at the great wrong done her, the ravenous need and will to be alive, to have what she was robbed of.

"Lisette," Selena said, and she took the *diakka*'s hand, the lost child's hand. "Your pain and your anger, Lisette. I want to know, Lisette."

Do you? Do you really?

"Yes."

All of it overwhelmed her, a crushing, smothering avalanche of overwhelming pain, psychic and physical.

Uncle, please Uncle . . . Oh, don't, don't you're hurting me . . .

* * *

abandoned

Mama? Mama, please come back. Don't leave me alone. Don't die . . .

the need for love,
a need that was exploited and twisted
and turned to something foul

. . . touch you, be nice to you, do what you want, do whatever you want, love me, lovemeloveme . . .

the tortured
last
moment
of
life

No! I won't die! I won't!

that should have been
the ending
but was
the beginning of
the diakka

Selena Lazone understood.

"It is all right, it is all right." she said, gratified she did not have to use clumsy words so that all she meant would be clearly understood by the tormented spirit, the lost soul, the lonely little girl.

There are moments when there are no meaningful differences between an act of the spirit and an act of the flesh.

Somewhere in a Void that lay between worlds,

a woman put her arms around a weeping child and hugged her close.

In the hall at the bedroom door, David Greenfield tapped his foot and rubbed his fingers on the ends of the *mulengi dori*. As tense as a garage door spring, David Greenfield waited.

Downstairs, in the kitchen, the room that would always mean assurance and stability, Vicki Barringer prayed and tried to tell herself that it would all be over soon, that God would deliver and protect. For flickering instants, she believed it; she had to or go mad.

And Selena Lazone, in the Void, very close to a house in Grove Corner yet at a distance that might not be measured in miles or inches or minutes or weeks, said, "Now, child, you must go on. There can be no place for you in the Nation of the Living. You belong . . ."

No!

". . . in the Nation of the Dead!"

But I want to live . . .

"You cannot. It is not your time."

The *diakka* turned and fled.

Selena pursued her.

He had to get home.

Later, there would be moments when he puzzled over the how and the why of that thought, trying to determine how that powerful obsession had sprung to his mind. He would sometimes think that she called him and he came.

But now, acting because he was compelled to act, he hurried from his university office, wiping off his list of concerns the appointment with a student he was scheduled for in ten minutes. He buttoned his coat as he ran to the parking lot and jumped into the Volvo.

"Your pain, Lisette. I will take it from you. It is your hurt that has kept you here, that has made you seek life that is not yours to have. Give me your hurt and move from here to a better place. Give it to me."

Lisette quizzically tipped her head. Her eyes were puzzled and suspicious.

Can you? Can you take away all my hurt?

"Yes," Selena said. "Give me your pain."

And the solitary pain of the *diakka* speared her, radiating throughout her being. Though she had no body, though she was just and only the soul of Selena Lazone, the anguish manifested itself as though physical, with a twisting of her guts and a brutal thrusting invasion into her sex and with dozens of dull thudding aches on her arms and legs.

The pain filled her. The pain consumed her. The pain flared, subsided, then attacked again more furiously as she said, "Lisette, now you are free to find peace. Go from here to the Nation of the Dead. *Akana mukav tut le Devlesa.* I give your soul over to God's keeping."

No! I will not die! He loves me! He won't let me die!

He burst through the back door, screaming, "Who is it? Who is in my house?" Vicki was terrified. She thought he had truly gone totally insane. She tried to explain, to tell him what was going on.

He heard the name Selena Lazone, and it registered faintly. He heard the name David Greenfield, and that registered with a reverberating clang. David Greenfield, the goddamn philandering bastard, the old hurt, the old fury, the long suppressed and nearly forgotten hatred!

And then he heard her, he was certain he did, heard her calling him!

"What are you doing? What are you doing?" Vicki tried to stop him. He pushed her aside. He wanted to smash her face in.

She called him!

He ran out of the kitchen, up the stairs, Vicki trailing behind, trying to hold him back and failing completely.

Face glowing like a madman, eyes bulging, he confronted David Greenfield. "You . . . in this house . . . *our* house!"

"Calm down, Warren," David Greenfield said. "We're here because of your daughter."

"You fucking sonofabitch!" Warren roared, and the punch he threw had all his weight powering it.

It caught David flush on the jaw. The back of his head thudded against the doorframe, and blackness rapidly pooled throughout his mind.

He ordered himself not to lose consciousness, but his legs couldn't hold him up, his knees wouldn't stay locked, and he was sliding down the wall, getting punched again.

And through wavering black puddles, he watched the *mulengi dori*, the Romany string, slip from his fingers.

Selena's words were Romany words, imploring and commanding. "Lisette, unhappy child, as the knot is untied, so may you be set free to journey beyond, *anda l thema*. As the knot is untied, may I be set free of your sorrows and pain and return to dwell once more among the living, *o juvindo*."

In a voice that was not the product of lungs and vocal cords and lips, Selena Lazone called to David Greenfield.

The *mulengi dori* must be undone.

Now!

Just before he blacked out, David Greenfield heard her.

He came to in less than 30 seconds to a scream that filled the world. It was Selena's agonized scream.

Groggily, he managed to stand and stumbled into the bedroom and into pandemonium.

On her knees, Selena looked as though she had just barely survived a terrorist bombing. Blood seeped from her ears and ran freely from her nostrils and the sides of her mouth. She was groaning, a throaty bubbling of blood and mucus.

The little girl sat at her table. She looked confused. She shook her head as though she'd just awakened from a wispy bad dream.

Kneeling by Selena, an arm around her, David saw the jagged red lines cutting through the whites of her eyes. The pupil of the left eye was the size of a dot, the right as big as a teddy bear's. She is dying, he thought, as she tried to talk to him.

"Pain, all her pain . . . in me. The pain . . ." Each "p" sprayed his face with coppery droplets of blood. Her left eye rolled up and disappeared.

"Gone . . ." she said.

"Let me go!" The little girl broke free of Vicki's arms and knelt by David and Selena. Gently, she touched Selena's graying face.

"The *diakka* . . ." Selena said, her voice thinning on each syllable.

"You saved me," the child said. "You saved me." Tears rolling down her cheeks, she whispered, "Thank you."

She pressed her lips to Selena Lazone's bloody mouth and kissed her.

With that kiss, Selena Lazone died.

FORTY-SIX

It was the second week of November, turning seriously and consistently cold, and when it turns cold outside, Vicki thought, it was fine to be warm inside. Eyes half-closed, leaning back, she luxuriated in the heat of the bath water and the fragile bubbles on her skin. She was not unhappy, nor could she say she was happy. There had been too much terror and dread, too much pain and loss, and so she could not trust any feeling of happiness.

But at last she was starting to think there would be a time when she would be happy.

Indeed, when they could all be happy.

The doorknob rattled and she sat up, putting her arms across her bosom. Curiously, she felt as though she had done something embarrassing. She'd thought the bathroom door locked. She liked, even demanded, her bathroom privacy, but . . .

"Melissa? What is it?"

"I've got something neat to show you. It is just totally rad."

"Couldn't it wait?"

"Uh-uh." A giggle. "It's something I want to show you now!" She skipped over to the vanity, stooped and opened the cabinet. "I saw this on a television show. It is just so cool."

"No!" Vicki said. Hands on the rim of the tub, she pushed herself up but knew she wouldn't be able to move quickly enough. Her knees were still bent, her buttocks brushing the bubbly water.

And the red plastic blow dryer was plugged in and a small thumb had pushed the "on" switch and a small hand and thin arm swung the slowly rotating dryer up and toward her—and it fell.

And Vicki was horrified, but, more than that, she was sad, she was just so sad, as one lucid and oddly comforting thought filled her mind: It is not my daughter who is killing me.

Then the hair dryer plunged into the bubbles and the water sizzled and the overhead light dimmed and Vicki Barringer's muscles jerked and knotted into tight cramps as she slipped down into the bath.

Her final sight, a placidly smiling little girl's face, was obscured by a watery film as her blood boiled and her brain burned.

Midnight approached, and the jukebox played Merle Haggard. The television showed a truly ancient rerun of *Hollywood Squares*, so old that Wally Cox occupied the center box.

He sat at the bar, drinking whiskey. He drank fiercely and steadily as he had been drinking for weeks. He drank because Selena was dead.

And he drank here because this was where he belonged.

The Pit Stop was a workingman's bar as well as a bar for those who got welfare instead of wages. Cigarette smoke, residual and new, hung heavy. No one ever ordered white wine. The Pit Stop was rough and raw-edged, a place to bring your sorrows, so that to jukebox accompaniment and the click of pool balls, you could feel that sadness in all its heavy intensity. It was no less a good place to bring your anger and to vent it in a fight in which you beat someone and perhaps got beaten yourself.

The Pit Stop was a bar of thick and dark feelings.

And David Greenfield belonged here because he had made a discovery.

Mandi Rom. I am a Gypsy. He was a man of feeling, a Gypsy man with a Gypsy heart.

And in all its varieties and permutations, the feeling that had filled him since the death of Selena Lazone was grief. Grief was an enfolding blackness that suffocated, then left off just so you could draw half a breath before it seized you once more. Grief was a taloned hand that clawed into your chest and tried to rip your heart out.

Grief was churning anger.

And it was regret.

It was the shattering instant when you knew you grieved because grief was the inevitable end product of the loss of what you love. Oh, yes, you loved, goddamnit, and damn that stiff-necked stupidity that would not permit you to feel, that denied you the pleasure of knowing the silly, comforting, warm, good feeling of being loved and that would not let you say, "I love you."

Selena, I love you. He said that often now, silently and sometimes aloud. He said it at her funeral. Said it, hell! It came upon him in the first wave of feeling he had ever known in his manhood, and he howled it when he threw himself on her coffin.

Selena, I love you. There were times he said

that and thought he was heard.

Because he was a Gypsy, *Mandi Rom*, he kept Selena Lazone's memory alive with the proper Romany rituals. He sponsored a *Pomana*, the traditional funeral feast for the dead. He anonymously contributed $1000 to the library at the University of Chicago. *Te avel angla tute*. This is done in your memory.

Sometimes, when he absolutely could stand no more, just could not abide any more grief, he consoled himself with the thought that the *diakka* is no more. The little girl, Vicki's child, is saved. There is purpose and meaning. Selena is dead, but her death has not been futile.

Suddenly, there was something on the television set that made him tell the bartender to turn up the volume. The midnight news was reporting "... a horrifying accidental death in Chicago's far south suburbs ..."

A grainy black and white photograph of Vicki Barringer's face shown on the screen. The nose seemed to be pressing against the glass of the picture tube. "... of Vicki Barringer ... bath tub ... electrocuted ..."

With a solemn newscaster's voice-over, the picture cut to a videotape of the husband and the child, the seven year-old girl "... who discovered the body of ..."

"Grieving ..." Warren Barringer. Melissa Barringer.

It couldn't be. Vicki Barringer, dead? It made a joke of Selena's sacrifice! It was too cruel a comment on all that happened.

Vicki ... Dead. For a dizzily spinning moment, he felt a new burst of grief, and it was for Vicki, and he wondered if perhaps he had loved her—or if he loved her now, now that he had learned he could feel.

Vicki Barringer was dead. That was the fact. But was it simply an accidental death?

"No," he said to the shot glass of whiskey in his hand. His voice was low. He could not believe it, could not accept that bad luck and a hair dryer worked together to kill Vicki Barringer.

And if that was what had happened, he needed to prove it to himself.

Outside, he did not zipper his leather jacket. The temperature was down to the low 20s, the lake wind sharp and stinging, and he wanted the cold to brace him, to clear his mind. The stars above were brilliant and the pointed slice of moon was burning silver. For more than an hour, he was a walker in the night city. Sometimes he tried to think and sometimes not to think. And it was in one of his nonthinking moments, a time when he had no thought of his own, that he heard faintly but clearly a voice in the night and in his mind:

It was not an accident.

He was certain, he did not doubt for an instant, that Selena had spoken to him.

It was three-thirty in the morning, and his fists battered the front door. He pounded, he rang the bell, hammered again, pushed the bell. He yelled, "Come on, come on!" Above, lights blipped on the second floor. As though thinking about the actions of someone other than himself, he realized he was creating a hell of a racket, and he wondered if even now hours later there were police still at the scene of the accident, or if they would soon be summoned—and he didn't give a damn.

Then the door opened, and he stood face to face with a bathrobed Warren Barringer. "What is it? What do you want here!"

"I want the truth," David said, and he pushed his way into the foyer.

There was a look on Warren's face that David could not quite fathom, but that expression was in addition to a look of fear—and David found satisfaction in that. David leaned back against the front door. He hooked his thumbs in his jacket pockets. "Tell me about Vicki," he said. "Tell me how she died. You tell me everything, and you do it now."

"You . . . You can't make . . ." David saw it then, saw it as cleanly and clearly as he would have had he been gazing through his camera's lens. Warren Barringer was a man with something to hide, something terrible.

"Let me say it for you so it all gets said and we get it out of the way." He took his hands from his pockets and ticked off the points on his fingers. "I can't burst into your home this way. I can't threaten you." He laughed. "You'll call the police. You'll see I go to jail for this. You'll have them haul me off to the asylum."

David lunged. He grabbed Warren by the lapels of his robe, and he twisted with both hands, his knuckles grinding into Warren's collarbone and throat. He slammed Warren into the wall. Then he did it again.

Warren's eyes bugged out. He gripped David's wrists. David cut his wind off, pressed him back, lifted him up, hanging him. Warren tried to bring up a knee into David's crotch, but David twisted a hip, blocking Warren's knee with his own. "This the way?" he said, and levered his knee into Warren's groin. "Like this?" He did it again, and crashed Warren into the wall and felt the whole house shake.

"How did Vicki die?"

Warren's cheeks were purple, and he was caving in, turning to putty. David cranked down the pressure of his hands a notch or two. "Tell the truth and you have no regrets," he said. "The truth will set you free. Let's communicate, professor."

Warren wheezed, and David turned it on again. "How . . ." He pounded Warren into the wall. "Did." He pounded him against the wall harder. "Vicki." He pounded him into wall harder still. "Die?"

Then he paused and waited as Warren tensed, bracing for another encounter with the wall. It didn't come. Warren sobbed.

"How did Vicki die?"

"Killed her . . ." A whisper, just audible, and it chilled David. And then, a whisper once more, but each word precise and crisply articulated.

"She killed her."

From above came a little girl's teasing and amused laugh. "Daddy, it is not nice to tell!"

In white underpants and undershirt, she stood halfway down the stairs. Her smile was the perfect smile of a perfect child.

David flung Warren to the floor and went after her. She tried to get away and nearly reached the top step. He stretched, fell, but snared her bare foot. He had her! His fingers crawled upward, and he tightly grasped her ankle.

She yelled, "Let me go, let me go!"

She kicked out. He yanked her down toward him. Her chin, forehead, knees and elbows thumped against each stair and she cried out in pain.

He pressed the flailing, kicking, screaming little body beneath him, rolled her over and pinned her with his weight. With the heel of his left hand braced on a stair, he raised his upper body and clamped his right hand around her neck. He felt the jittering pump of her pulse in the slim column of warm flesh.

He squeezed.

You are murdering a child! The voice of reason suddenly shouted within him.

But another voice spoke, the voice of *tshatsimo*, and he knew it spoke the truth. This is not a child. Not anymore. Not now. This is *diakka*. You must destroy it!

Her eyes rolled back. Like a hungry baby bird, her tongue stabbed the air. Her jerks and wriggles weakened, no longer voluntary attempts at escape but waning reflexes as he choked the life out of her.

He had her.

Then he felt an inexplicable circle of pressure on his back.

He turned his head and saw Warren looming over him.

Warren pulled the trigger of the .25 caliber pistol pressed between David's shoulder blades.

The report was the loudest sound David had ever heard. It was as though a bomb had gone off inside him. He was vaguely aware that he was rolling down the steps, that an ankle twisted painfully, that his lips were split and bleeding, and then he was on the foyer floor.

He got to his hands and knees and then, try as he might, he could not find the strength to rise to his feet. He heard a delicate wet sound and realized it was blood leaking from the exit wound in his chest. He had to get up, he had to . . .

Warren came up behind him and shot him again, low in the back.

David crawled toward the door. By gripping the knob, he managed to pull himself up. He opened the door and staggered outside.

Above, the stars and moon shone in the clear sky. It's a fine night, David thought, cold, so cold, but fine. He could walk no farther. He lay down on his back in the front yard. A Gypsy death, he thought, the sky overhead, and it is all right.

It is all right.

I am a Gypsy.

Mandi Rom.

EPILOGUE

It is Wednesday, the middle of February, a few minutes after four o'clock. On either side of the four lane highway, Route 57, irregular islands of dirty snow melt into the muddy, southern Illinois fields. The ebbing sunlight is misty but still bright and penetrating.

Days are always too bright now, bright and condemning.

The Volvo travels south. The child sleeps. The man drives. There has been so much traveling these past months—up to Wisconsin, Michigan, Iowa; over to Indiana, down to Missouri and Kentucky.

Why the Midwest? Why only the Midwest?

Perhaps because he is crazy, fixated, locked into psychotic patterns of irrational but precise and regimented behavior.

Or perhaps because he sees the Midwest as his maze. And he is The Rat, and The Rat must run the maze.

He realizes with crystalline paranoid awareness that they cannot stay anywhere, any one place, too long. They are fugitives and so . . .

Oily perspiration polishes his blotchy, alcohol-puffy face. He squints, his hands a tight grip on the steering wheel. Concentrate on the driving, he tells himself, as he checks to see that the speedometer needle is set at exactly 55.

He is driving well.

He reaches down. The uncapped pint bottle of vodka is angled upright in his crotch. That is what he needs. A sip. Maintenance dosage. Just enough to keep him steady, to center him, to keep him focusing.

Listen to the tires on the road. Listen to your snuffling ragged breathing. Listen to the voices in your mind, the voices that will not cease.

Drive . . . drive . . . drive . . .

Must get away.

Cannot stay anywhere too long. Cannot take a chance. They will find us.

It would be all over for them.

It would be all over for . . . her.

And if he turns his head now, will he catch her sleeping, truly asleep and genuinely unaware? Will he therefore really see her, behold the face of a monster/demon or the face of The Rat, his own Rat face.

Around and around we go. A maze. Survival, perhaps, but not life.

A drink. Now.

To keep away the shakes, the convulsions that want to send all his muscles into spasm, to keep terror and revulsion and anguish from exploding inside him. Without liquor to keep him going when he needs to keep going, to sedate him when he needs sedation, oh, Jesus, he just might start to scream.

What she is . . . What I have become . . .

So vodka, then, is the fuel that burns within him, that burns like the fire eating away the interior of a log.

I am burned out, a burned-out case.

Nothing left. He no longer has substance. His only reality is drinking and her.

He drives and drinks vodka. Clear liquid. A clear bottle.

He feels colorless and smooth and brittle. He is glass. Light passes through him and reflects off him in angled glints. He is a glass ghost.

And he is tired. He knows that without actually feeling it. Must stop and rest. How long since he has slept? A day or two?

Must keep moving.

But surely it is safe now. It must be. They cannot still be pursuing.

Who are they? Who? The Furies on his trail? Demons? Oh, no, not at all. Your demons are within you; it is futile to strive to elude them. Something else then. It is vengeance in pursuit; vengeance seeks them. It is justice. In a way he could never articulate, he knows this, has known it since that late night when he packed a few things—clothing and credit cards and cash and liquor—and they fled the house.

But I am innocent. I have done nothing wrong. The courts, yes, the American system of jurisprudence has found no guilt. A man invaded my home, tried to kill my child, and I saved her.

He sometimes talks this way to himself, and knows he lies.

Sunset. Soon it will be night. Hard to believe that, hard to believe it is winter. Mild weather here, so far south in Illinois; could fool you, make you think you're in springtime.

But he no longer believes in springtime as reality or metaphor. There is no hope, no possibility.

There is only need.

And so, he must stop soon. Rest. Sleep.

One mile, a blue sign promises Food-Gas-Lodging. One mile to the next exit.

He takes the off ramp, drives to the Mt. Vernon Ramada Inn and produces his Mastercharge card. A room for his daughter and him. The little girl has hold of his hand. Her eyes are open, but she is not fully awake.

He does not like the way the desk clerk, a young man as bland as a Disneyworld employee, looks at him. In a vague way, he thinks it is because he looks like an alcoholic ruin, that his pores are seeping vodka sweat.

With the door double-locked and dead-bolted, everything is better. A drink. This bottle is empty, but there are suitcases with other bottles. He is all right. They are all right.

He needs to rest, but first get rid of his dirt, get rid of his stink.

He is going to shower. He is going to get clean.

That is what he tells her. She sits in one of the two chairs by the drapery-covered window. She has the television set's remote control. Without turning up the volume, she runs the channels. The television's picture is too green.

When he is finished, he tells her, they'll go to the restaurant. She can order a hamburger, like always, and a kiddy cocktail.

With the shower's hot water pounding him, a welcome assault of clean heat, there is a brief time in which he feels alive, as though he is again a man of flesh and bone and blood.

He stays under the pounding spray a long time. Then, in the steamy bathroom, he stands on the pile of the clothing he has shed. He takes a deep breath, then another.

And he is all right, he thinks, until with his palm he rubs a clear space on the fogged mirror.

There is nothing there. No reflection. He cannot see himself.

And he knows he has ended. He does not exist.

Then a face appears and glares at him. The Rat!

He looks in the mirror and sees nothing but the sad simplicity of what is—the red-streaked eyes, the bloat, the spidered capillaries in the nose, the shaving cut on the chin, the bitten lip.

This is what he is. Not who. What.

He starts to weep.

A towel wrapped around him, crying, the sobs hot and bubbling as they tear up from his chest, he emerges from the bathroom.

She nods, rising from the chair. She turns down the bedcovers. He lets the towel fall away and slips into bed.

He waits.

Then she is with him in bed.

She is naked and touching him, and he does not think of The Rat, does not think of what was or what might have been, does not think of loss or degradation, does not think at all . . .

. . . as she touches him and touches him . . .

The woman drives the specially equipped Ford Aerostar. Its headlights wash the night, creating shadow specters. For several weeks, since beginning this mission she has not been certain of her destination. But she has never doubted. She has passed beyond doubt. She is going where he tells her to go, and that is where God wants her to be.

Her life is in the hands of God. The Lord has brought her health and wholeness.

The man who brought the Lord into her life is waking now. He groans and coughs. He has little strength and less endurance, so he sleeps frequently. And sometimes, in his dreams, God speaks to him.

Perhaps God has just given him, given both of them, a dream message, because the man says, "Take the next exit."

Ten minutes later, they pull into a numbered slot in the parking lot of the Mt. Vernon Ramada Inn.

They wait.

There are two men in the front of the customized ruby red Cadillac Eldorado. In back is an old woman. Her seat belt prevents her from toppling when the auto turns onto the off ramp. On this journey she has not said more than a dozen words to the two men. She has passed the trip in a dazed sleep, or in talking to ghosts and memories, or by watching the five inch, color television with which the Cadillac's passenger compartment is equipped.

And constantly she has been commanding the death inside her, death that is impatient now, to leave off; she will be ready soon enough, but there is a task to be accomplished.

The *diakka* must be destroyed and its wickedness destroyed. There are spirits who can find no ease or contentment, souls who can take no rest, until this is accomplished.

When the Cadillac is parked, the two men gently help the old woman out. They seek to support her, but she gestures them away.

I have the strength to stand, she tells them, and because she is the *Rawnie*, Pola Janichka, they cannot dispute her.

And she has the strength of others.

The side door of the Ford Aerostar opens. A hydraulic ramp whirs and clicks into place.

Emerald Farmer carefully rolls Evan Kyle Dean's wheelchair out of the van and onto the concrete of the parking lot. There is a blanket over his useless legs. He may never take another step, as God wills, but always will he humbly walk in the way of the Lord.

A way that has brought him here.

A way that has brought Emerald Farmer here, a child of God, to aid him and serve God.

Pola Janichka feels the power. There is *draba* with her, with them all, an intense magic wrought by those who have united in a good cause.

And there are not only the three of them. In her right hand, Pola Janichka holds two strips of cloth, each tied in a simple knot. She has *mulengi dori*, the magical Gypsy strings. One cloth strip has been cut from the cotton length that took the measure of Selena Lazone's coffin, the other that of David Greenfield's. Both *mulengi dori* have been touched by her tears.

As she walks to the crippled man and the woman, her comrades, Pola Janichka feels the presence of David and Selena. They are here, now, *mule*, no longer flesh and blood but as real as ever they were in life.

"*Devlesa avilan*," Pola Janichka says to Evan Kyle Dean and Emerald Farmer. "It is God Who brought you."

"It is God Who has brought us together," Evan Kyle Dean says, "to do His holy work."

"*Bater*," says Pola Janichka. From somewhere, somewhere else but somewhere not so faraway, she hears Selena Lazone say, "*Bater*."

Bater.

May it be so.

AUTHOR'S NOTES

There might be a linguist or two who finds fault with the Romany terms and phrases.

When one speaks Romany, one speaks *tshatsimo*, the truth, but when one writes Romany—lots of luck. Or lots of *bahtalo*. Or *bact*. Or *baktlo*. Not until the 19th century did Romany become a written language. Romany spellings vary from reference book to reference book to reference book. *Marhime* aka *marimay* aka *marime,* etc. The spellings I employed were chosen by the lingual postulate, "Eeny-meeny-mynee."

As for Romany rules of grammar, well, the *Gaje* seem more concerned with such concepts than do the Rom, and I got into the Romany spirit as I worked on the book.

Finally, while not all the ceremonies and rituals presented are authentic Gypsy practice and custom, I have tried to make them true to the spirit of the Rom. As Pola Janichka would tell you, there are times it makes sense to create an age old tradition on the spot.

SPEND YOUR LEISURE MOMENTS WITH US.

Hundreds of exciting titles to choose from—something for everyone's taste in fine books: breathtaking historical romance, chilling horror, spine-tingling suspense, taut medical thrillers, involving mysteries, action-packed men's adventure and wild Westerns.

SEND FOR A FREE CATALOGUE TODAY!

Leisure Books
Attn: Customer Service Department
276 5th Avenue. New York. NY 10001